Jack's Blues

By

James Darby

Maverick Publishing

Houston, Texas

2012

Acknowledgements

Katherine Darby, Hugh and Cindy LeVrier,
Margaret Stuart, Sarah D. Johnson

Cover Photography and Design by J. Bryan

September, 1971

Chapter One

Walk Away

Jack Clifford looked up for a moment, as he carried two foaming mugs of beer into the nightclub's office.

He stopped in his tracks.

"What the hell are you doing, Travis?"

Travis was standing on top of the club owner's desk, gazing ahead, staring at the far wall. Random papers and pink invoices were crinkled under his worn Dingo boots that sagged a little at the ankles.

"Lord help us," Travis moaned to no one in particular, "I think we're screwed."

"No shit?" said Jack,

"Not you, Jack." He didn't look down. "I mean the band! We're screwed, blued and tattooed!"

"So what are you doing, looking for a way out?"

"I know it in my bones, I can feel it." said Travis, not really listening to Jack. "Now, don't interrupt me."

Blackplanque's lead singer spread his arms wide above Jack and the beers. His palms turned upward and his head drooped low to his chest. His eyes closed. Then, Travis' face rose slowly and his eyes opened and gazed up toward the dirty ceiling. "Lordy, lord, lord," said Travis, "ain't I suffered enough?" Travis stood chest out, praying or meditating, crucified, a slave to rock and roll, seeking the Almighty's justice. "This is the cross I bear."

Jack Clifford was the band's photographer and a friend; free-lancer who had known Travis and the group for over a year, he had recently finished their new album's photography and artistic layout for the album cover.

"Well, when you're done playing Jesus, I've got the beer," said Jack, interrupting the plea from Travis. He wasn't going to cut this country-boy rocker any slack or pity. He figured Travis Montague was a long way from martyrdom, and a long way from the small Texas town he grew up in. Travis ignored him and worked his way toward rapture. A single fluorescent fixture in the ceiling of the small room bathed Travis in a soft, dirty, pale green light. Nearly impressive, thought Jack, looking at the arms stretched out, a lonely figure standing alone on the desk.

Travis suddenly gave up looking for salvation and looked down at Jack from his mount. "I ain't Jesus, Jack. I'm just trying to get a handle on his blues, you know.

Trying' to get in touch with his soulfulness. I think I've got similar feelin's too. My life has turned into a total bummer you know. I've nearly lost hope."

Jack flashed and realized that here was the perfect pose for their next album cover, if there was one. He framed the scene in his mind and took a mental picture of a musician's crucifix. Jack knew why Travis' was feeling frustrated and where it came from.

"Well, I guess Jesus did get the blues, what with all the sinners around him. Especially toward the end," said Jack.

"Well, horseshit," said Travis. He exhaled fully and let his arms fall down to his sides. "That didn't help one damn bit. I do regret that, Lord," he confessed. "I am forsaken in this quest" He looked at Jack and the beers, knelt and jumped off the desk. He landed with his boots making a gritty thump. "But, I think I know how that old boy felt."

"If you'd told me what you were into, I'd brought nails."

"Very funny."

Travis plopped down into the office chair and pulled at the collar of his tie-dyed

T-shirt, stretching it to his shoulder. He let go and it snapped back to his neck. Jack sat the beers down on the desk and settled on the couch. Travis stretched way back in the squeaky, wooden office chair so that he could pull a pack of Winstons out of his front jeans' pocket. A silver Ronson lighter was on the desk and he snatched it, flipped open the top with his thumb and lit a short joint he had tucked inside the pack's cellophane wrapper. Jack could hear the jukebox wailing the blues next door. He was in the club practically every week visiting with the band and meeting other musicians who would drop by and sit in with Blackplanque.

"I almost never do dope you know," Travis said to him as he took a long hit. "Not anymore, but, thanks for the beer." He held the number out to Jack, who waved it off.

"No thanks, I'm cool. I'll just stick with the beer." He'd probably get enough of the drifting smoke to pick up a contact high.

Jack knew what was on Travis' mind, seeing the singer's white face was flushed with frustration. Actually, he'd been waiting for something like this to happen. Jack knew the band, Blackplanque, was in trouble, mired in their musical career sludge. The blush almost made Travis' hundreds of faint freckles disappear. His dark red hair was parted in the middle and puffed out above his ears like a mini-afro.

"Are things that bad?" said Jack

"Oh righteous Jesus, yes," Travis continued in a biblical vein. "When is success going to rain down on us, Jack?" He took a long, last hit off the joint, dropped it on the floor and ground it into the linoleum. "We've written songs, done recording sessions and played a thousand gigs, but the Promised Land is still out there." He shook his head.

Jack wasn't surprised at Travis' deal. Jack had been involved in the Houston music scene for a while and had quickly learned about the wheeling and dealing that went on behind the stage and studio. Blackplanque was fighting for their record producer's attention, and striving to create their own sound--their own contribution to rock. Jack believed in their musical skill, but realized they had not found the magic. They were creative but unfocused.

"Aw Travis, it ain't that bad, it's not the end, no matter how you feel."

"You blame, Louie?" Jack asked, leaning a little toward him. Louie Thibodeaux was their record producer. "You know he wants Blackplanque to make it. He loves you guys. You're just paying your dues, playing in this bar five nights a week. Lee told me you're disappointed in your new album."

"Disappointed," Travis shot back. "It stinks! I don't blame Louie any more than us. Hell, nobody likes it but Mombo. What the heck does that redneck know? If he had any taste, he'd probably be in another band. I don't even know why we did another album except it's in our contract. But, I got a feelin' it's gonna be our last. We can sell it at gigs, 'cause they ain't going to be in K-Mart. It's one dead mullet, Jack."

Jack understood his black mood. It was a slow Tuesday night and the band was playing to a nearly empty club. It made the evening just another session for songs they had played a hundred times before. Jack had heard the new album. The songs were a classic rock on one side and original material on the other. It was not bad, but it also was not memorable. He couldn't recall the melody or lyrics of a single original song. They hadn't found their own groove and that disappointed him.

"Jack, if I didn't love the music so much, I'd jump out the window on my head!" Travis said.

"That would be pretty damn hard to do Travis, we're in a basement".

"Oh yeah, dammit, ain't nothin' going right." Travis smiled despite his mood. He took a sip of the beer in front of him. "Thanks again for the suds."

Jack felt tempted to say something to Travis about what he knew was Blackplanque's big problem. Why they probably didn't have a shot at the big time with their current producer, but he kept quiet. He considered the band members to be friends and clients, but he had other conflicting confidences that had to be kept. Life isn't always simple, he told himself. Being a part of the music business in Houston was tricky. Jack had found there was always a complex set of hidden schemes or agendas involved in every scene. Good guys didn't always finish on top. The boys in Blackplanque were just going to have to figure out their deal by themselves. He decided to keep these complexities to himself and maybe time would provide their answers.

"It's 1970. I'm getting to be an old man…I'm so tired of this," said Travis. He had calmed a little after the smoke; worn down by his own rant. He leaned in toward Jack. "I'm sorry, man. I've been playing since I was twelve. Lee and me's been making' music since fifth grade. We would have won that first talent contest in seventh grade if Lee hadn't got stage fright and peed down one leg when we hit the school stage."

He laughed at the memory.

"'Copy the Everly Brothers she told us," said Travis. "My sweet ass! That music teacher didn't want us to rock out," he paused, "and I guess nobody still don't. Maybe we're at an end of this thing." He paused, and the memory formed a faint smile in the corner of his mouth. Jack knew Travis was only twenty-two, but tonight there seemed to be years of frustration emerging. Rock 'n Roll, Travis's first love and craft, was something he had studied, first as a hobby and now a profession. They lived it. Jack felt Blackplanque was a rocket, ready to launch off the pad, with no one to light their fuse.

Chapter Two

Down on the Corner

Travis Montague slumped back in the office chair again. He and Jack continued the rap in the manager's office of the Basement Blues nightclub. A long breath slowly escaped from Travis' lips as if he was practicing his yoga. He was trying to cool down. The office was decorated in a cheap Sixties nightclub office motif. He sat behind the big second-hand walnut desk. The walls were faded, scarred pine paneling with a couple of windows with heavy, dusty wooden, Venetian blinds. Through them, the manager could peek out and see the nightclub floor and bar, but Van, the owner was seldom there at night. Actually, the head bartender Malcolm ran the place. Van would show up now and then when his stripper girlfriend pressed him to dance. They'd usually have a drink and then he'd slow-dance her around the floor a few times with one hand firmly placed on her butt. Then they would split without a word to anyone.

Jack sat on the front edge of a well-stuffed leather couch that was against the opposite wall. A woven Navajo blanket covered most of the dozens of cigarette burns on the cushions. Its Native American Indian geometric designs competed with the wavy, flowing letters on the psychedelic posters covering the walls.

Travis jumped back to the present. "What we need is to write a hit record, a monster, that's all there is to it. Something Louie could run with. Then we could do a nationwide tour; get some exposure on the road coast-to-coast." He fired up a cigarette and took a draw on it.

"Look at the facts;" said Jack, "Johnny Winter came out of the club just down the street. The 13th Floor Elevators made it big on the West Coast. There's Fever Tree, and The Moving Sidewalks, a lot of talented artists breaking out of Houston. Even straight acts like Kenny Rogers and B. J. Thomas. That's where your head should be at."

"I guess" Travis replied. "It's not all Louie's doing, but we're still screwed, and I think we need a new agent. For god's sake, if Louie can push out two gold records for Hidalgo Martin, a Mex'can even, what about us. Something's wrong here." He was more right than he realized. Maybe Blackplanque was screwed. All of Louie Thibodeaux's attention was on Hidalgo these days.

Basement Blues was a cellar nightclub at the bottom of a deep maroon and black- light lit stairway. The "club" was in Houston's Market Square district at the far north end of Main Street. The Square was getting a little long in the tooth, with a few creepy retail stores that catered to an older Negro clientele, selling antiquated clothing and shoes. In the late Sixties, a surge of nightclubs and bars had revived the area around the one square block park. A new nightlife had come to the north end of the Bayou City's downtown. The park wasn't much more than a hangout for winos during the day.

From Market Square, further up Main to Buffalo Bayou, was a scattering of head shops, hippie clothing stores, and biker nightclubs. All of this culminated at Allen's Landing on the Buffalo Bayou and the coolest psychedelic club in town, *Love Street Light Circus Feel Good Machine*.

"Travis," Jack said. "Listen man, success doesn't come quickly. Sometimes it takes years to be an overnight success. That's a cliché, but it's true, man. Sooner or later you guys are going to get into the right groove and it won't be luck. You get lucky when you work hard at it and you do."

"Yeah, I appreciate your confidence and hearing me out, but Jack, Louie really doesn't help us shape the music or give any creative ideas when we're in the studio," said

Travis. "I don't think he understands what we're trying to do. Hell, sometimes I'm not sure we do either. I've been with him for six years and here we are -- nowhere. Our albums just ain't getting any better."

He was right. Louie's production values were not keeping up with the new sounds, but he still knew how to pick and promote a hit record. The basics hadn't changed since the early Fifties. That was rock and roll, now and maybe forever.

Travis Montague was lead singer and rhythm guitarist for Blackplanque, a rock band he put together with his musical partner Lee Lewis who played lead guitar. Both were East Texans and the band's heart and soul. The two had settled in Houston from Lufkin at the suggestion of their long-time producer, Louie Thibodeaux.

Lee was the quieter of the pair, a little withdrawn, slow to speak to anyone other than Travis. He had light brown wavy hair and was medium height with a middle weight boxer's build. He had a level of skill that Travis, although a very good player in his own righ, readily admitted he could never reach. Travis considered Lee the artist and himself a craftsman.

Conversely, Lee felt he was carried on the coattails of Travis's voice and stage presence. He was an intense lead guitarist who would stand like a statue with his cherry Gibson SG, stone-still at Travis's right, and stare down at a spot on the floor, about fifteen feet ahead. Largely expressionless, his head would cock slightly, hearing every note from guitars, the organ and the bass with clarity beyond that of most mortals.

On stage, Lee Lewis could duplicate practically anything another guitarist might play on a hit record. If he were an actor, he would have been called an impersonator or mimic.

Jack sat for a while listening to the piped in music which filled the minutes between sets. At the corner of the office were two doors. One opened into the alcove at the bottom of the entrance stairs and it was kept locked, the other to the poolroom that held a couple of tables.

Mombo, the bass player strolled in from the poolroom with a cue in his hand. He filled the doorway.

"How long 'til we got to play?" Mombo asked. He sniffed the air and smiled. "What you boys been up to, huh?"

Travis looked at his watch …"Five minutes."

"Should've invited me in. I think I smell something sweet." He looked back at the game for a moment. "Say

Jack, where's your little Mex'can lover been? Ain't seen her with you lately."

"Aw, we kinda broke up."

"Too bad, man. She looked like a hot chick."

"Yeah, sometimes a little too hot."

"I'd take some of that," Mombo smiled and smacked his lips.

"You're disgusting," said Travis

"Easy, man, I'm just talkin' about a little taste." Mombo said, giving Jack a nod and went back to the game. Mombo never seemed to be too bothered about anything.

Louie had introduced Mombo to the pair of guitarists two years earlier and they welcomed him in as the band formed. The three had meshed musically from the beginning. He played a mean traveling bass that would not take a backseat to any instrument in the band.

"That old boy claims his wrists are too big for a watch. He's just fat and lazy." Travis said. "He sleeps 'til noon and then spends a couple of hours in his garage building speaker cabinets for churches and other bands."

Mombo was a sight to behold. He was about five feet, ten inches and 350 pounds on the hoof. He had a round, baby face with a chew in his lip, shoulder length, stringy black hair always topped by a flat, black wide-brimmed hat. The hat looked like it had been run over by a tugboat. He changed clothes at least a couple of times a week and woke up rumpled. But he could play and was strong as a musk ox. The only lead bass Jack had ever heard. He had told Jack that he had attended Julliard after high school. He was good, thought Jack, but he was also full of good natured bullshit.

Travis was getting restless and idly pulled open the middle drawer of the desk. He dug around a little among the papers and lifted out a small nickel-plated revolver.

"Damn!" he looked surprised, "I didn't know this was in here. I might need it someday. You never know when some crazed nymphomanic fan or her boyfriend might attack me." He cranked open the cylinder and peered in the chambers. "Loaded," he said. He flipped the six-shot cylinder back in place, leaving the hammer down in a safe position. He slipped the gun back in the drawer, pulled some paperwork over it, and got up to hustle the band back on the tightly packed, elevated stage behind the dance floor.

"But now it's time to rock," said Travis. God knows I love it!" he admitted this with enthusiasm; and put his earlier blues on a shelf.

Travis let out a Tarzan yell to warm up his voice as they entered the alcove. His singing voice was unique, schooled in the Southern Baptist church back home. Now it had a raw Rod Stewart-like edge, with great breath and range that could peak in incredible highs. It was not a sound he developed up in Summer Bible School but worked well singing the lead vocal in a rock and roll song. In the nightclub, Blackplanque was a cover band, playing live rock and roll that the crowd wanted to hear. They could rock the house whether it was Eagles, Procol-Harem, Cream, the Stones, James Gang or Chicago. The boys could hear a song a couple of times and play it elegantly, leads, vocal, backgrounds and all. They seldom did their original work on stage. The management wanted them to stick with Top Forty hits.

Mel Mobly, an English drummer who specialized in Bee Gee vocals, high harmonies and double-base rolls, provided a strong beat for the group. Louie called him the band's 'token Limey'. Then there was their soulful, top-hatted organist, Jacob Constant, who had cut his teeth with East Coast Jersey rockers and also sang backup. Jacob came from a bee-bop vocal ensemble that had actually had two top-ten hits before their fame and infighting blew them up. He fled south. They brought some outside flavor to a basic Southern rock sound. Only Lee, Mombo and Mel were married.

The walls of the nightclub were dingy, smoked tones of blue, maroon and grime. Small tables that sat about one hundred and twenty people surrounded the dance floor. In front of the band stage was a dance floor of polished blond oak with revolving, multi-colored stage lights and occasional bright flashing strobes. To the right of the band and along one wall was a bar where Malcolm, bartender and night manager, held forth. Usually three or four waitresses worked the tables on a busy night.

Jack watched the band take the stage casually, plug in and check their tuning. He felt comfortable in the club. After a brief look around the room Travis raised his right hand and on a single drummer's tap, they launched into "Walk-Away", a current James Gang hit. Always amazing to Jack, who had now witnessed this many times before, each member was looking in a different direction when they struck the raucous first chord perfectly in sync. The few couples responded immediately and began moving toward the dance floor. "How'd they do that," Jack yelled to the bartender who had no idea what he was talking about. "How do they all kick off the song together when they aren't paying any attention to each other?"

"I don't know," Malcolm replied not really giving a damn. "Must be practice, man."

Their playing was tight, tight, tight--one of the keys of a potentially great rock band.

October, 1970

Chapter Three

I Just Want to Celebrate

Jack Clifford first stepped down the maroon carpeted stairway leading to the Basement Blues Club about twelve months before the night of Travis's plea for divine help from the office desk top. There he would first meet the boys in Blackplanque, Louie Thibodeaux and Angie.

Just inside the door, his friend Rudy Trevino greeted him and led Jack past the cash box where Rudy's partner, Pancho Cruz was collecting three bucks a head from their friends coming in. They'd been doing this every Thursday night for about a month.

Rudy had an infectious personality, very funny, but his partner was serious, almost sinister as he collected the money at the door. A very silent, mysterious character, Jack thought. He later wondered if he did a little dealing on the side. By inviting their
friends and friends of friends, they had built a predominantly Chicano night of rock and roll at the blues club. Most "Latin" clubs in Houston played *Tejano* music,

which no longer suited many collegiate and young professional Hispanics. They were increasing in numbers in the Houston, and every week the crowd was getting larger. In addition to their day jobs, Rudy and his partner were making a fine amount by keeping the door receipts, while the club's owner enjoyed the extra bar sales on an otherwise off-night. The Basement Blues' owner discovered early on that rock filled the house more often than the blues, but he still brought in notable blues artists for the die-hards each month. The Latin Night was a good deal for both parties.

"Hey my brother," said Rudy to Jack, "I am *so* glad you brought your cameras." He gave Jack a South Texas *embracio* hug and a big smile, which seemed always to be on his face. "Just shoot all you want of the people and we'll put their pictures on the wall next week. They love that shit, club celebrities you know. I'm covering all your costs and your drinks. Might even fix you up with some fine ladies. Maybe my sister," he laughed. Rudy was raised in the small town of Tivoli, a hundred miles or so south of Houston and moved to the big city after high school and a year at the junior college in Wharton, Texas. He was a natural salesman.

Jack couldn't help but smile. A photo job where he could have some fun, pick up a little cash, and maybe meet some new chicks, that was a great combination. Jack had a day job selling sporting goods, but was ready to quit retail as soon as his free-lance work could support him. Rudy worked there as well. He figured that every opportunity to shoot pictures and meet more people improved his chances of success. Jack slid through the crowd. He was a little smaller than average with mid-sized frame and about five-foot, seven in height. This, plus his photo-journalistic background made it natural for him to shoot candid shots without drawing attention to himself, unless he asked for a pose. Jack worked to catch people off guard and enjoying themselves, rather than smiling group hugs or cheesy shots of lovers smacking each other over their drinks. It was a more journalistic style of shooting he was especially good at, but he figured this job demanded some of both.

The band was rocking and it caught Jack's attention. They were a strange assortment, a real mixture of shapes and sizes. The band, Blackplanque, according to the marquee at the door, were getting heavy into *I Just want to Celebrate* and it was moving from the chorus into a multi-synchronized beat-thing using all kind of sounds.

Canastas, tambourine, guitar scratching, cowbell-- all working off a great drummer. It went from a basic rock beat into African tribal drum rhythms and then transcended to an American Indian-like chant. The crowd on the thence floor was going tribal also. After about five minutes of this unusual rhythm jam, the band slid back seamlessly into the actual song. They had the dancers excited and the listening crowd mesmerized as they closed the song. There was a burst of applause that normally didn't come from a young, hip nightclub crowd. Vibrant reactions to bands and their music were usually not to be considered too cool in a nightclub setting, never in a psychedelic place like *Love Street,* down the block. That was really smooth he thought, and they deserved the applause.

"How do you like the band?" said Rudy as he moved up beside Jack. A big grin showed Rudy's modified Poncho Villa mustache. He had noticed that Jack was listening intently to them. "They're called Blackplanque."

"They sound pretty damn good," Jack shouted into Rudy's left ear as the band cranked up the Eagles' *Already Gone.* "I think they may be a key to your success. Wonder if they need a photographer?"

"I'm gonna set you up my friend," shouted Rudy in reply. "They told me they are into recording an album for some big time producer."

"Sounds good. Say, in the meantime, where's this sister you told me about?"

"Later, man." He walked off to flirt with a covey of chiquitas that had just come in the door and Jack went for a beer.

"It was about 9:30 when their break came and the band retreated to the club manager's office and poolroom. Rudy led Jack in. "Hey guys," he said to the group in general. "I want you to meet a friend of mine and a most righteous photographer. This is Jack Clifford."

The bartender was bringing the band a tray of cold beer in pitchers and mugs, and that grabbed their attention for the moment. The band members were steaming at the break, especially the refrigerator who had been playing bass. He was panting slightly; sweat pouring down his face and hair looked like he had just come in from a rainstorm. He dove for the nearest mug. He looked like he was nearing a stroke.

"Howdy," said the big one between gulps. The others nodded a greeting. He took a swig that emptied half the mug. "My name's Mombo" as he sat down his beer and stuck out a wet hand." Jack got a Texas style/Masonic grip and a side fist-bump from the other hand. Mombo had big strong hands and fingers that reminded Jack of chunks of an industrial steam hose.

"This is Lee, Jacob and Mel," Mombo said, gesturing toward the other three. "Travis is in the office over there, contemplating life."

Jack nodded in their general direction and said, "Howdy, good to meet you. You guys sounded great out there. I liked your version of *Whiter Shade of Pale*, Mombo."

"Thanks, man."

They were setting up for a foursome around the pool table so Jack held onto his drink and sat down on a stool and leaned back against the wall to watch. The game was intense with the usual patter among men as they kidded each about the shots and made a few comments concerning a couple of women on the dance floor.

Rudy directed himself toward Mombo, "If you guys ever need some shots to help make you famous, he can get 'em down. I mean, he does some great work." He hung around a minute and then went back out to work the crowds.

After the first game, Travis came out and shook Jack's hand.

"Evenin'," said Travis, "I overheard you guys. My name's Travis Montague and we *do* need a photographer. Our producer is helping us do the final mix on a live album we cut in one of them LSU bars in Baton Rouge. Something we can sell here and at gigs, and a demo he can take to the big labels. We haven't figured out a cover design or had any publicity shots done. Not since this gang's been together, at least"

"I can dig that," Jack replied. "Let's get together and kick it around. Throw out some ideas about where you guys are at."

"If you're looking for a gig, you ought to meet our producer and our agent. They might be able to turn you onto something," said Travis. "He'll be the one paying you for any album photographs."

"Who's your producer?" Jack asked.

"Louie Thibodeaux."

"Oh, yeah?" Jack had never heard of him although Travis had dropped the name like it was important. Jack didn't know if there were any major music producers in Houston. He had followed several local bands' progress for a few years and he thought he knew the local music scene. More than anything else, he wanted to get deeper into shooting around the local music scene, the artists, bands and studios. With luck it would lead to album covers, magazine assignments and more.

"Our agent's name is Jocko, Jocko Dove," said Mombo. "He books a mess of bands around town. He's got a little cubby-hole office down on Alabama in Montrose."

"And Louie always got something going on with his acts. You got to meet him," said Mombo. "Louie is a big time producer. Me and him used to run a studio in Gulfport 'til a fuk'in hurricane blew all our shit away. That's when he moved to Houston. I came over later. He's big time, lots of gold records. Buildin' what's gonna be the best studio in Texas, too!" He said it all with a round faced, six-year old's wonderment and wide-eyed sincerity.

"That sounds like a deal." Jack replied. "Thanks for the leads." Blending the music and his photography would be a dream come true.

Later, Travis gave him some phone numbers and hints on how to get through to Louie at the studio. Their talent agent, Jocko Dove was another contact he could go see. The prospect of meeting a producer and talent agent could be a good leg up on shooting PR photos or album covers for local bands.

Jack found Rudy outside the poolroom in the alcove. He had followed the band out from the poolroom as they returned to the stage. There, in the hallway, next to Rudy, stood a five-foot doll. Rudy grabbed her hand and led her up to Jack. She was a Hispanic girl, very petite, lighter skinned than Rudy. Jack was immediately captured by something exotic and beautiful about her face.

"Jack," Rudy said, "This is my sister, Angie." Jack was shocked silent for a moment.

"You really have a sister?"

"She's a lot prettier than me, ain't she?" Rudy laughed. Angie had a light Spanish look, but with a touch of Oriental in her eyes. "Angie, this is my good friend Jack Clifford. I've been keeping you away from him so don't take advantage of the boy." He paused as the couple looked into each other's eyes.

"Ain't she a dream!" said Rudy. "We got the same Momma but different Daddy's. 'Fraid she came out with the college brains and the good looks. Jack, I hope you are prepared to provide for her, be true and raise your family according to our Christian heritage. Otherwise, why don't ya'll get out there and dance. I'll hold your gear."

"Hi Angie," said Jack. "It's good to meet you. Rudy's been keeping secrets." Angie stood before him in tight, black hip-hugger jeans with flared legs and a short, beige cotton peasant blouse. Several strands of love beads and a thin, gold chain hung around her neck. In her ears were small, gold peace symbol earrings; very much in style for a post-hippie coed.

"Jack," she said, her dark brown eyes sparkling with intelligence and interest. "I'm afraid this brother of mine doesn't tell me anything either. I'm glad you're here tonight." Long, silky black hair fell down her back, almost to her waist. She smiled, it was like a flash of sunlight in a mirror, and Jack was in love, or at least in lust. She took his hand and led him to the dance floor.

Angie looked too good to be true. They danced and he felt there was something developing between them. During the evening, they had a couple of drinks and she told Jack her Dad was from Brazil and she had a wider ethnic bloodline than could be traced. "I think I've got that Spanish, Oriental, Mexican thing all stirred up in me," she said. Mom's *puro* Chicano and Dad says he's a Portuguese and Asian mix.

"Very international," said Jack. "I'm afraid I'm from much less exotic stock. Just an Irish and British mix of Texan. They do say my ancestors were run out of Ireland for stealing horses. At least that's something notable."

He had a difficult time concentrating on his photography, but broke away a few times to get plenty of shots of individuals in the crowd.

"Are you in school or do you have a job?" Jack asked when they sat back down.

"School. Mom and Dad are supporting me while I'm in school. I only work in the summers. I'm pursuing on my Master's in Spanish literature at Rice University."

"Wow, that's some serious academics." Rice University had the reputation of an Ivy League level of education. Only top students were accepted and the courses were rigorous and demanding. Angie must be a brain, Jack told himself.

"I guess. I use my spare moments working politically to end the war and help with migrant worker's causes. Have you heard of United Farm Workers or La Raza? I have to tell you, I'm very passionate about the cause. I'm just to the right of Che and the left of McCarthy, if you can dig that?"

"I definitely can. I came that close to getting drafted last Christmas. I've had friends leave for Canada and even fake being queers to keep out of Vietnam. We've got to pull the troops out and leave those poor people to themselves. The establishment has got to be stopped from killing our brothers. Lyndon or Nixon, even Kennedy, it's all the same scene."

"Right on," she said. "I volunteered in the Valley near Harlingen last summer helping organize with Cesar Chavez's people; forming migrant worker's unions. It's not much but maybe it will make a little difference in the end. Anything to stop the oppression of our poor people, the victims. Viva La Raza, you know."

"You're obviously very compassionate. Right on!"

It was a time when students at most universities were working for "change", and waiting for the coming "revolution." The Vietnam War had driven them into new consciousness. The fallout from the *Summer of Love* had left many moving toward what they now considered "radical" action against the establishment. Jack was tuned into that effort from his time at the university. They had a few more dances during the evening and he got her phone number. Jack was very interested, captivated by this sharp and passionate girl and thought she felt the same about him.

Two a.m. seemed to come too quickly for Jack. The band was leaving, bar closing and Jack asked Angie if he could walk her to her car. She had arrived with two of her friends who were pretty well gone, and folded themselves into Angie's Falcon. Angie led Jack to the driver's door and turned.

She pulled him closer.

"Jack," she looked up at him. "You're someone special, baby, but I'm not going to sleep with you tonight."

This was out of the nowhere and he wasn't sure how to reply.

"You shouldn't be so shocked, Jack. We're just not going to have sexual intercourse tonight."

"I really didn't ask."

"I know, it just sprang into my mind and sometimes I'm just very straight forward. After all, we just met, and then there's my brother. But I might like to…someday."

"I like your thoughts that spring up, Angie.

"Me too, some are my best. But right now I think I'd better get my two drunk *muchachas* home to bed. Remember, maybe someday, but not the next time we meet."

"Now I'm getting a little confused."

"Think about someday," she said as she slid into the seat, shut and locked the door. Jack waved good-by through the side window and they pulled away. He turned and left without a kiss.

Chapter Four

Moving Down the Highway

Early the next morning Jack dialed Louie Thibodeaux's office and a woman answered the phone on the second ring. She had a young voice. He explained who he was, why he was calling and who sent him.

She was sweet, professional, and said Louie was in New York and wouldn't be available until next week. It sounded like a charming Southern bluff to buy time, but not a dead end. Jack called Travis and found out that Louie's current office was way out west on the old Hempstead Highway. Travis said Louie was there temporarily while the new studio was being finished. He also gave him the location of the new studio that was out in North Pasadena, just south of the old Washburn Tunnel that went under the Houston Ship Channel. That was on the other side of town to the east.

Jack had the morning off from his regular job at the Oshman's store and decided to investigate by driving out to Pasadena. It was about a thirty-minute trek from his apartment in the Montrose area near St. Thomas University. He loved the neighborhood and its mix of artists, hippies and students.

The Pasadena location was very obscure, almost hidden, but not far from the old "downtown" area of Pasadena. Compared to Montrose, it was another world. The new studio was just south of ship channel's row of refineries, steel and paper mills and other port industries that stretched for more than thirty miles west to east, along the channel. Not an environment to improve your vocal chords. Pasadena in the late Sixties had a reputation for polluted, smelly skies, unions and rednecks. There was an open air Icehouse bar and donut shop on every other block for the shift workers to visit before going home.

The studio building was a little rough looking, dirty and it seemed to have been a big two-story retail furniture store. Bricklayers were replacing the broken glass windows at the front with cinder block walls and closing in the front door entrance. Around the corner, behind the building, was a fair sized parking lot with plenty of loading space in the rear. Jack decided not to stop since Louie was out of town anyway and he didn't have an invitation. He headed back west toward central Houston.

Since he had nothing better to do, he decided to check out Louie's current address. From Pasadena he drove across a good part of Houston to the far northwest side. Twenty miles later on Old Hempstead Road, there wasn't very much to look at out there either. Along the semi-rural road was a string of welding shops and junkyards. Jack spotted a ratty strip center with a few occupied office spaces. One had the correct address on a yellow door with black letters reading *Thibodeaux Enterprises Inc.* On the spur of the moment, he abandoned his previous plan to only reconnoiter and pulled in.

Jack turned the aluminum door knob and walked into a very plain lobby. No celebrities in sight, no glitz or gold records on the walls. The walls were bare and painted in sort of light, cement green. No carpets on the cracked linoleum floor. There was a Formica paneled counter on the right that would be more in place in a laundry mat. A dinky radio was playing a country station in the background. Behind it was a decent looking brunette about 30 years old who was sitting at a steel desk and slitting-open mail. She turned and looked up at him and flashed a big smile.

"Hi," she said. She was wearing jeans and a blue bandera-patterned cowboy shirt.

"Afternoon," he said. "I'm Jack Clifford, the photographer. I think I talked to you this morning."

"You're a little early darlin'…like 10 days. The boss is still in New York."

"I know, I believed you the first time, but I'm on my way to College Station to see my cousin," he lied, "so I thought I'd drop in."

"I'm Mona Sinclair," she said, "like the filling stations." She giggled lightly and held her right hand out for a quick shake. "I'm Louie's office manager." The hand was hand crème soft. "Things aren't exactly swingin' today. It's been pretty quiet around here except for phone calls and the mailman"

She smiled. "So the boys in Blackplanque sent you. Bless their hearts. They are so sweet. I've known Travis and Lee forever."

Mona had a solid Texas country accent; definitely an East Texas twang. He'd put it a little East or Northeast of Houston. She put down the mail and the letter opener, and turned to the counter placing both hands on the top, folded together, as if she was ready to pray. "They just finished their live album and Louie's up there trying to sell some distribution. You like music?"

"Oh, yeah," Jack replied. "Blackplanque's a tremendous rock and roll band--way above average and nice guys. Have you heard the new album yet?"

"No, but I'll get to it sooner or later, honey," said Mona. "Everyone around Louie hears just what they are supposed to hear, and just knows what they need to know." She paused and tilted her head a little. "And I know the most." She smiled coyly and winked her right eye. "Louie is gonna want to meet you," she said. He could use some shots of the new studio construction. I'll tell him you came by, but it may be a couple of weeks before we get back to you. We'll be moving over to Pasadena and the new studio by then, I hope"

"How long have ya'll been here?" he asked.

"Oh, not long, but I've been working for Louie about nine years. We've only been here about four months. Louie's owned this shopping center dump since 1962. His business kinda got interrupted a way's back, sort of a temporary bump in the road you know. So we are looking forward to getting into the new studios."

Jack didn't mention that he had visited their new location and couldn't think of anything very positive to say about the place anyway.

"So you're ready to move out of this place," Jack said. The reception area was nearly bare. Boxes were stacked in the corners and one old office chair sat near the door. He could see a back office door but it was closed so Jack didn't know what might be beyond. He stood at the counter. "What's in the back? Do you have more room there?"

"You really don't want to know. It's a big, fat mess." He knew she had cut him off. "Pasadena isn't exactly Disneyland you know, but I'm ready. I live in Pearland, so it's gonna be a lot closer for me to get to work. Gonna save me a lot of time and gas. I had to pay nearly forty cents a gallon this morning. Plus I'll be closer to my little girl and Momma." Jack noticed she wasn't wearing a wedding ring.

"Sounds good," he said. "I'm looking forward to visiting the studio. I understand it's going to be quite a place."

"Yeah, it's a little rough right now, still a lot of work to do. I don't think he'll get it really finished for a year. We'll have three separate recording studios and a real reception area and office. Louie is finally gonna get to do it his way, like he's always wanted. Lord knows they owe him that much."

"They do?"

"You better believe it. More than you know."

"Well, the studio sounds impressive. I'll let you get back to your work," Jack said. "Good to meet you, Mona.

I'm glad I dropped by. Please give me a call when it's time."

"See ya, Jack. I'll be in touch. We could use a cute photographer around the place."

He bid her good bye and headed for work, wondering who "they" were. Jack thought about her, the strip center and what other things Louie might be into. She seemed a little flirty one moment, and mysterious the next. Nice, pretty attractive, but not exactly his type. Whatever the case, Thibodeaux Enterprises didn't look very "big time" at the moment. He had a sense that he must be missing something

It was the following Thursday when Jack's phone rang.

"Morning Jack, this here's Mona Sinclair, honey. You available today? Louie is heading over to the new studio this afternoon and wondered if you could meet him there about two 'o clock."

Luckily, it was still early enough that Jack could call in sick. "Mona, what else could be more important in my life than meeting Mr. Louie Thibodeaux," he replied.

"Hell, if I know smart ass!" she said laughing. "But you just get ready for that coon-ass, baby. You just stay in the saddle and it will work out." She gave him the address. "He's one of a kind, that Mr. Louie Thibodeaux. Now you two have a good time if I don't get there first." Jack got a kick out of her noting his sarcasm and decided Mona was smarter than she let on.

At two, Jack turned the corner in front of the "new" Pasadena Studios. No name on the front. Only an address painted on the upper left, front corner of the building. The exterior was being repainted a baby blue with a two-foot black stripe at the top. The address was in white. A few painters and other craftsmen were hard at it, finishing up the exterior. They had made quite a bit of progress since his initial drive-by.

He pulled into the back lot where he saw some other cars, and noticed a new eight-foot chain link *Hurricane* fence with a rolling gate had been built along the lot's street side. The fence continued all along the broken sidewalk to the back property line with a few tallow trees providing spots of shade. Jack parked his old Mustang convertible and saw that the same fencing went completely around the large scruffy concrete lot. Several pick-ups and a new beige Cadillac coupe were parked nearby. The back lot was now looking very secure. Apparently this place wouldn't have a front door on the street. He walked inside the open double back doors and into the large unfinished room with a high ceiling.

Jack's eyes immediately fell on a man sitting on a tall, chrome barstool in the middle of the room. He was under bright work-lights with a Coke bottle in his hand. The slouching guy was facing away from Jack, wearing green, flared polyester trousers with a white belt, white Beatle boots, and what looked like a full-cut, red short-sleeved silk shirt. His long brown hair was combed straight back to his collar, which was oversized, and stood up high. Jack stood there a minute taking in the scene with the sounds of hammering and electric saws filling the room.

One of the workers in front of the guy saw Jack and motioned that he was there behind him. The man spun around smoothly on the stool and smiled.

"Jack? Is that you brudder?" he said.

"Good afternoon," Jack replied showing him his most winning smile. "Guess the camera bag tipped you off.

Before Jack could say more, the guy hopped off the stool and opened his arms as he neared him.

"I done been waitin for you man." Jack approached him and they shook hands; first with a traditional Texas Mason's handshake, which then slid into a *hip* wrist to wrist clasp, a soul brother move that was very cool at the time. Jack went comfortably along, just like he'd been doing the past few years in college. It was the tacit sign of the times that both were cool, and anti-establishment; a brother or sister of the new culture. The guy briefly slipped his left arm around his shoulder in a semi-hug.

"I'm Louie Thibodeaux. Comin' at'cha live, in stereo and Technicolor. Man, I'm very glad you done brought your shit." he said looking at the camera and bag slung over Jack's shoulder. "I been needin' for somebody like you to show up, and here you is. How 'bout dat! The Blackplanque boys told me de liked you."

"Glad to hear it."

Louie had a hell of a Cajun accent, thick as cane syrup, like something in a movie. It was one hundred percent pure South Louisiana and Jack didn't know for sure if it was real or he was just acting the part. Whatever the case, it had a warm entertaining quality like boiled crawdads and McIlhenney Tabasco.

Mona, who had apparently been somewhere in the back, walked up to them and said, "Louie, I have your lunch. They got a phone put in and a new door for the reception area. It's a lot quieter back there."

Hi, cutie" she said to Jack. Louie turned and winked at him.

"Le's go see." said Louie, "I ain't quite hungry yet. We got enough   fo' my new friend he'ar?" Jack followed him into a finished room that looked more like a motel lobby. It had vinyl furniture, couches and chairs with end tables. Cheap, but serviceable stuff with a big purple shag rug in the center of the room. There was a chest high wooden counter of varnished blond ash off to the side. Some office desks and filing cabinets stood behind it. Jack didn't notice the closed circuit TV camera in the ceiling corner behind the counter.

"'Dis is the only'est room we got done yet," said Louie. "When we get finished," said Louie, "you gonna haf'ta go thru an armed back door to get in. Rung in you know, den travel the hallway that leads in he'ar. We got us a camera comin' that'll show Mona who's visitin'. I dun got eleven thousan' square feet down here, and sometin' or 'nuther more upstairs in the attic."

"So this won't be your office? Jack inquired.

"Oh shit no," said Louie. He put one finger beside his nose and sniffed hard. "My place is gonna be tucked way in the back, away from things. I need my privacy for bidness. If you ain't figured dis out yet," he gave Jack a grin and a squinty eye. "I'm a Cajun from up around Grosse Tete, Loosiana. See, back in dem swamps, we like to have privacy to tend to our bidness. I ain't never los' dat."

Later, Jack looked it up on a Louisiana map and found Grosse Tete, just south of Interstate 10, at the edge Des Ourses Swamp, on the Bayou Tech. That was big time swampland. He'd always heard stories about the crazy Cajuns that lived way back in that country, the swamps. Private didn't even come close to the way those folks lived. A good number of them only spoke the Cajun French. They were as far removed from the rest of American society as the Navajos in the upper plains of New Mexico or Eskimos in Alaska. It was a unique Arcadian-French culture that had survived hurricanes and alligators for two hundred years.

"We lived way back off the highway and my Daddy raised frogs for money. Send dem long green legs to restaurants in Na'Orlans. He had already done been hurt workin' for the railroad when I was borned. Got his leg a little crippled, so he got dis piddlin' pension. We'd make do with Mama packin' frogs and workin' the truck garden. Somehow dey got me thru school. Pawpaw had a little Cajun band and we'd play at church parties and joints. That's how I started in da music bidness, playing a drum and washboard. But I really wern't no good."

He waved one arm out from his side. "Dis hears gonna be Mona's spot, her parlor. Den we gonna have two studios to begin wit, one very modern you know, ladest recorders and a board from California. And the others gonna have an old fashioned tube-board. I like dat old sound. Dem tubes done break up the bass like transistors, dey got more smooth soul. Good shit."

Jack nodded his head appreciatively as if he understood every nuance and why it needed to be that way. He was trying to keep up while wading through Louie's accent.

"That's going to be nice."

"Dat's right, brudder, we're gonna call dis place Acadia International Studios, the Sound of Houston. We're gonna do some bidness he'ar. Gonna be a monster like Muscle Shoals. It's got the feel."

Louie shut the door behind him, which muffled the contractor's noise and flipped on a tape recorder that was already primed and after a couple of beeps, some soul song kicked off. He leaned on the counter next to it and looked at Jack. This guy had some eyes, Jack thought. Like a pit viper's, a crafty pit viper. He reconsidered; maybe that's too serious an evaluation. Louie seemed like a nice character overall, but he seemed to drill right through you with those eyes. That couldn't be unintended. Jack was thinking they were sort of smallish -- green and sharp as diamonds. Louie had large, wide forehead and a lot of hair. Not quite parted in the middle but a sizeable Fiftyish dark brown pompadour that was immaculately combed. His skin was a shade of an indoor-white with not much of a sign of a tanning. This was a middle-aged man, Elvis era, who was not prone to exercise. He was a little too pudgy around his middle for his medium height. They both listened to the song.

"You dig da sounds?" asked Louie, his eyes never breaking contact with Jack's, who returned his stare. "Dis is King Edward's latest R&B cuts we did in Na'Orlans last month." Jack had been taught from early on to look another man in the eyes and he was determined not to look away from the snake eyes. He'd never heard of King Edward, at least not outside of a history class, but it didn't sound bad.

Before he could reply, Jack heard the door open behind him and turned to see an over six-foot steer-wrestling type in a plaid cowboy shirt at the door. The guy was holding a hammer in his hand and looking a little sinister. But, sort of pasty looking face for a big guy, he thought. He had straight brown hair; cut short and overly neat for a Texas carpenter. He looked too slick and uptown, plus he was clean-shaven, no scruff. He had a carpenter's apron around the waist of his jeans, but he looked more like a misplaced stockbroker.

Jack looked up at him when he came in and said "Howdy." The guy looked down and through him like he was an aquarium full of dead fish. Very controlled, Jack thought, considering my winning personality. Still, he didn't look like a guy to be messed with.

"We got a problem," he said seriously to Louie. "The electrician says there's a steel beam where we want to mount the backyard security camera. It's going to take three days with a jackhammer to drive in the screws in there." He seemed pissed.

Louie paused before he spoke. His thoughts had been temporarily derailed "OK, Buck. Go out der and see if der's any other place for it, but up high, its got the look at the goddam door and gate."

"I'll take care of it, Louie." The guy nodded, and went away. "Just wanted to let you know." Louie, a little annoyed at the interruption, started back up.

"Dat's Buck Smith," Louie said before Jack could ask. "He's an old college buddy of mine. Very smart but he's done mislaid his balls. I'm lettin' him help me put dis place together 'til he finds dem again. Buck's kinda in between jobs. Good man, used to an Army Ranger, but he don't trust nobody."

"Where did you go to school?"

Louie paused a moment. "Up north…but like I said earlier we can use a really good photographer 'round the studio. I know Mona likes ya, and the Blackplanque boys… but Jack, remember dis is the music bidness and a lot of people's emotions get thrown out der on the floor when we work in a studio. Sometimes der's pressures, hurt feelin's you know. Creative people, well known acts, artists you know, der personal, private stuff is kinda hangin' out. If you gonna work with us, you gotta keep that stuff in tight. We don't put our bidness on the street." He paused, "Not on the street."

"I've kind of been on the inside before Louie," Jack answered. "A while back, when I was at the University of Houston, I worked as a journalist. Any business here is gonna stay what we called 'off the record'. Don't worry about it.   It's their private lives, right…making music brings out deep emotions, and they deserve respect." He was trying to sound sophisticated and confident of himself. "You can trust me."

Louie's pit viper rays bored into him again for a few moments. During the pause, Mona stopped shuffling the papers she was sorting and looked up. "Lots of letters and tapes are piling up Louie," she said nervously. "This move is gonna put us way behind." Louie continued staring without acknowledging her words.

"Jack, der's not too many around a studio a fella can really trust. Or in life for dat matter. Me and Mona's got trust between us. Lotta years and personal shit. Der's lots of fast money out der for secrets you know, tryin' to hustle a leg up. Desperate people do desperate things sometimes," said Louie, still keeping his eyes locked on Jack. "You gonna learn about that hangin' around dis place. I've been in the bidness a long time. But you strike me as sharp…knowin' bidness is bidness. You're a salesman I think, and I hope you're a good photographer. I've seen a lot of talent in my time, and a lot of jokers."

"Sales," he continued, "Dat's my old job…still is, but now I sell talent and sounds 'stead of boots. Boots was easier. I get you and I think dat's why I gonna like you fine brudder. You got facets. I think we are gonna get along jus' fine."

He paused and looked back at the tape deck, which was still playing King Edwards songs.

"I sure hope so, Louie."

"So do you dig R&B?" He smiled at Jack, brightening up, and like a co-conspirator, Jack nodded yes.

"I love good music, any kind." Jack said. "Play a little bad guitar, but I have to say I favor rock 'n roll and old gut-bucket blues a little over soul music or rhythm & blues. But, I like most anything, as long as it's played right."

"So you dig the sounds, dat's too much. Dat's cool. You're gonna like it he'ar." he said. "I do mostly R&B, some country and a little rock. Dat's where my big label contacts are at, and what I can sell up the bayou in New York or Nashville. Got to feel it to sell it you know. Sometimes I'm in the studio and some song a cat is singin' just makes the hair stand up on the back of my neck like a woman's touch. Dat's the magic. You feel dem hits if you blessed with the soul for it. Some folks done ever feel nuttin' and you know, I feel sorry for dem."

"I dig the sounds and I know what you mean," Jack said. "If you haven't listened to the blues when you were drunk and beat down to your knees, you'll never understand."

"Dat's it, brudder."

Jack felt like he was in, the connection was made but he didn't know who had sold whom. Maybe it was the music.

Louie took Jack around the construction site and pointed out the things he was most proud of and told him more of his plans and the studio construction fine points. Jack took pictures of just about everything. The work was nearly done on the walls and electrical. Louie said he needed photos for his bankers and they would take more next week and every week until it was finished. Jack gave him what he thought were his best prices and Louie declared it a deal.

Louie said, "You know da talent, da stars that have come out of dis area, Jack? The Big Bopper, Lightnin' Hopkins, George Jones, Doug Kershaw, Johnny Clyde Copeland, Archie Bell... man, I could go on for the next ten minutes. People up north don't realize what East Texas and dem Louisiana swamps flushes out. But dat's ok wit' me; don't get as much competition to sign dem acts."

Upstairs, Jack met another friend of Louie's. Randy Sun, a young black guy who told Jack he was a percussionist and R&B singer. So was his wife, Suze, who wasn't around. Randy was friendly and extended a soul brother handshake like Louie's' and gave Jack a brief hug.

He was working with the carpenters, but mainly as a gofer. He had one of those hyper positive, enthusiastic personalities and could have been hustling at a carnival.

It turned out Randy didn't know which end of the nail goes in the wall, but in a brief couple of minutes with him, Jack learned he was in from Watts in LA. Another soul pulled in by Louie's new studio, hoping to follow this light to stardom. Louie was paying him a little to help out construction and run errands.

While Louie talked with the electrician, Jack visited with Randy. "I'm a singer, a screamer like James Brown," he said. "I do some stuff like James, but I got my own style. You got to be different--Elvis said that. You got to do your own thing. That's what me and Suze are working on. We're going get a band together, get a bus and tour." He was cocked and ready to promote himself to stardom. Full of fast talk and dreaming dreams.

"We're going make some hits with Louie. It's all out in front of me, I can see it," Randy said.

Then he spoke to Jack quietly, in confidence. He shook his head slightly as he spoke. "You know Jack, Louie Thibodeaux's the most soulful white cat I've ever known. Me and Suze just love him. He's mostly a black like me, way down in his heart. You'll see."

Chapter Five

Spinning Wheel

Jack Clifford was back at the Basement Blues about a month after his first visit to the new studio. He was there at eight sharp to show photo proofs to the boys in Blackplanque. It was a Wednesday night and there were just a few patrons in the club. The band played Tuesday thru Saturday each week.

They had met before noon the previous Sunday at the base of *Love Street Light Circus* for a photo session. The club was on the third floor of a freestanding building near the Buffalo Bayou and next to a ratty park. It was a hazy, drab area of gray and brown on an early Sunday morning. The entire band had made it, despite a late Saturday night, but they were dragging. Their live album was in final production and nearly ready to be pressed. They were short on time to get the cover shot. Jack figured it would be painfully early for the group so he brought some coffee and donuts from Shipley's. He approached Travis first, the most talkative of the group.

"Them hippies can sure leave a mess the morning after," Travis commented with a laugh. Remnants of the previous night's revelry were scattered over the nearby park and along the street's shop fronts in the area.

"Outside of us and a couple of abandoned cars, there ain't anybody on the street."

There was no Love Street at *Love Street*. It was actually Commerce Avenue that fronted the bayou in that area -- the center of the 'Love Generation's' downtown society. These few blocks and the Montrose neighborhood a few miles to the southwest made up the co-epicenters of Houston's hippest and Hippy-est enclaves in the late Sixties and into the early Seventies. The boys in Blackplanque weren't really hippies by any stretch although they were in the right generation. They had tried marijuana and a few other hallucinogens in their search to find a higher level of artistry or amusement. They couldn't say it had hurt them and they were still occasional pot smokers. But, they didn't get too deep into the love and peace thing, since their leaders were basically country boys with conservative, rural backgrounds. Both Travis and Lee thought drugs interfered with the music. The rest of the band weren't so emphatically convicted of their conclusion. Mombo would smoke, drink or eat just about anything that came within his reach.

There were a couple of city employees drove up and began picking up the litter. Some winos were emerging from their slumbers in the alleys.

"I guess everybody's still sleeping it off." Travis continued.

"Shor it's peaceful," Mombo said in a monotone. "All the Baptists are in church and the Mex'can's haven't got their cars started yet." Everybody laughed.

"Well, I see you guys all made it. I really appreciate that." Jack said. "I don't exactly know what ya'll had in mind for the shots today, but we can try some different stuff. Let me know what you're thinking.

"I think I'm still hungry," said Jacob. He always had his top hat on, which he reset on his head constantly between shots throughout the morning.

"I've told you time and again mate," Mel said in his lowest English accent. "You can eat me." Mel also had an offbeat sense of humor along with his uncultured English accent. He had the most well balanced disposition in the band. Mel just flowed, "like the English countryside," he'd say.

"I think I'll just whip your royal ass instead," replied Jacob. He was tall and slim and was wearing union soldier trousers and an old cut-away tux coat.

Mel's wife and Jacob's girlfriend showed up about that time to check out what was happening. It was the first time Jack had met either of them. Mel's wife was a slender

Australian with a Judy Collins look. Mel said she occasionally would drop by late at the club for a cold beer and to listen to the band. She told Jack she worked as a waitress in one of the better restaurants downtown. Jacob's girlfriend drove a cab. He met her when he first got off the plane from the East Coast. Jacob had hired her to drive him around the Houston area. They started talking, and she drove over 135 miles that evening, costing him $79. Houston was a big sprawling place. Jack hadn't met Travis' girl who was a co-ed at Texas Women's University in Denton. Mombo's wife Dee Dee stayed home, cooking, Jack supposed.

It was an overcast day with a little low mist that Jack considered perfect. A bright, sunny day in Texas would mean deep shadows that were tough on faces. Soft lighting was hard to come by along the Texas coast. They had convened a brief meeting at the blues club a couple of nights before and decided the grubby streets and alleys around Buffalo Bayou might be just funky enough to give them what they were looking for.

Jack decided to do a series of shots along the bayou in the reeds, bushes and brush along the bank. It was a good place to start because they could horse around and get it out of their systems. They were nervous and helpless in setting up the shots. There was no model potential for any of them.

They shot later in an alley stairway where a wino wandered up, stopped and stood just behind Jack's shoulder, occasionally offering his direction to Jack or the boys as to how to pose. He smelled like the streets and a serious hangover and Jack inched away from him as he shot. But the wino, who called himself Sonic, wasn't going to let him disengage and would immediately resume a position looking close over Jack's shoulder whenever he paused to shoot. He could tell from the band's expressions, that they thought it was hilarious. When they paused to change location, Jack turned to see him still close behind.

"Pretty good shots weren't they," Sonic said. Jack couldn't figure how he could see anything from behind those blood shot eyes.

"Yeah, I think we got some good ones," Jack replied.

"You bet'cha," Then he held out his hand. "You think I could get a little something for helping out?"

"Well, I guess," Jack didn't even try to question his efforts and they all gathered up about four bucks and he went on his way with a "good luck" towards all and 20/20 wine on his mind.

"You ought' a hire that Sonic guy as an assistant" said Mombo.

"You bet'cha."

The final location was on the street where they borrowed some trash receptacles and pick-up sticks from the curious street cleaners and the band took various poses leaning against buildings and street lamps, while other members posed as the workers. Jack was fairly satisfied with the results and felt he would like the alley shots best. Maybe Sonic had talent.

Late that night of the following week, they sat in the club manager's office and surveyed the results. They were "gassed" with the photographs. Over the coming months, Jack discovered that most performers seldom saw photos of themselves that they didn't swoon over. The women might be skeptical of their hair or dress but they would still inevitably dwell over the shots and ask to keep the proofs. At first it was flattering to Jack but he soon realized they were either feeding their own egos, or bargaining for a lower price. Most of the *artists* would appreciate any photographs of themselves in their musician's role. The realities of the business made them cautious hagglers.

Blackplanque was surprisingly professional about editing and selecting the picture they wanted for the album cover. For the back cover, Jack suggested that they get some additional live action shots of them playing in the club, and that really turned them on.

Travis and Lee were to take the color shots to Louie the next day to get his opinion and listen to the mix-down of the live cuts for the album. Mombo had been in the AIS studio the past week with an engineer, trying to finish up the mix for the record.

The band had agreed that his studio experience made Mombo the man for the job.

Sunday night, after he had spent the morning shooting Blackplanque, Jack went over to Angie's apartment. There was a movie, *Blow-Up* that she wanted to see. It was about a hip British photographer who witnesses a murder, so Jack was interested. Angie answered the door in a long-sleeved, red silk blouse and black mini-skirt. Her black leather boots and gold look earrings completed the effect and Jack was again mesmerized.

"We are becoming an item," she said. "Do you realize we are seeing each other almost every day?"

"I believe you're right," Jack said. "And don't forget the nights." They were spending more time together each week and their relationship had grown over the past month. They had taken it slow, making an honest effort to get to know each other. Both liked what they saw and were feeling closer with each conversation and kiss they shared. But, these feelings were heating up the relationship.

"You're exceptional, Angie. You've become an essential part of my day. I'm not sure when that happened, but it's the truth. You look great," He took her hand and they walked to the car.

"Thank you, baby. I'm very happy being with you. I love the time we spend together. You're pretty special to me also. *Pobrecito* you."

"*Pobrecito yo?*"

"You'll see. My family says I'm a hand-full."

"I bet they're right about that. But I don't mind, as long as they're my hands."

He had gained in admiration for her and determination. She was a little radical and more into her politics than Jack. Partially due to his friendship with Rudy, he hadn't wanted to get too involved unless there was something there to take seriously. But, Jack liked everything he had discovered about Angie, and it seemed that she felt the same. There was something serious and something fun developing between them and it felt good.

The movie was tremendous. They analyzed the story afterward and the underlying symbolism, as they drove back to her place. Jack told her more about his photo shoot with Blackplanque. She thought his story of the wino assistant was hilarious and put her own twist on the event.

"You should have given that poor old thing more money," she said. "Society has just cast people like him aside. The system just beats them down and keeps them there. He's just representative of the oppression in society."

"Aw, he would have just got that much drunker," Jack replied.

"I would too if I was sleeping in an alley. It's not right."

They arrived at her place and stepped inside the apartment.

"Do you turn on?" she asked as the door shut. "It's strange we haven't really talked about that. I mean we've been dating over a month now."

"You mean grass or something stronger."

"Oh, just a little marijuana, sugar. I stay away from the other junk. Just a little pot now and then to relax out. I like to smoke a little and listen to music or read poetry. It puts me in a new place with art."

"I know what you mean. It's about as far as I've traveled up that highway."

"I've got brownies in the refrigerator," she said. "Magic brownies for the *high* way."

"You're kidding," Jack rolled his eyes. "You bake?"

"Just for special occasions and holidays."

She went to the icebox and took out an unopened bottle of *Boones Farm Apple Wine* she had cooled as well as a covered bowl of the brownies.

"This is a good year for apple wine," he said staring at the label. "1970 from the Vineyards of Boone's." He unscrewed the metal top and filled a couple of small jelly jar glasses.

"These guys I shot are really good," said Jack going back to the conversation about the band. "But, I'm not sure what it would take to get Blackplanque to be a big-time act. Probably a lot of luck to go with their talent."

"It sounds like you really like those guys," said Angie. She handed Jack a brownie. "The drink of university champions," she said and took a swallow of the apple wine. Angie coughed and followed with a laugh. "This shit is terrible! It cost me a dollar and nineteen cents at the 7/11."

"Well, you can't beat the price."

"Well," he toasted her glass with a click, "To Rice champions and their friends." He took a sip. "It is a little sweet, but soothing. But, yeah, they're really good musicians. You've heard them. Did you hear anything exceptional?"

"I'd like to see them be successful," she said, "I've sure never heard any better in a club. But Jack, I don't think I've got much of an ear for music. I like the beat, the rhythm, I can get into that, but I'll tell you a secret, I'm more tone deaf than not. That's why you'll never hear me sing," she laughed.

They stepped through the beaded curtain between the kitchen and living room.

"You care," she said. He followed her to the couch. "I like that. Your passion for your photography, music, your musician friends."

"Don't forget my passion for you." He squeezed her hand and they sat together on the couch.

"I won't," said Angie. "But, I imagine there are a million bands out there like them. Just like there are lots of talented writers and actors and poets. I suppose some artists are just lucky to be in the right spot at the right time."

"Yeah," said Jack. "I'm beginning to see that there's a lot of talented people in the business, but maybe only a few talented and lucky people. Maybe that's the way it is all over."

"Maybe I'll be the talented and lucky Spanish lit student who wins a Fulbright Scholarship and a year studying in Spain," she said. "That would be so groovy." She took a long drink and went back into the kitchen for the bottle.

"I hope you will be that student. You make me proud, Angie," said Jack. He refilled both of their glasses again and they toasted each other again and followed that with a quick kiss and another brownie. He looked in her eyes and could see she was starting to get a buzz on. "So here we are, young and alive in the land of the free."

"Oh yeah," said Angie, "I've got my bachelor's degree; I'm matriculating at Rice, quasi-liberated. All that shit, but I'm still frustrated or lost. I think it's one or the other. Working on my Masters and still dependent on my parents despite the scholarships. I'm not really free am I? I need to find employment eventually and support myself some day. But even that's still not real freedom."

"I don't know how free or liberated any of us are," said Jack. "Everybody's working for somebody or something." Angie moved up to the front edge of the couch. There was a long silence, or so it seemed. Jack wasn't real sure; the pot was seeping into their thoughts and distorting time.

"It's our society... America," she said. "The civilized world. It can't let a truly *free* man or woman survive. We're all just Play-Doh being molded into the system. That's what pisses me off, man! I just put my finger on it." There was an obvious break in her thoughts.

"You know what pisses off," she said and turned to Jack. She didn't wait for an answer. "What a liberated woman means in society. I'll let you in on the conspiracy. I've been taking these women's history classes about the growth of women's rights through the ages. See, there's a movement building in the universities and in big cities right now. Women's Rights. But you know, despite all of our apparent progress, nothing elemental has changed in America."

"So you don't have equal rights?" said Jack "There are more women in universities, science and business. Hell, you can vote and pretty soon women will be marrying each other for all I know. At least the disagreeable ones."

"Now you've stepped in it!" she smiled. "Jack, I recognize that you're just trying to provoke me. You're on."

"I am?" Jack was trying to feign innocence but he knew he had stepped off a cliff and could do nothing to save himself. He might as well enjoy the fall, he told himself. "On what?"

"You know what I'm talking about!" Angie was instantly torqued up, not mad, but exhilarated. "The Civil Rights Movement isn't about just the blacks in our society. The women's movement is a reality. But our quest for rights is still defined by men." She was on a run. "Men run the media and the universities…and business and politics and everything else on earth. And they see women's liberation as just something sexual. They demand that it be defined on sexual terms, not social or political. They are the power pigs. Always sex, first, foremost, forever. Anyone in the movement must be a lesbian, *right*? The critics go right for the sexual instead of the content of the message. Now we're being called women's libbers. What the hell is that? We want an even chance in society, not to sleep with each other. We're fighting the system just like the blacks and the Chicanos and Indians. Most men must be idiots!"

She had exhausted herself and spaced out; she picked up a brownie and began to examine it closely. "Look at all those pecan chips, all broken."

Jack reached for the glasses.

"I don't know if I need more wine," Angie said. "I'll just have this brownie."

"Men are only idiots to the women around us," said Jack. "We have our reasons behind everything we do. Most women just don't understand us."

"To hell we don't! And that makes no sense."

"You're right. I'm not sure what I meant." For some reason he smiled at his confusion. "Broken nuts."

"For men, there's not much understanding of needs, needed. It's just to get us in bed, to dominate us, which is the ultimate double-edged sword." She was on a roll.

"Why?" Jack was fighting a little to keep his train of thought on the tracks. "Which needs?"

"Because nowadays if you're liberated and you act liberated, it's almost by definition that you're an easy lay or gay. Men assume that it's either, or."

"Hadn't thought about that, but right on"

"Don't be sarcastic! Of course you hadn't thought about it, you're a man! But if a woman is liberated and she likes a guy, then there it is. She has to submit to him. That's the paradox."

"Submit to him! What kind of archaic thinking is that? Look around us; I think most people are submitting to each other voluntarily. This love generation that we're part of is so busy *submitting,* they'll never get around to the revolution everyone is singing about."

"You're hopeless my dear," said Angie. "I love you, but you're not changing my opinion that everything, every movement in the United States is defined by men. Mostly rich, white men by the way, and the mass media they run."

"That's me, except for the rich part. It's *The Man,* man."

"You're right, in more ways than one. The pigs run the world."

"You got it." He took another sip and Angie reached out and got a brownie for Jack. Angie held it in her hand and gazed off for a moment and then looked back to Jack.

"Nuts," she said. "Held together by fudge." He took it from her hand but set it down. Things were getting very spacey for each of them. Angie managed to unzip her boots and kicked them off. She leaned back into the couch and tucked her feet under her. She looked at Jack, still poised on the edge of the couch in case of more intense discussion and staring at a candle burning on the table.

"Come here," she said. "Relax. I don't know what got into me." Jack slid closer and she reached out and pulled him over on top her as she leaned back on the pillows. She put her hand behind his neck and pulled him close. They kissed and cuddled for a few minutes and the intensity built. She eased herself up from under him and looked in his eyes.

"Sorry about the tirade, must be the chocolate. You said you were proud of me earlier. I'm not sure what you meant. Are you still?"

"Of course, I think you're fantastic."

"Thank you," she said and smiled. "You sound like your taking ownership." She awaited a response. None came. He wasn't sure what this liberated woman was thinking and didn't want to rekindle the liberation debate. "You know, parents say their children make them proud. So do brothers and aunts and teachers. How would you describe yourself--why I make you so proud? What is our relationship?"

Her words sounded serious but before he could worry, he noticed the teasing sound in her voice and saw a sly smile on her face.

"I'm the steady boyfriend, I hope."

"You are the very steady boyfriend, if you wish to be," Angie said with certainty. She stood up carefully.

"I do wish to be." He stood and kissed her.

"OK." She thought for a minute. "Don't' think this is the wine and weed talking, Jack. I like the sound of very steady boyfriend, straight or stoned. I like the feel of it too, like right now."

"Yeah."

"Very steady boyfriend, would you mind if I go take a shower? It's been a long day and I feel a little grimy. I need something to brighten me up." She gave him a quick peck. "You just sit tight and finish your wine. Just watch TV or something. OK?"

"All right Angie. I think I'll just listen to some music and investigate your women's history library. Maybe I'll learn something."

"I'm looking forward to that!" she laughed and walked toward the bedroom, unzipping the back of her skirt as she went. "We'll figure out the rest of the evening when I get back."

"Alright, baby."

Angie bumped lightly into the door jam as she went into the bedroom. "Wow," she said. "I guess I must be a little ripped. You better go easy on those brownies, they're loaded too."

She giggled, straightened and shut the door. Jack went to the kitchen and dumped out the remaining wine in his glass and refilled it with tap water. He took a drink and decided he'd had enough wine and brownies. Back in the apartment's living room, he dropped down on his knees to peruse her book collection. I've got to get straight, he thought. He wasn't nearly ready for the short drive home on Montrose's streets. The Houston cops were everywhere at night, and looking for someone to hassle.

The bookshelf was typical student furniture. A series of stacked cinder blocks with unpainted one by eight pine boards serving as shelves. They were slightly warped in the middle from the weight. She had a generous collection of Spanish textbooks about the language, history and several dozen novels and novellas. Apparently she had sold or traded off her books from the undergraduate years except for economics and accounting textbooks. There was also the usual student collection of classic novels that every student plows through on the way to a degree. He pulled out an art survey book and sat on the floor, skimming the pages for interesting paintings.

In a few minutes she reappeared in a navy blue silky bathrobe. Small gold ball earrings peeked through her brown hair. Her makeup was gone but it didn't matter with her dark features. She looked refreshed but her eyes were closed slightly more than usual. Still a little high, he figured. Despite her shower, her hair was dry and flowed down her chest. Just as the first time he had seen her, she reminded him of a perfect doll with long deep, almost black, hair and enticing eyes. Again, Jack was stunned at the view.

"Please stand up," she said. He did and she walked up to him.

"I think I need a little more time before I head for home." he said. "I'm still a little wasted. Do you mind?"

"It's ok. Jack, the brownies aren't the only surprise I've got for you. Since that first night, I've been saving something for you. Something I've thought about often since that night. You remember?"

"I try not to forget anything about you." He looked in her brown eyes and could see a soft mellowness that the evening had instilled."

"It will tell you all you need to know about our relationship."

She took his hand and led him into the bedroom. Her bed was turned down with a plush quilt at the foot. She drew him near to her. "You are my boyfriend," she repeated the words, and whispered in his ear, "My very special, steady boyfriend -- I love that and I think I love you."

She pressed her body against him and whispered. "And, Jack…I would like it if you also became my lover. I am a liberated woman and all that, but I'm giving myself to you for as long as you might want me."

"I understand," he said. He looked into her eyes. "I want you too, completely. I think you know that. I want you more than anything."

His hands went down to her hips and they kissed. The smooth fabric across her bottom felt slightly damp to his touch.

"I guarantee I'll be a lot to handle. But, I don't want to wait any longer for you," she said. Angie pulled back and began to unbutton his shirt.

"Just be mine. I'll see just how hard to handle you are."

"I never told you this Jack, but I'm on the pill."

"It certainly takes the worry out of being close. You're full of surprises this evening. So we can just relax and enjoy each other."

"Yeah." She was excited and laughed. "Well, may have heard about us liberated Rice gals. We take care of ourselves. I want all of you tonight."

"I want you too." His shirt came off and her hands went for his belt. He pulled the sash on her robe and it opened to him. There was nothing underneath but Angie.

"But don't think we'll let a man get off easy."

"I won't."

Her head tilted deeply to the left and she dipped down, taking him with her onto the bed. He folded in beside her. She rolled away briefly and turned off the table lamp on the other side of the single bed. They met in the middle and began to discover more about each other.

Jack spent the night and they both sprang up the next morning fresh with this new romance, despite a major loss of sleep. Angie had an early class and Jack needed to be across town to a photo shoot at an electronic manufacturing facility. She jumped in the shower while Jack made coffee. After a few minutes of hurried conversation, they kissed and told each other of their happiness with the previous night and their delight in waking up together.

"It is a new day for us Angie," said Jack

"I love it, bye lover," she said. "I'll call you tonight."

She did.

Chapter Six

In The Heat of the Night

The new studio was located in a neighborhood that was intimidating enough in daylight. At night it was a strange, dark trip that sort of spooked Jack. Mona had called him that morning to see if he could come in about 10 pm and shoot a late night recording session.

The area was spotted with old houses occupied by poor Hispanics, rednecks, blacks or an occasional old, white couple who seemed to have lived there forever. Shotgun shacks and occasional ratty trailers were on weedy lots amid small businesses and the steel warehouses that completed the area. Most of the homes and buildings dated back to at least to the Thirties and Forties. The blocks were away from most traffic and Pasadena's main streets and neighborhoods. Street lamps were few and scattered randomly on the streets. It was not far from the ship channel's turning basin in East Houston. The Houston's ship channel ran for miles thru Channelview, Pasadena and Texas City and finally into Galveston Bay. Pasadena was a town built on the tough jobs in the refineries, paper mills and freight docks of the port. It could be rough.

Before oil and chemicals swamped the area, Pasadena had been a thriving land of strawberry farms.

Acres that were now criss-crossed with pipelines that ran through blue collar neighborhoods.

Few people chose to live in this area if they had other options. Pollution and the threat of nearby refineries exploding didn't do much for property values. Even patrolling cops usually skipped these streets unless a disturbance brought them in.

Jack wheeled into the studio's back lot, after seeing that the rolling, chain-link fence gate was open. It was moderately well lit with a few yellow "no-bug" lights above the back wall and doors.

Inside, Jack had to search for a minute to find the crew. Louie was busy directing his entourage in Studio A. Almost everything in the studio was cleared to the walls except for the grand piano and the big Hammond B-3 organ. A Leslie speaker and Moog Synthesizer sat against the wall. A dozen microphone stands were already set up around the room with another half dozen mics wired up and lying on the floor with their cords snaking to plugs in the walls. The ceiling work lights were up rather than Louie's "mood" lights, which were set on the walls and in the ceilings. Along the back wall of the studio were four sound-deadened booths where a singer or instrument could be isolated. The big one, left-center could hold a sizable drum kit, if needed.

All of the studio walls were composed of the same cushy, deep padding and peach colored burlap fabric floor to ceiling. Inside was eight-inch cushioning of batts of a synthetic straw-like material. It had a deep, dark brown patterned rug. The dead sound of the room was incredible. Walking in from the hall made your ears hurt from the lack of echo, like negative sound. It was always disconcerting at first. Notes and voices went into the walls and ceiling and disappeared. The sound of silence.

Louie saw Jack come in and said, "Glad you could make it brudder, Lucinda's on her way. Her bus is limpin' in on I-10 a few miles out. We're just about ready he'ar."

Jack didn't know who Louie was talking about but he assumed it was the band that was to record that night. He'd find out who they were soon enough and didn't need to ask. This was the first full recording session that Jack had been invited to attend.

Jack went into the recording booth and Louie came in and sat down behind the board with a tall, skinny dude to his left. Jack hadn't seen him before. The new guy stood up and extended the hand without the lit cigarette. He had a long ponytail tucked into the back of his jeans and a scruffy beard. Jack also noticed there was a pair of chubby legs in khaki shorts and tan moccasins sticking out from under the console on the far end.

"I'm Shingles Malone," the skinny dude said to Jack with an unusually resonant voice. The name rang a bell with Jack but he couldn't place it immediately.

"Good to meet you," Jack replied, and introduced himself. They did the soul man handshake and he sat back down.

Louie spoke up next.

"Shingles is helping out a little this evening with the engineering. You've probably heard him on KLUG." That was it. He was one of the wilder DJs on Houston's hottest underground FM rock and roll station. He played the latest, hottest and most acid laden rock. The fine line of his patter on air was laced with drug and sexual references that tread a tricky path, considering Nixon's FCC.

"Now, Shingles," Louie said, "Moonie done told me that he'd heard about you in Nashville. He special asked for you to do dis tonight. You buildin' a reputation as a studio engineer, brudder. You know that."

"Oh, yeah?" said Shingles.

"But *you* done it. The trouble with a good reputation is you got to live up to it every time you sit down behind dis board. People gonna always expect the best, the greatest from you."

"I'll do my best tonight, Louie."

"I know. I just wanted you to know what was happenin'. You got a shot at doing some recordin' gigs in Nashville if you keep pleasin' Moonie. Moonie is a king big shot wit' the record company. You come to his notice."

Jack snapped to the transaction. He pondered Louie's ability to get the best from those around him. Or at least what he wanted. And he realized he was as susceptible as the guy sitting at the board to Louie's persuasion. Flattery, veiled threats or the promise of a bright future, were all in his bag of tricks. Shingles was glowing although he kept it somewhat covered by his laid back, cool slouch.

"Shingles, Jack here is my doctor of photography. I didn't know it 'til right now, but dat's who he is. He's got what de call the da demeanor. Must be the college in him dat done reminds me of a doctor."

"I guess, I'll take that as a compliment Louie," said Jack.

"Damn right!" said Louie.

"Queenie!" Louie suddenly turned and shouted. There was a dull thump followed by a shrill yelp, which seemed to come from further up the legs under the mixing board.

"Louie," there came a soft, but pained voice from under the console. "You scared me and I banged my head. You must stop that! I insist. I just can't work like this if you keep making me so nervous."

"Aw Queenie, jus' tryin' to find out where you was," said Louie. He smiled at Shingles and Jack. "You know I get worried when I can't see you ass," Louie purred.

Louie winked at Shingles and Jack and continued. "You get that thing fixed down der. Keep you hands on the wires and off your din-a-ling. We gonna get started pretty soon. And you be careful. I don wan' to drag you' electrified self out from under the board."

"Yes," said Queenie. "Just leave me alone for a minute and I can finish. You're making me nervous as a bonnet of bees.

Louie turned to them. "Dat's Brucie Berg down der," he said. "Finest electric engineer that money can buy. I flew him in from LA dis week to make sure the board is got all dem transistors is wired up good. That's where I got it from, out in LA. I jus'calls him Queenie, out of affection. He kinda come with the deal. You're da genius, Queenie," he said.

"Love me all you want Louie, but you know I'm taken." Queenie replied.

"Yeah, yeah. You know fellas; he's got a boyfriend, Brad, out der in Hollywood."

"Bradley has a major role in *All My Children*," said Queenie. "And I'm missing it. That's why I'm so frustrated and lonesome."

"Don't worry, dear, I think we gonna get you back home to you sweetie tomorrow night."

Queenie emerged from under the board and they were introduced. Jack and Shingles received a soft handshake; an inquisitive smile and a sweeping look from him, head to toe.

I'm Bruce Berg," he said. "And I wouldn't be here if I could be back in LA, but one has to do certain things to survive in this business. I hope we can be friends. He was a peevish five foot two and a couple of hundred pounds topped by short, curly bleached, blond hair that reminded Jack of a California poodle. He had that west coast, oily tan that gave him a funky Hollywood touch along with carefully shaped eyebrows.

"Certainly," Jack said. Shingles gave him a quick smile and sat back down. Queenie retreated to a stool in the corner of the booth to await Louie's next command.

"I just feel like a slave sometimes," said Bruce quietly.

Louie spun around.

"Lookie here, Queenie." Louie flared up at him. "You know why you here and why you gonna be here as long as I need you. You know what I'm talkin' about."

Bruce jumped in place. "I want to go home."

"You gonna go home when I tell you, you can go home. You done fukked up and my friends saved your ass from jail. You da one dat can't leave da schoolboys alone. You remember what de done for you? Now you gettin' me pissed."

Louie left the control room and went into the studio and lay down on the deep carpet. Jack looked over at Bruce.

"I've never seen Louie that pissed," Jack said to him.

"I am doomed, mere chattel," said Bruce. "They'll own me forever."

Louie lay on the floor a few minutes with his eyes shut. Getting up, he came back in the mixing booth. Jack was worried about what was about to happen to Queenie. Louie was steamed and had a sinister look in his eyes when he walked out. Jack didn't look at Bruce who was trying to make himself disappear into the corner of the room. He felt like he could hear him sweat.

"Tell you what's goin' down tonight, Jack," said Louie to Jack. "Lucinda Black is comin' in to cut a few songs. Dis evening kinda what you said a while back, 'off de record'. She and her band ran a little cash short 'cause the bus blew its stack in Louisiana couple of days back. So I'm gonna slip dem a little help tonight and we're gonna cut some tracks. Get'em back on the road."

"That sounds good," Jack said. Fortunately, he knew enough to know that Lucinda Black was a legend in the black rhythm & blues clubs across America. She had only had one crossover hit in the pop charts back in the late fifties, but it was enough to give her name recognition beyond R& B fans, black and white. She did pretty well in Europe as well, not that unusual for American black singers with blues or jazz roots. This would be a chance to hear blues from a great blues lady in a very intimate setting.

"Trouble is dey is under contract to Knighthawk Records and der in town to do an album for 'ole man Knight. See, he won't give dem shit until the record gets done and released, but dey got to get back on the road and tour in Illinois. So, Lucinda called me and we gonna do a little arrangement where I won't do nothin' with the stuff from dis evenin' until she gets in between contracts."

Jack nodded. Blackhawk Records, he hadn't met him, but Douglas Knight was a renowned black record producer who was now in his seventies. He'd been recording music in Houston since after World War II. He had recorded some of the best of gospel, blues artists and rhythm and blues bands in the nation.

"Dem old black motherfukers like Knight treat their acts bad," said Louie. "De don't never give dem a break. See…a white producer wouldn't think about doin' a Black act like dat. And a Black artist wouldn't take that kind of shit from no honky. Dat's the difference you see. It's jus' the way it is. Everbody understands dat!"

"Lucinda's stuff's like gold," said Louie. "A few years from now I might sell it off to a major or release it myself on a new label. Maybe break even. She'll sign dis little contract letter and I'll just leave the date blank. You know I wouldn't do dat usual, but the sister needs some help."

Jack was impressed by Louie's plan and that he seemed to be sympathetic to Lucinda's plight, so he put this event "off the record."   Whatever "front" money Louie would give them tonight would keep them on the road where they could make their money from shows. Lucinda was rarity in blues music. She was one of only a few black women who had balls enough to tour with her own band in a bus. Jack had seen her once or twice on TV and she looked attractive, but a little tough.

Louie finally looked over at Queenie.

"You done?" asked Louie.

"Yes."

"Get out of he'ar," he said. "Jus' go back to the motel and we'll talk tomorrow. Maybe 'bout you going home."

Queenie nodded and slipped out of the room.

"Damned crazy faggot," said Louie. "But he's da best."

Chapter Seven

Rollin' n Tumblin'

Lucinda Black showed up about an hour later and her band piled off the bus where most had apparently been sleeping. These guys were the real thing. Living, barely breathing bluesmen and a lady. This old black rhythm and blues band had no one under forty or fifty years old. A couple of the horn players looked like they might be WWII veterans. Musicians that were beat up, scarred, and worn from decades on the road. If this group, road weary from too many one-night stands in a row, didn't have the blues, no one would. They looked resigned to another late night.

The first musician stumbled off the bus and walked up to Jack who was at the door of Studio A.

"You got a smoke, man?" the musician asked. He stood slightly stooped and his hand with two cocked fingers came up to his lips but there was no cigarette.

"No, sorry, I don't smoke."

"Shee'it," he moaned. "I could sure use a smoke. How about a couple of quarters for a Coke? I seen a machine in the lobby and we've been 600 miles tonight, all the way from Baton Rouge."

"I didn't think that was but a couple of hundred miles," Jack said innocently.   Jack was either testing or teasing him, depending on the reply.

"Yeah man," he paused for a moment, and then grinned. "But you see...we got lost." The old guy grinned widely. The whites of his eyes were a golden jaundiced yellow against his ebony skin. The combination reminded Jack of drapes his aunt in San Angelo once had in her front room.

"So you ain't got any smokes?"

"No."

"Lucinda, my lady, it's great to see you...long time baby." Louie said sweeping into the room. Lucinda was taller than Louie or Jack with a strong, but feminine build. She looked like she was in her forties. She smiled at Jack and said, "Hey man."

Jack nodded a reply.

"Lookie he'ar," Louie spoke to the group. "I got some drinks, barbeque, all dat shit in parlor down der. Show my boys your drums, instruments, amplifiers, whatever and we'll get started settin' up. Let's get 'em in before dos mosquitoes get to dem an' carry 'em off." The studio crew helped with the gear.

"How'd you make out in Baton Rouge?" Louie asked Lucinda, pulling her close.

"Oh, I cleared a couple of few hundred from the gig. I need some new fans that ain't sitting' in wheelchairs."

It didn't take long to get their instruments, drums and couple of personal amps off the bus and into the studio. Two engineers started setting up for the session, all of it under Louie's watchful eye. Jack enjoyed watching how Louie's natural handling of the people around him nearly always got the results he wanted. Charismatic; he moved them without anyone being aware of his persuasiveness. He had just the right words or body language to reach whomever he met.

Lucinda's stage band, the Blacksmiths, consisted of a drummer, keyboard man, guitar and bass for the rhythm section. Then she had horns: a sax man, trombone, and trumpet, seven in all. They traveled in an old band bus that was black and silver and had a red blaze of type sown each side, *Lucinda Black and the Blacksmiths, Tuscaloosa, Alabama. U.S.A.*

After some barbeque, potato salad and cherry pie, the band eased back into the studio where Louie and Lucinda were going over some lyric sheets and tab pages that were to be distributed to the band. Her hair was cut short, not much over a half-inch long. Jack figured she wore wigs on stage. Must make it a lot easier on the road. There were about a dozen proposed songs to record. About half were blues standards that the band was familiar with. Jack figured that they could knock them out in their sleep and probably had on some nights. Louie was explaining to the engineers that the horns might or might not be used from song to song. Later, Jack realized that Louie owned the writer's rights on about half the songs. He had cut many of these songs before, with different artists, to distribute on their LP's, to build up his royalties

Louie explained to Shingles that the most important thing was to wait for the rhythm section to find a groove for each song and get those tracks down. The vocal would be recorded along with them but might be overdubbed. An arranger would add horns, strings and back up voices sometime later. He was coaching him, and teaching Shingles his style.

Jack discovered later that neither Lucinda nor the band would hear the finished product until they had the album was on the stands. An album like this was beyond the artistic control of the face on the album cover. The record would probably show up years later on bargain racks or ethnic record stores. There would be no sales royalties for Lucinda, just the front money and the good will of Louie. That was the deal. Any profits after tonight would be all Louie's. He was just placing a bet tonight to cash in down the line.

After tuning up and running through a couple of their regular set songs, they were ready. Rough sound levels for each instrument and the vocal had been set in the studio. Just to improve things, a couple of bottles of whiskey were cracked open and every one got their first taste after dinner, although a couple of the members looked like they had started getting their "thang on" a little earlier. Lucinda took a shot along with the band. Louie had Jack shoot some photos of Lucinda and him for PR purposes before the session started. Jack had the same problem he always faced with Louie's black acts. Louie, who was a pale white, had on a deep red shirt and black Lucinda was wearing a white blouse thus making his best shot at a correct exposure for the flash impossible. He'd tried to explain it all to Louie one afternoon but got him confused. Louie intended to promote some of his first visitors to the new studio in the industry magazines. The reason for the visit wouldn't be mentioned in the press release for the record and music media.

Jack's first illicit late night blues session with an old blues artist in need of fast cash was about to start. In the control booth Louie asked Lucinda, "How much for da boys?"

"$100 apiece will make them happy."

"So that's $700 for them and $2,000 for you. Lucinda, jus' sign dis and I'll stick a date on it later. As far as you and me remember, we did dis little thing four years ago when you way between Ozone and Knighthawk labels. OK?"

"You got it Louie. It's a pleasure doing some business with you."

Louie took a large roll of bills out of his pocket and counted over 27 one hundred dollar bills to Lucinda who folded them up and put them in her back blue jeans pocket.

"I ain't givin' them nothin', until this night is over," she said.

"Dat's up to you, sugar. Here fellas'" said Louie. He gave Jack and Shingles a hundred each. "Dis is jus' for you time."

Louie cut the studio glare by cutting off the work lights and turned up the blue and gold mood lights on the walls. A few classics were first on the bill. There was finer tuning on the control board for the drums and vocal compression and echo were set. In the semi-darkness of the "mood" lights, they began rolling from song to song and finding the groove for the night. The muted lights softened the studio and made it more intimate. Louie could not have cared less if Lucinda had recorded the same songs before on another album, although that surely violated a prior contract somewhere. It was all the better if fans recognized a favorite hit song on back of the cover of a future album. Some buyer might realize later that the song was not the same cut as the original hit, just a minimalistic version, but that would be too late.

The drummer was working with the bass and the guitar punctuated the rhythm with tasteful licks. It didn't take a music critic to know this was a real blues take going down. They had found their groove. These were guys that lived their lyrics, old time pros.

Lucinda had a soft, mellow voice that could move from a melodic whisper to a frustrated scream like a caged cougar. Jack could hear the reason she was a star in R&B. She had something special, magic even on an off-stage night like this.

"Dem strategic screams is what makes it," Louie said and shook his head from side-to-side in sympathy to the blues Lucinda was singing. "Der ain't nuttin' like it.

The session continued along with the shots of booze between numbers. The first bottle died a quick death and another was cracked open. After about an hour, the whiskey and the groove came together and the band hit their stride. It was beautiful as they laid down a half a dozen tracks, which included some old standards like, Lowell Fulsom's, *Trouble in Mind*, *Georgia* and Janis Joplin's *Piece of My Heart*, just to prove Lucinda could do the modern stuff as well.

Three hours into the session, after a short break, things started to change for the worse. It was well pushing two am. Lucinda started getting on the drummer for dragging the beat. Her energy seemed endless, probably assisted by the little black pills and BC Powders Jack saw her swallow after midnight. The drummer was a skinny guy, one of the youngest of the group, but seemed to be getting a little too mellow up from the booze or fatigue.

Lucinda suddenly held her hand and stopped the band in mid-song and turned to the drummer, shouting at him, "Man, would you get it going. Wake up, you lazy bastard! We got work to get finished here. Don't just keep the beat, push it man." She looked around the room to see if the other band members were listening. "Let's get this finished and we can get some rest before tonight. It's almost morning man. We got another session coming on. We got to be extra sharp tonight for the Knight! They paused and then Lucinda counted off the same song again.

It wasn't two minutes later when she suddenly stopped singing. Lucinda was mid-verse when she spun around, jumped over, and kicked the stool out from under the shocked drummer. He seemed about half her size and he fell against the back wall, bumping his head on the doorframe. The top hat flew away and cymbals crashed against the bass amp. The drummer rolled sideways and into a fetal position with one hand over his head as she charged at him.

"You lazy son-of-a-bitch!" Lucinda screamed. She was an imposing figure when mad. Tall enough with a long build to be intimidating. She stood over the wiry drummer. She kicked his leg hard, just missing his crotch. The drummer rolled further away into the booth. He was flipping around behind the drum kit, trying to avoid another strike and still holding his head with one hand and his privates with the other. "You ain't gonna fuk up my song and my band by getting drunk and sloppy." Lucinda screamed again. "You keep this shit up and we're gonna lose your ass in Illinois." Lucinda was mad, almost out of control. She seemed ready kick the drummer into a corner.

Louie didn't move from his chair in the control room. Shingles smiled and reached over to lift his Coke off the console. They all watched through the booth's glass window as Lucinda continued to shout. The rest of the band on the recording studio side of the window watched complacently and the guitarist reached over to the piano to pick up a pack of cigarettes.

The drummer started to get up and Lucinda stuck him a glancing blow on the ear with her open palm, knocking him back to the ground.

"Are you hearing me, Sam?" Lucinda said looming over him. "I'm Lucinda Black and I don't put up with this shit in my band. You hear me nigger! Use your good ear!"

Sam, the drummer nodded a yes, wide-eyed and waited for another blow, but Lucinda walked back across the room to her mike stand. The drummer cautiously got up and began putting the kit back together. Then he resumed his former seat and rubbed one hand down his face.

Lucinda shook off her anger and had a drink from the bottle on the piano. After a moment she put her lips to the mike screen. Her voice came into the booth through the studio monitors. "I'm sorry about that Louie," she said in a soft, calm voice. "Sometimes the boys just have to be reminded of who they be working for."

The session went on another hour without incident; another three songs were recorded before Louie said he had enough. After the last cut, Lucinda went over to the drummer and said a few words and then cuffed him playfully on top of his head.

It was about three in the morning when the band packed up and loaded on the bus. Louie hugged and shook hands all around with the musicians as the left the studio.

"You mind if we stay parked in the lot until mid-day everybody can get a little sleep. We're expected to be at Nighthawk Records on Dowling tonight for our yearly sessions." They owed Douglas Knight another album this year. Louie told her to hunker down there as long as they liked, but he would not be back in the studio for couple of days.

"What's with you and your drummer?" asked Louie. He had a mischievous twinkle in his eyes.

"Oh," she paused. "That little bastards tellin' everybody I give bad head."

"Ain't that the way it always is, darlin'. It's always a little turd that ain't getting' any dat's talkin' out of turn. Take it easy on the road, baby."

He gave her a hug and she walked out to the bus. The bus door shut behind her.

Jack packed up and drove home with his ears ringing from the playback speaker monitors in the control booth. He got home and happily found Angie sitting up in his bed, wearing one of his t-shirts and studying. Her books and papers were all around. She had her portable typewriter in front of her and she looked bright-eyed. She welcomed him with a smile and a long kiss.

"You look tired," she said. "It's almost four. That must have been a long session."

"Well, you look beautiful. It's nice finding you here. It was long," Jack said. "I'm not that tired, but I've got this high pitched frequency between my ears. Adrenalin I guess. It's going to take a little while for it to wear off."

They cleared off the bed and he talked on, telling her about the events of the night. Angie yawned after a while and folded her books and papers up, setting them on the floor beside the bed. She jumped off the waterbed and went across the room to turn off the ceiling light. Jack shut up, but his mind still raced, remembering the more dramatic moments of the night.

"You too wiped out for some loving," she said.

"I'm never too tired for you."

She happily snuggled into his arms.

Chapter Eight

Louisiana Man

Jack was at Acadia a few weeks later to check on any upcoming sessions or potential photo jobs. Jack had quit his day job a week earlier and had money in the bank to get started with his photography business. It was time to step out and try to make a go of it as a full-time, freelance photographer. He had talked to Louie about the move and he encouraged him to let the dice roll.

"Shit, Jack," you're a young guy, you've got talent and a lot of heart," Louie said. "Ain't no way you gonna be happy 'less you follow it. Der's gonna be lots of stuff goin' on he'ar and der's some other shit gonna go down soon that we can move your way. You getting' to be one of the family here and I'm personally tell you that I'll visit wit' Randy and Buck to get dem pushing bidness your way."

"I really appreciate that Louie," Jack said thinking that his support that could make a difference. He wasn't surprised by Louie's words, but they were welcome.

Louie even loaned him a room upstairs in the studio that had running water and a drain. Jack built some shelves and a counter in the small space and converted it into a reasonable darkroom. He installed his safelights and enlarger. It was nothing fancy but it worked. Jack was considering offering to build out a larger space upstairs for a photo studio. Louie was only using a storage room near the front stairway for his files and tapes.

"Like I said," Louie said making a throwaway brush with his right hand. "You one of us, man. Dis just gonna get bedder."

It wasn't unusual to run into some of Louie's acts or new artists hanging out with Mona. Not unlike other people with common careers-- musicians, writers and singers like to congregate to visit, bitch and tell stories. They weren't any different from teachers, nurses or lawyers. For Jack, they were often opportunities. Somebody was usually around the studio to pick up a check or bum some cash from Louie. Almost all of them needed a photographer to shoot promotional photos of themselves or bands.

But today the place was quiet. Louie had disappeared on one of his out of town trips to Nashville or New York. Paranoid or secretive, he never told any of the gang except Mona, when or where he was going. He would just be gone, leaving Mona and Randy holding down the fort. Protocol was not to ask. Jack visited with them a while and had a cup of coffee while they kicked around the latest studio gossip. Jack needed to get across town for an afternoon appointment so he said his good-bys and shook Randy's hand before leaving.

Jack had developed a couple of other Houston producer contacts and had a few album covers under his belt. He was picking up other free-lance jobs from weddings and portraits to occasional light manufactured product shots. Jack also was shooting for a little city magazine where one of his former journalism classmates was now an assistant editor. The other record producers were not majors, but made a good living doing "custom" work. One of the producers focused on Texas polka bands and small country and western bands around Texas and actually had some notable Grand Old Opry musicians under contract. They were small production runs and the artists or bands sold their albums at musical events, fairs or concerts. Some albums were distributed to hard-core country and western or bluegrass record shops. Since they weren't big stars or bands, their albums were small runs in the thousands, not millions. The work didn't bring in a fortune, but it was profitable.

Mr. Piedmont, the producer Jack was working for that day, was an old man who owned a number of traditional record stores scattered around north Houston and east to Baytown. His main store was on Fulton Avenue and even had 1950's style listening booths along one wall. His store was fascinating, with hundreds of records from obscure country singers and bands. Some of the records had years of dust and looked to be fifteen years old or more.

In the back of the store, he and his wife had their residence and a small but efficient recording studio with a couple of two-track recorders. His console looked more like something out of an AM radio station and they had stapled what seemed to be thousands of egg cartons to the walls for sound deadening. Low budget, old equipment, but it worked for what they needed. He told Jack that he had once owned stores in Tyler, Lufkin and Beaumont as well and had a passing acquaintance with Louie Thibodeaux that dated way back to Louie's first success.

Jack arrived for the session and rapped on the glass on the backdoor of their shop. Mr. Piedmont let him in and they went into the studio and sat down. The band was not there yet. Mrs. Piedmont brought him a coke and they shared some homemade chocolate chip cookies, as they waited.

"You're doing some work for Louie Thibodeaux I understand," said Mr. Piedmont.

"Yes sir. I do all kinds of free-lance work around town. A lot of it with studios."

"The Stallworths in Waco gave me your name. Have you worked with them?"

"No sir, I don't know how they found out about me."

"Louie probably told them. They told me you were available for session shoots, album covers and such. Louie must think a lot of you."

"Who are the Stallworths? I don't think I know them."

"Oh, you don't know. They have a record pressing plant up in Waco, been in business since a little while after the war. Good folks. About every producer in Texas has done business with them. Good folks, like I said. Have you known Louie for long?"

"Only a few months, he's some character."

"He's done pretty well for a poor kid from the Louisiana swamps," he said. 'First time I met him was in a coffee shop in Lufkin. He was selling boots and shoes out of his trunk of a red '53 Buick, traveling all over East Texas. Sharp kid, just out of the Navy and couldn't been over twenty-one or so. But man he was a slick charmer with that accent. Never heard one thicker, not even in Louisiana. Way he throws in that Cajun French. The good-natured cussin' he mixes in like it was spice. He did all right with those farmers and lumbermen in East Texas."

Jack thought the story was getting interesting and encouraged him to continue. Facts or even rumors about Louie's history were hard to come by. They were sitting comfortably on a couch in his studio waiting for Pomp Havelik and his Polka-Polka Boys to arrive and they were late. Mr. Piedmont was enjoying his storytelling and didn't need much prompting to continue. Mrs. Piedmont sat quietly, also hanging on every word from her husband.

"When he started promoting his records, Louie and a nigger boy who was a DJ in Baton Rouge started using the radio station sound booths on Sunday mornings to record their acts." Jack withheld a winch at the term; it wasn't said with any animosity. "They'd get in there and set up two mikes, one for the singer and one for the band and just record it all live" said Piedmont. "The only mix was setting the levels between the two mike lines. They used all kind of tricks to improve the sound and they got pretty damn good results. Sometimes they'd run a speaker and mike into the bathroom to build up an echo. Had one guy sing into an empty galvanized Kelly garbage can. That's some sound effects."

"When was this," Jack asked?

"Oh, I don't know, maybe '57 or '58. Elvis was big then, Chuck Berry and such. His first big act was Venus Blue, little East Texas nigger gal out of Orange"

Mrs. Piedmont frowned. "Edward," she said sharply. "They are Negroes now. I don't like that word."

"Yes, dear. Anyway, she had this voice that you couldn't forget. Kinda a *Negro* Brenda Lee, if you could believe that. Anyway they cut a little 45 record named *'Any Time'* and pitched it to all the stations in East Texas and the Louisiana border and they latched on it. The DJs started playing it. He took Miss Blue to Houston and she did on-air interviews. He introduced it around here and into Louisiana and the Deep South. Louie had three thousand more copies pressed after it caught on and took off on a fast round trip and sold the top thirty record stores 25 records each. He gave them the other 75 records free, under the table. Off the books you know. Quite naturally they really pushed the song to the kids coming in 'cause they were making pure profit on the forty-nine cent record. Back then, the top DJ or station manager in lots of towns also owned the city record store. That's back when local

DJ's were big shots, star makers. Record stores were where kids hung out back then…record stores and the local drugstore fountains. Most small town drug stores had a soda fountain and a jukebox. You wanted to get your records in the jukebox and sometimes there was wheeling' and dealing' with the distributors."

"I decided not to accept his free records," said the old man. "Nothing wrong with that. He paused, thinking back. "Don't misunderstand me, I've cut a few corners with the IRS in my day, but I'm not greedy. Never wanted to get involved with that kind of payola and I never had a taste for the penitentiary. We did do an autograph day in Beaumont where Venus Blue came in and signed records for the kids. We had one heck of a crowd. She was real popular. Nothing wrong with that, you know."

"By the time he got back home, they were ordering more. Louie had a regional hit, just like that. Course he hadn't made a dime yet. They ordered another 10,000 copies with Texas Sun Records in Waco. The Stallworth's shop. Then he took a mighty leap of faith or foolishness. He took twenty-five records and booked a flight to New York City," Piedmont chuckled.

"Apparently he had succeeded in making an appointment with a junior talent acquisition guy with

Saturn Records in Manhattan. They had a number of hits with black, rock and roll artists. That took some kind of Cajun balls."

"Mr. Piedmont, you'll watch you language," his wife interjected.

"Yes dear. Excuse me." That was the first and last time Jack heard Mr. Piedmont use what might be considered impolite language.

"Well," said Piedmont, "he gets off the plane and doesn't have anything but an address, his records, sixteen twenties, and a return flight ticket for the next they-- or at least that was how he told it to me back then."

"He gets a taxi into Manhattan, khaki pants and a plaid wool jacket and a cardboard box of records. Louie Thibodeaux goes right up and into some skyscraper and into the office of some guy named Lawrence Levine, now Louie calls him 'Moonie.' They were both young men with ambition. This Lawrence doesn't know what to do with this hick and his bizarre accent but to go ahead and listen to the song and Louie's spiel about how hot the song is in the South. This Levine wasn't any fool so he makes a couple of calls on the spot to Houston, New Orleans and Atlanta. The kicker is he thinks the song is great and has nationwide potential."

Piedmont continued, "Levine's was an up and coming young exec, and on the make in the music world, so he calls his boss who comes in to listen to the song. This guy is an Artist and Recording vice-president there, and he takes Louie on a tour of the spacious headquarters of Saturn Records, which actually occupies six floors. Then they show him the largest of the three studios and it looks big as a tennis court to Louie."

"They go straight into the Executive Dining Room for lunch, which is New York elegant with French waitresses and Louie falls in love more than once. Lucky for Louie he reads a little French, so he could order from the menu without looking like a fool.

So Louie asks, "Say, that big-ass studio that you took me to. I'm quoting Louie dear, if I was to just bring an act up here to cut a record, book it you know, how much would you charge me? Kinda as, just as an independent producer."

Levine tells him, "Two thousand dollars an hour, but you'd have to use union musicians and engineers so that's going to cost you about $75 each, per hour. That's just an average of course"

Louie wasn't anybody's fool so he just kept his expression flat and didn't say another word. But then the

VP says, "You've got a great record Louie, great potential, and we want it for Saturn Records. We'll put our national marketing muscle behind it if you sell us the distribution rights. I think it's going to go gold my boy. How much did it cost you to cut it?"

"Louie looked at him and for once, he told the truth," said Mr. Piedmont.

"Twenty three dollars and eighty-nine cents." says Louie quietly. "We just set up in our radio booth and the can."

"A week later, Louie walked into a bank in Sour Lake and deposited $29,000," said Piedmont. "Not bad for a shoe and boot salesman. The bank president called the cops. They brought Louie in for questioning. Heck, they never had seen anyone deposit that kind of money unless they were bootlegging or selling dope. It wasn't until he finally had them call the Saturn Records in New York, that the police regretfully let him go home. That little town spun on its heels for a month.

Chapter Nine

Hurdy-Gurdy Man

Jocko Dove showed up at the Acadia International Studios one morning soon after Jack arrived. Jack had dropped by to pick up some money for a PR shoot he had done for Louie the previous week. Louie was turning a little work his way. Jocko was a strange character, even by show business standards for an agent, but he had been nice to Jack. They had met before at the Basement Blues and he was still booking Blackplanque. Jack had shot some promotional black and white eight by tens for a couple of his other bands. Jocko was a little on the short side with roly-poly walk, black frame glasses and a toupee which sat square on the middle of his head. A bad toupee that looked like some dusky Spanish moss had fallen out of a local live oak and landed between his ears.

Fortunately, Mona had the check ready for Jack and he stayed to share some coffee. Louie had been in New York over the weekend for the Grammy awards. When Jocko was buzzed in, it was still early, at least by studio time, and he announced to Mona, Randy and Jack that he was there to "get Louie on track" in regard to Blackplanque. Jack was amazed and stayed to watch. Mona was standing behind Jocko as he made the announcement and she rolled her eyes. Jack sat down on the couch to see how Jocko planned to get Louie straightened out.

As Mona put it later, "Jocko got his game on early in the day. He was loaded by nine." Louie normally didn't really get rolling until the afternoon.

"Jocko's pretty alcoholic," she had disclosed to Jack. "At one time he was quite a promoter. I think he taught George Jones how to fall off the wagon. You know, I don't mind if he's a little gay, but he's such a bag of it. He gets bands clubs jobs around town, he's got those connections, but that's about it. Blackplanque needs to find an agent with a larger reach. Get out of Texas and Louisiana you know." But that was going to be hard to do without a hit record.

Louie had only been in his office for a few minutes and although Jack hadn't seen him, Jack knew he hadn't made it back to the parlor for his second cup of coffee.

Jocko stood in the reception room wearing madras, corduroy coat cut like a Nehru jacket and peach colored polyester flared slacks. Mr. Dove was quite a sight that day and he had a head of steam up. Louie came into the reception area from his office for more coffee. He wasn't looking for a meeting with Jocko and didn't acknowledge his presence until after he had filled his mug.

"Mornin' Jocko," said Louie. "Hi Jack. Did Mona get ya dat check you needed?"

"Yeah, thanks Louie." Jack and the group waited expectantly to see what would happen.

Jocko immediately jumped into the conversation and broached the subject of Blackplanque's new record, and whether Louie had had success in pushing it in New York. Before Louie could respond, he then asked whether he was going get a cut from the live albums that Blackplanque sold at gigs.

Louie wasn't in the mood to deal with "a piss-ant agent" that morning or his silly questions. And Louie never talked business in front of a group. He dealt with people one-on-one and usually behind closed doors. Witnesses made him nervous. He had given the band 1,000 copies of the album for free without informing Jocko. Jocko had found out and asked him what his cut would be from the sales.

"I don't give a shit," said Louie. "Dat's just a little extra taste I give dem 'cause dey is my boys. Don't want dem to starve to death workin' off da jobs you bring 'em. Why should you wanna cut of der record sales at the gigs and shows," said Louie. "Why you wan'ta be such a chicken shit. You're gonna to have to talk to dem. You get fifteen per cent of their gigs anyway for a few telephone calls. What the fuk do you expect?"

Jocko dropped the subject for a moment and reset his aim.

"Louie, did you sell them to any labels in New York? What about your buddy at Saturn."

"Don't press me Jocko!" Louie said emphatically. He was now talking in a much louder voice than usual. A voice Jack seldom had heard and he could tell that he was getting irritated with Dove's grilling. "Besides, Moonie's in R & B mainly, not rock. Look Jocko, we can do a little bidness together," said Louie. "I don't mind dat." He stiffened and stared down at the agent. "But don't think you're gonna ride my ass about my bidness. The recording side...der records is my bidness! I don't haf'ta to tell you a fuk'in ting about that. You do the bookin'. But no, the boys just ain't commercial enough. De play and sing good, but der original material just ain't turnin' heads up in New York. Rock's a hard sell; the labels are looking for acts that write stronger stuff. What's wrong wit you today?"

Louie was getting more intense, staring at Jocko and definitely getting very annoyed with the conversation.

"Anyway, you know I'm mo' of an R&B or country producer. Dat's where my contacts is. You got any acts like that?   The money in publishing and writer's royalties. I love the boys, de's all good kids. Don't get me wrong, de's a bunch of good boys, soulful kids, but de ain't der yet in der careers.

Now Jocko was getting angrier than he should have. He didn't want to hear this. He raised his voice.

"Aw Louie," he squealed. "They're better than that.   You don't know what you've got. I don't think you've got them right on a record yet, not their sound, not the right kind of production."

Louie didn't like that at all. He took a long sip of coffee before answering in a calm, serious voice.

"You keep 'em workin, suffer'n and de might make it yet. I been recording acts and making gold records 'fo you discovered your tally-whacker," he said.   He was keeping his anger under control. "Dey ain't der yet Jocko," he said quietly. "Dem boys ain't foun' the groove. Let's you and me drop dis an' we'll get together next week to talk about the boys."

Jocko went back to shouting. "Dammit, you've had Travis and Lee under contract for five or six years. Mercy, they were damn near babies. Let'em go Louie, give 'em a break! Let'em get out of the recording contract!"

Buck had been working in the studio and heard the shouting and came into the room to see what the hubbub was about. He had on his carpenter's apron and held a claw hammer.

"Yeah," said Louie. He was really mad now and wanted to shut Jocko up. Jack could see his face flushing and he set down his mug. Louie had heard enough and said too much. It was getting intense. "I know your game, Jocko. You wan' me to dump 'em so you can shop'em with other studios and labels and maybe get some front money for a new contract."

"No dammit," said Jocko. "Christ! I can do more for their careers than you can. I have this vision."

"Oh, I can see that," said Louie sarcastically. "Why done you start by visioning up some tours or big show dates? You ain't done dat! Why don't you get dem out of that fukin basement where dey can be seen by mo' people? Dey'd be a great opening act for somebody on the road. You're der talent agent, you dumb bastard! You ain't got shit! I've heard enough of your crap for today, Jocko. You better leave fo' I get permanently upset wit' you."

Louie turned away and walked toward the door leading to the back rooms.

"Buck," Louie said. "Why don't you show Dovey here the back door so's he can fly home. By the way Jocko," he finished, "Luv yo' jacket."

Louie left and Jocko trotted down the hall toward the outside door with Buck; hammer still in hand, on his heels.

About half an hour later Louie came out of his office and into Mona's reception area. Jack had been hanging out with Buck and Randy while they re-hung some studio monitors in Studio B.

"That dumb son-of-a-bitch made me hungry," said Louie setting down his coffee cup. He turned to Jack. "You ain't said much dis morning."

"Didn't figure you needed any help, Louie."

Louie laughed. "It's just some of the shit you gotta put up with." He shook his head and smiled. "Let's you and me go get something to eat Jack, I'm buying." They went out and got into his new Lincoln Continental and set out for Luby's Cafeteria. The car was a beautiful emerald green Lincoln with a light green top and sunroof. The interior was light beige leather and the car was loaded.

"Did you get rid of the Cadillac?" Jack asked, trying to start a conversation about a new topic.

"Oh yeah," he said. "That car was nothin' but trouble. I wished I had never bought that piece of junk. Got it to celebrate my college education. It's not even worth givin' to my wife in Sour Lake. I was parked up at the North side at one of dem malls one night, and somebody stole it. Cops found it burned to the ground up near Hempstead. Think maybe I accidentally left the keys in it." He turned to Jack and winked.

"Something like that could happen up there. I didn't know you were married, Louie."

"Oh yeah," he said. "Been married since 1958 and got a little girl. Well, she ain't so little now. Anyways, we ain't lived together since 1960, but Nadine won't divorce me you know…good Catholic gal. You won't never see dem 'round the studio. But I support dem and dey do all right. She works for a car dealership in Beaumont. Her Daddy's a rice farmer. Dey gotta good life up der livin' on dis little spread I got dem outside of town. You know, I do my thing and she does hers, but she'll never divorce my ass."

Mona had told Jack that Louie was nuts about this black Bahamian girl who was his attorney's secretary in

New York. She had actually emigrated from England where she went to a private and then legal aide school. Mona said he had been trying to get her and her young daughter to move down and live with him. He had a house in the Heights area of town. But she wasn't ready for that kind of change in her life. Mona said that the girlfriend wanted to go on to law school in New York and Louie had put her on the task of researching law schools in Houston.

After they had gone through the buffet line at Lubys and picked out more than enough to eat, they sat down at a corner table. Louie sat with his back to the wall. Jack watched him as Louie constantly surveyed the room for anyone suspicious. It reminded Jack of the story of Wild Bill Hickok getting shot in the back. Apparently Louie wasn't going to let that happen to him.

"I tell you someting about the music bidness, Jack," he said. He spoke softly even though no other diners were nearby but an old couple. The old man had leaned his cane against the table after allowing the waitresses to carry his tray to the table. His wife helped him and then sat with her handbag in her lap throughout lunch.

"When you're a successful producer like me, wit' a track record of makin' hits, gold records, dey's everybody on you all the time with der stuff. Not jus' da acts, you know the singers and bands and writers, but den you got the agents and half-ass promoters. Dey all wants you to be der ticket to make dem rich and famous. De all got big ideas and de tink you should front the money so de's can get rich."

"That Jocko Dove is just like a little swamp rat, scurrying around tryin' to scramble up some crumbs. Ain't never had an original thought in his life. He ain't never getting' nowhere 'cause everbody see right thru him. Plus he's a drunkard."

"Here's da thing. Jocko's never snapped to dis. Der's thousands of great acts out der. Folks like Jocko don't realize that Louie Thibodeaux ain't gonna run out of talent. Der's more talent on this earth then I could ever use up. People think it's only der son or der cousin that could be a star. Lord, I've seen so many talented people, special people."

"Der's thousands of stars out der. Der in the churches and nightclubs and jus' singin' wit' der friends. But der's only a few who are lucky, or smart or maybe big enough whores to ever make it. The rest is jus' as good and talented, maybe a lot more, but just missed getting demselves into the net. Da music business jus' has dis fishin' net that scoops up a few ever year out'a the lake of talent. Da rest get washed down the bayou an' to the sea. You'll see that in time."

"I'm sort'a like Jesus, you know," he said. "I 'member dem nuns at the Immaculate Heart of Mary tellin' me da story. And 'I jus' go walkin' cross that pond and haul up a few myself in my net each year."

That's some simile, Jack thought.

"You see, I got the recordin' and management contract with ever one of my acts," said Louie. "My New York Jew lawyers draw 'em up jus' like the one's the big labels use, coast to coast. And dat's the first thing ya gotta get, some powerful New York Jews on ya side. Mine is the Milstein brothers. Dey got der work cut out for dem keeping me straight. I didn't think dis stuff up you know. I was in the bidness a while before I figured dis shit out. That's just the way you do bidness in music. I got stolen from many a time for I got smart."

"My contracts usually say that I got to put out sometin' like three albums over three years for the act," said Louie. "Sometimes it's a singles. And de got to make demselves available to record. I got choice over the material and I own da publishing rights to der songs de write. I gotta put out sometin' like a minimum of 1,500 records each time or somethin' like that. And I got to do my best to sell and promote dem. Make my best efforts; it's in the contract. I can't sign 'em and foget 'em. I got to get off my butt and do sometin' and so do they. Ain't that fair?"

Jack shook his head acknowledging the reciprocity of the deal as Louie saw it.

"Den," he said. "I got to build or rent a studio, front the recording expenses. Buildin' AI ain't been cheap! Don't cost my artists nothin' up front. I got to use my telephone and time promotin' and sellin' them. Got to pay musicians sometimes for the cuts, arrangers, backup singers, all that shit. Got to pay for masters and dem records or albums and ship 'em out to DJ's and promoters and such."

"I got to admit," said Louie, "when dey sign dem contracts I own their asses, but dey also own a piece of me. Course I can sell dem off for a profit if I want. I seldom do dat. We both gotta perform to make it happen. And dey know I've made it happen for a lot of stars. Dat's why dey sign. "

"You know, they all have a dream," Jack said. "I think that's what makes most of them a little crazy. They want the fame, money, power and all that goes with it so bad, but most of them can't cope with the dues they have to pay."

"A lot of dem just ain't got the chops or the discipline to make it work. Ain't no different from the bank president and his counter clerk. One makes it to the top and da other don't. Who de gonna blame? If de's singers, de blame der producers and agents, I guarantee you that"

"You see Lucinda Black, how come she's comin' to me for cash?" said Louie. "'Ole man Knight ain't gonna help her and Lucinda knows it. He'd slap her around like Lucinda slapped that drummer. I mean he may not hit her, but he'll abuse her somehow. That old man's too mean to *hit* any of his acts. Lot's of dem black producers treats der acts worse then I do mine. Dat's why so many sign with me in de first place. Now Lucinda knows that 'ole black bastard gonna screw her worse then me, her own people are gonna do that. Lucinda's been robbed of her money in bars and clubs and her producer that she's been wit' forever do it too. But she won't leave Knight 'til the old man dies."

"I ain't no angel, but I got some feelin's for my acts," said Louie. "I know most of dem ain't gonna make it big time. I'll make mine in time. Play along and make my moves at the right time. It's taken me a lotta years to figure something. It ain't finished. I need to get these down to the main Post Office downtown and I wondered if I could get you to take me down there to get them mailed."

"No problem. Hank, do you need a ride downtown?"

"Sure," he said. "The mission is on Texas Street. Sure beats riding the bus"

So the three of them loaded the envelopes into the trunk of Jack's Mustang and Hank crawled in the backseat. Mona took shotgun. As she slipped in Jack took a moment to glance at her smooth legs beneath her black skirt. Attractive, he thought. He looked up to see her watching his eyes and realized she had caught him gazing at her. She just smiled and looked ahead.

"Let's get it on, cutie," said Mona. "Watch the road

Jack was an embarrassed and blushed slightly as he put the car in gear. They dropped off Hank at the Star of Hope Mission where he was living temporarily. His roommate had booted him out of their apartment a week earlier. Hank was an old WWII veteran who had come home years ago with a drinking problem that still haunted him. He and his roommates had gotten into an argument earlier in the month over some liquor, so Hank had lost his sleepover privileges.

Louie had met Hank at the VA Hospital when Louie went in for a checkup. Louie had served two years in the Navy during the Korean War. He never left the states during his two years of service and took advantage of the Houston VA hospital now and then.

"I try not to remember none of it," Louie remarked in the office one they, "My Navy weren't nuttin' but getting' drunk and chasin' pussy around San Diego."

Louie had gotten into a conversation with Hank in the hospital waiting room a couple of months earlier and felt sorry for this fellow ex-swabby. He wound up offering him a part-time job as janitor and general helper around the studio. Hank usually had to hitch a ride or climb on a bus to get to the studio. He seemed to keep himself sober, at least during the days, and enjoyed being around the characters in the studio. On late nights he would often sleep in the studio overnight. They all had a soft spot for Hank; he was good-natured and blended into the group well.

After Jack dropped Hank off, Mona and he went over a few more blocks to the Post Office. They carried the mail in and left it on the counter for the mailmen to pick-up. Back in the car Jack began to back up and stopped. He turned to ask Mona where she needed to go next.

"Tell you what," said Mona. "My Momma's cookin' fried chicken, corn bread and green beans tonight. How'd you like a home cooked meal for a change?

"That, I couldn't turn down!"

"I didn't think you would. Let's head home. Why don't we just jump up on the 45 freeway and head for Pearland. I really do appreciate you givin' me a ride home tonight."

"No problem," he said. "I'll get to meet your little girl and Momma?"

"Oh yeah, she's almost seven now, Samantha, Samantha Sinclair."

"She came along not long after you went to work for Louie didn't she?"

"I was lucky to have a job through it all."

"Was Sinclair your married name?" Mona had never mentioned a divorce but he knew she wasn't currently married.

"No, I wasn't lucky enough to have a husband when I got pregnant. Wasn't really even in love. Not the kind of love you have for a real marriage. Just enough in love for some lonesome sex. I guess I was just lonely and her dad is persuasive guy. He didn't have to push that hard.

But she wasn't really a mistake so much. I wouldn't give anything for her."

"I'm sure it hasn't been easy."

"No, raisin' a child ain't easy no matter how many people you have involved. Thank God I had my Momma and she was pretty accepting. She's been divorced from my Daddy for more than twenty years. She'd made her mistakes too. So it worked out all right for all three of us. Samantha's brought some refreshing joy into our lives."

"You ever see him?"

"Yeah, I see him pretty often but there's no more messing around. But, I get a check from him regularly. He's been responsible in that way.

"It must have been hard."

"Still is."

They drove on in silence for a while, commenting occasionally on the traffic.

"Working for Louie all these years must have been a real experience," Jack said. "It's not like a regular office at that place.

"Yeah," said Mona. "It's a zoo all right…a real trip. I was working for an accountant in Deer Park the first time I laid eyes on Louie. This CPA I worked for had his account for a while and Louie stole me. Louie bribed me with charm and a lot more money. Then, my boss got mad at him and that was the end of that. I don't think they would have made it long 'cause the firm was real conservative and Louie likes to push the rules to the limit, with his accountants and attorneys. Doesn't make a major move without them, which is probably smart. They're all in New York and mostly kept him out of trouble."

"Only mostly?"

"Mostly, mostly," she said. She paused. "I tell you what, we'll go eat a bunch of Momma's cookin' and we can get into that later.

"OK," Jack said. He dropped Louie as a subject. Jack was interested in Mona's story. He didn't feel a romantic or sexual tension between them, but he liked her and her honesty. He was sensitive to the five years or more age difference between them. She seemed to have a good head on her shoulders and had a natural intelligence. They had formed sort of an alliance.

"What's your background, did you go to school here?" Jack asked.

"I grew up in Pearland and went to a couple of years of business school training after I graduated. After that, my first job was with that CPA. I guess in the back of my mind I never figured to work in an office all my life.

Me and my sister were basically raised to be housewives you know."

"Things don't always work out like the plan."

They drove on out I45 and went south to Pearland. Their place was out among ranches and small truck farms on the southeast side of Houston, about 15 miles from downtown.

The home was a one-story ranch style on about two acres of land, a little off the highway. The yard had a couple of dogs, clothesline and open three-car garage, very typical of the area. Her Mom was not expecting company but took it in stride and she set an extra place at the table and invited Jack to sit down in the kitchen with them and have a beer. She went back to cooking supper and kept complaining about the stove not getting the grease hot enough to suit her. They visited about all of the wet weather they had been having. Pearland fields were standing in water after a six inch rain storm a couple of nights earlier.

Mona brought Samantha in to say hello and then the little one disappeared back into her room to work on homework.

"Mona said you're a photographer?" said her Mother.

"Yes Mam," Jack said. "I've been taking pictures and wrote for newspapers and the like for a few years. I majored in journalism at U of H."

"So now you're doing pictures for Louie?" she said. She wiped her wet hands on a cup towel she had tucked into her apron.

"Yes, him and some other clients. Just trying to get my business going. I also write a few publicity releases for the Acadia."

"Well, I wish you luck." she said. "It's hard starting up. I work part- time for a florist in Pearland and he's only been around a couple of years. I do his bookkeeping. I like it because I can do some of it from home and watch Samantha after school. I know he struggles to make ends meet. Maybe some Sunday you can drop by and take a few pictures of Samantha. I don't have near enough good ones."

"I'd like to do that Mrs. Sinclair," Jack replied. "She's a little beauty."

"You watch out for Mr. Thibodeaux. He's a strange one as I'm sure you already know. The man leaves both joy and misery in his wake. I hope someday Mona will see her way to get away from him. But that's just between you and me, OK. She's a grown woman and it's her business. But I wish she had never gotten involved with the evil SOB."

"Yes Mam," said Jack, "I will."

Mona came in and started helping her Mother, putting things on the table and called in Samantha when all was ready. Her Mom was a good cook and they all enjoyed the meal while the trio listened to a chronicle of Samantha's day at school. Jack hadn't been around many little girls and thought she was charming. Mona got a kick of how she flirted with Jack.

After dinner, Mona told Jack to go on in the living room and watch some TV while she helped her mother wash the dishes and clean up. He sat down on an Early American couch with walnut trim and one of those too busy patterns that always reminded Jack of Thanksgiving. Family photos covered most of the walls along with some china plates and figurines. Jack noticed there was none of Samantha and her father. It was only about ten minutes later when she came in with another couple of beers.

"Two's my limit on work nights," she said.

"That sounds like enough for me too," he replied.

They began watching an old movie for a while, sitting on the couch. Her Mother stopped by the living room and announced she was meeting some friends for

Bingo Night at the Knights of Columbus Hall in Pasadena and left. At eight she went in to put Samantha to bed.

It didn't take long until Mona was back to work on her beer. Jack was curious about their earlier conversation about Louie.

"I wonder some times," he said. "Why have you stayed with Louie for all these years? His studio and the music recording business are kinda crazy?"

"There's something about it I must like," she said. "You have to admit it's exciting. I mean, I have never had two days the same for nearly nine years. Like I told you earlier, Louie pays me way more than I could earn anywhere else and I've got Samantha to think of. Louie and I have a special relationship. It's a strange trust. We sort of depend on each other."

"He's quite a character," Jack said. "I have to say I can't get over what he does; the way he does it. I've never seen anyone who can handle people like him. It's not just charm or that accent. He just has an uncanny ability to persuade. He doesn't sell them you know. He moves them to do what he wants, while they think it's what they want."

"Sometimes I've thought maybe he's the devil incarnate. But then there are times he does some really nice things for people, really unselfish. You know, nobody knows this, but every Christmas he takes several thousand dollars out of the bank. Then he hits all of the Salvation Army stores around town and just gives it away, bit by bit, to folks he finds shopping there. I went with him one year and it's quite an experience. The poor folks are just shocked when he hands them twenty or a fifty dollars out of the blue. It makes a difference in their Christmas I guarantee. Takes him all day. Nobody knows. Later, he's a scoundrel and he loves to get the best of the folks he does business with.

"That's pretty amazing. But, he's no fool," Jack said.

"Nobody's fool is more like it. He always seems to know what everybody's after and he's always one step ahead of them," said Mona. "I found that out early on and from then on, I just started telling him exactly what I think about everything. I'm completely honest with him in private. When he asks me an opinion or question, I give it to him. No bullshit. And you know, I think he trusts me to do that. I'm about the only one who will, or can. But I never question him about the business or anything else in public."

"I'm sure you're right about keeping your opinions to yourself when others are around. I've never seen anyone like him.   Buck's pretty good himself at persuading people."

"Yeah, you got to watch him, Jack. He's an ex-drunk from what I know. If there is such a thing. He spreads it way too wide and deep. I don't trust him. I know Louie doesn't. He'll work with him whenever it's to his advantage or he can see something in it for him in the long run. I think Buck's got a real mean streak inside. He doesn't give a damn about anybody and you won't ever him doing anything decent just 'cause they might deserve it. Louie's got a heart but I haven't seen one in Buck yet; he's an angry man.

"Why's everybody so paranoid in the studio. So secretive. I mean there's always something going on under the surface." Jack took a chance. "There's something people in there are afraid of. It's like being in a house where somebody has drugs and everyone's constantly looking out the windows or making sure the door is locked. What's the secret? Is there something hidden behind a door or not"

She smiled and looked over, into his eyes. "You little rascal," she said. "I'm not surprised you've picked up that."   She reached out and grasped his hand lightly. "There's a body buried under the studio. Well, it's not really a body and it's not a real secret. Lots of people know the story, but nobody but Louie ever has the nerve to talk about it."

"I don't know what I feel, Mona." But there's always something rippling under the surface when you and Randy and Buck, even Louie talk. "She turned more toward him on the couch and tucked her nearest leg under her. She reached out for his other hand. She seemed ready to open up to him.

"Can you tell me?" said Jack.

"It's probably a feeling, a bad vibration from Louie and Buck's time up at college,"

"What could have happened in college that cast such a cloud over the studio," Jack said.

"It wasn't what happened at college," she said. "It was college itself," she said. "It's public knowledge but nobody mentions it."

"Why not?"

"College, it's what Louie and Buck call the federal prison in Oklahoma. They met there after both of them were given a vacation from the citizens," said Mona.

"Oh," he hesitated a moment. "They spent time in a federal pen?"

"Nothing deadly, Jack. Louie is still humiliated by the conviction. I think he came out a changed man." She squeezed his hands for a moment and let go. "Buck was there for three years because he had swindled his partner out in Lubbock over some oil pipeline deals and Dairy Queen franchises they had opened together. Apparently they got him dead to rights. I think he's got a better lawyer now. He's still on probation for another year. It was pretty hard on his family out in Katy and I know his wife is gonna be giving him hell for the rest of his life. But, she stuck with him. She's a natural bitch anyway. 'About big as he is, but they've got a pretty teenage daughter in high school."

"What was Louie in for?"

"More complicated. It seems that he and a co-producer got in trouble up in Arkansas while his partner was taking one of their young gal stars on a radio station tour. Apparently she was really into the "I'm a star" thing and wound up trying to boost her career by pulling a few "nooners" with several station managers and DJ's at radio stations here and there. Louie wasn't even there when this happened, but his partner was. Her Dad found out and the shit hit the fan. It got pretty hot because Louie had been sleeping with her Momma. I told you it was complicated.

The partner caved after he was arrested and turned state's evidence against Louie."

"OK, so he wound up in the can?"

"It's a little complex, but all I can say is that his partner was a nobody. Louie had all these big time record business connections in Nashville, New York and LA. This was back when the payola scandals had died down but the feds were always out there sniffing around. So the FBI and the Federal Trade Commission got wind of it and landed on Louie. Basically they told him he was gonna spill all he knew about any illegal activities like payola or bribes or was going to jail for violating the Mann Act. They wanted Louie to implicate and testify against these record company big shots. You know these were some powerful people."

"What's the Mann Act?"

"Well, it's pretty obscure, but it's taking an underage gal across state lines for immoral purposes. Dates way back. She was not quite seventeen and that made it a felony. The Feds declared that Louie organized the whole tour and encouraged the girl to screw those guys. Let me tell you, she didn't need any encouragement. That apple didn't fall far from the tree. His partner got off without charges."

"What happened?"

"Louie kept his mouth shut and that really pissed off the Feds and they prosecuted him. He never gave them a thing about anything illegal, although he knew a lot I'm sure."

"So Louie bit the bullet. He didn't tell them anything he knew?"

"Nope, he kept his mouth shut, they threw the book at him and he did the time. The Feds were pissed and even sicked the IRS on him. He did sixteen months, until a Senator pushed through a parole with the board."

"Now, there's a whole bunch of important people in the New York, Nashville and LA who owe Louie their butts. Ever now and then he needs a favor and collects. They helped him borrow the money for the Acadia International, which is hard for a convicted felon to do. But, it really hurt him in his heart. Louie's no angel, as you know but it wasn't what I'd necessarily call justice. That little tramp who thought she was a star caused a lot of tears. You can't tell me she didn't know what she was doing. She's a waitress at a Beaumont IHOP now. That was a little justice at least"

"Wow, that explains a lot. I can see how that would put a scar on Louie's soul."

"Enough about Louie. Why don't you tell me about your girlfriend, cutie," said Mona.

Jack gave her a brief rundown of Angie's best qualities, how they met and the last six months with her.

"What about you Mona?" said Jack. "I've never heard you talk about any men in your life. Is there one?"

"Yeah, now and then, but no more in the music business. No produces, musicians or writers. No way. I've tried all three over the past nine years and that ain't working for me. I am star-strucked out. I'm looking for a tone-deaf lover. Seriously, I'd like to find some guy and get married. Samantha could use a Daddy. A good Daddy; maybe a cowboy."

"Sounds like a plan."

"But I can't marry until I find that guy. Maybe he'll show up in my church someday."

"I hope so," said Jack. "I really do."

Chapter Eleven

I'd Love to Turn You On

Jack and Angie went to their favorite Mexican restaurant a week later. He had been tossing around the idea of whether he should tell Angie more about the characters at the studio and their felonious backgrounds. He felt compelled to go with the truth, although he knew it might scare her.

"Angie," Jack said over dinner. "You know how I've told you how strange it is around the studio sometimes. Something a little weird in the air."

"Yeah?" She was tentative.

"I think I found out why a couple of nights ago. It seems Louie was in prison a few months before I met him." That got Angie's attention and brought a frown to her face.

"How long ago was he in? What the hell did he do?"

"A little over a year before they let him out on parole. That's where he met Buck."

"Great. So they're both paroled felons or something."

"Yeah, I think the governor or somebody pardoned Louie."

"So who did they kill?"

"No one." Jack told her the basics of the story that Mona had spilled. Angie listened calmly and asked a few questions, most of which Jack could not answer.

"Well, Jack, I don't like it a bit." said Angie. "I know most people wouldn't think violating the Mann Act, is the worst crime on earth. Apparently the feds thought it was serious. That's *if* Mona's version is the whole truth, which I doubt. You make her sound like an innocent, but I don't believe it. She's in too deep. I don't think you're dealing with the most truthful, open kind of people there. You better not believe or trust anything Louie or Mona tells you, or Buck either. "

"I know. I don't know very much about them. I don't even know where Louie lives. Buck never mentions his family. A lot of their stories I only know through gossip and most of that's from Randy. They don't tell me more than I need to know most of the time. Maybe they're afraid I'll be captured by the FBI and spill my guts," he told Angie. He laughed at his joke. That was a mistake.

"But you're still going over there and working for them aren't you!" she continued with more intensity. "I don't know how you can consider them friends!" She was getting fired up.

"It's just business," said Jack. "They're not friends. I don't think they have real friends, either Buck or Louie. They don't have that kind of trust in anybody. You've got to give something away of yourself to be a friend. They don't let that happen. I guess they've seen the worst when they were in prison."

"Maybe they *are* the worst," she said. "They are paranoids, neurotics or sociopaths! I don't know! Maybe they've got good reasons for all that. Who cares? You don't know what they're up to most of the time, do you."

"Nope."

"They are just symptomatic of the people who make all the money. The greed. The older I get, the more I think all business is like that. I mean, I think big corporate executives are all crooks. Look at the creeps at Brown and Root and how they're making millions off the blood of our soldiers in Vietnam. You think I don't know they're crooks? Hell, look at our President, Nixon. What do you think is going on behind those murdering, beady eyes? You want to see a paranoid, just watch him on the evening news with Cronkite. Our corporations have exploited South American peasants for years. We're no better than the British in Africa or India."

"Maybe they're all crooks on some level," said Jack. "I don't think you expect me to go into a monastery to get away from this kind of reality. I'm not an academic like you."

"Even academics have their politics and frauds," she said. "But other people's jobs aren't like that," said Angie. "I mean you don't need to go out there and do business with convicted felons intentionally do you? You're not like them. I worry about you Jack."

Maybe you're right," Jack said. "But they've been good to me while I'm trying to get my photo business started up. You've got to admit that."

"I'll admit they've used you. But look what they take," said Angie. "You're getting compromised just being around them. These guys are bad news."

"I haven't broken any laws, and I'm not going to. I'm not going near any questionable deals they may do. Who knows? Anyway, I'm getting out of the scene as soon as I can."

"Is that a promise? I'll believe that when it happens," said Angie. Both planned for Jack to stay at her apartment that night and both were ready to end the argument. It was going nowhere at this point. He had no solution and she was getting tired of bitching at him.

"I mean, I'm all for you baby" Angie said. "I really want you to be able to do your own thing with the photography. I know you love it. I know you love the music also. But Jack, tell me, at what point will you break off working with these guys? This is slimy, creepy and for all I know, dangerous. They sound like professional crooks and thugs to me."

"I know what you're saying. The music business is corrupt and they didn't get into trouble by accident."

"Jack," she said. "Enough of this. She leaned across the table and whispered. "Rudy left me a couple of fat joints when he was by today. I think it's time to go home and relax." Angie pulled back with a devilish smile, her eyes bright. The prior subject was dropped.

They drove home and Jack poured a couple of glasses of a decent chardonnay while she checked the door locks, drew the curtains tight. She pulled a small cigar box from under the couch. He could usually sense a little paranoia when there were drugs present. It ran rampant throughout university parties and most of the *love generation*. Inside her box were some love beads a small alligator clip and some matches. The two joints were in a Rosary pouch.

"My Mom gave me this," she said, holding the pretty woven pouch in her hand. "Isn't it sweet? She bought it in Monterrey and had the Mexican priest bless the rosary. I keep the rosary beads in my jewelry box. You know, I think I'll go back to church when I get out of school and get settled. It's sort of comforting and passive at mass."

"Yeah, I think there's a lot of people I know who believe in God, but they just don't believe in churches. They're into this 'nature is my church' kind of thing'. That doesn't even cover their fantasizing over Far Eastern religions. It's like they're zooming into Zen. Become a Master in three easy lessons. That's lame. It's just rebellion over their parent's beliefs."

"Maybe, I mean, who do you know that trusts institutions? They're all screwed up from the federal government to organized religion."

"No wonder so many students are just dropping out and moving into communes. Going to the country. You get older and you see the truth, the politics, it sucks."

"Your right," said Jack. "But tonight it's just you and me. I'll put on some music. He went over to the record player and pulled out the Moody Blues' *Days of Future Passed* album and Iron Butterfly's *Ina-Godda-Da-*

Vida. "This some prime head music" he told her. He put on the Butterfly's album first and set the second side of the Moody Blues on top of the bottom LP. "It's so beautifully mellow at the end. I love it."

Third on the spindle went Big Brother and the Holding Company with a new singer named Janis Joplin. "How do you like this Big Brother album?" said Jack.

"I love it too. I just got that record yesterday, baby. She's too much. I listen to her and I say, woman, that's liberated."

He flipped the automatic player switch. They turned off the lights and sat down on the corded rug in the center of her front room. Both had crossed their legs and faced each other. She lit several drip candles and then the jay. Her largest drip candle covered a gallon wine jug and sat on a small cable spool table in one corner of the room. It was the results of dozens of previous candles, dripping down the sides the bottle, which was barely visible beneath the wax. It was magnificent and the colors and shapes were fascinating when stoned. After the second joint was finished, she wet the ash ends of both with her tongue and swallowed the bits. She put the alligator clip back in the cigar box and slid it back under the old couch.

"Down the hatch with all evidence," Angie said and giggled. The weed was beginning to take effect. Both kept to their own thoughts, letting the music take them away. Angie shut her eyes and hugged a big pillow, swaying slightly back and forth. The record player's LP's progressed from the Butterfly to the Moody Blues and finally to Big Brother. Time spaced out until they both suddenly realized the silence. No more music. Jack stood up slowly and dealt with the record player and Angie went into the kitchen to refill their glasses. Janis Joplin was up first on the flipped record stack. He sat back down and took the glass from her hand. "That's some good dope," she said and they got quiet again. Less than an hour or so passed.

Angie stretched and got to her feet. It was late. "Bedtime," she said. Jack flipped the stereo from records to FM and classical music came on. He left it on, but turned down the volume, leaving the channel softly playing.

"My throat's really dry," she said and swallowed the rest of her wine. Angie went into the bedroom and he joined her near the bed. The weed had worn off but they were still buzzing. "I feel like that joint had some speed in it. Is that possible?"

"You got me."

"Well, I have to compliment you on your choice of wines tonight."

"The good stuff."

"Big Brother makes me horny," Angie said. "And I just don't know what to do with myself," she said in a swooning southern belle imitation. The back of her right hand went to her forehead.

"Horny? What would your mother say about that kind of language?"

"She'd say, quit thinking about that *caca* Angelina, and say a Rosary," switching back to a heavy, South Texas Mexican accent.

"You should be ashamed of yourself."

"I know. I'll probably go to hell if I die tonight."

He was close to undressed but she stopped him. Angie was down to her bra and panties. She grabbed his right hand.

Look," she said and hopped onto the waterbed. He sat down on the edge facing her. From her previous mellowness, she was now wired. She started jumping up and down on the waterbed as the bed waves almost rolled her over. She was laughing hysterically as she tilted from side to side, nearly losing her balance. Jack was lagging behind in coming back from his relaxed, dreamy state, and smiled at her antics.

"You're very funny tonight," said Jack. "Doing characters and voices."

"Yeah, yeah, but you should try this," she said. "It's great. Makes you feel like kid again."

"If we both jump on this thing and it breaks, it's going to be a mess."

She rode it to a stop. Whoa boy. "I've got some cards," she said taking a deck off the bedside table. She was a little breathless.

"You want to play a few games?" said Jack

"Let's play strip poker," she said laughing. "I've never done that. What are the rules?" She reached out and popped the elastic on his underwear.

"But," said Jack. "You've only got your bra and panties on and I've just got my shorts and an undershirt." He laughed. "It's gonna be a short game."

She giggled hysterically. "That's just the way I want it. Besides, it's too hard to get dressed again just to take it back off."

They both were feeling silly and began to laugh. With classical music in the background, Angie fanned the deck straight up into the air and all across the bed.

"I win," she said and reached out for him.

"You cheated!" he replied and pushed her flat on her back. "And I demand a recount." She rolled him over and lay on top of him. He slid his hands down, into the back of her panties.

"I demand satisfaction!" she said.

The waves began to roll again and luckily, waterbed seams held fast.

They slept in, the next morning and Jack finally got up and made coffee. He brought a couple of mugs back to bed and she welcomed a drink. They sat in the middle of the bed, sipped from the mugs and surveyed the cards scattered around on the sheets and blanket. The previous nights romp had been hard on the playing cards. Angie picked up a bent ace. She held it up so Jack could see the damage.

"I see," Jack said. "It's marked forever."

"I won?" Angie asked.

"I think it was a tie. It was a tie game."

"You can't have a tie in poker," said Angie. "I definitely won"

"I don't know if that was poker, according to Hoyle, but I feel like the winner." said Jack.

"Me too," she said and leaned over and gave him a passionate kiss. He took the cup from her hand and sat it down on the floor next to the bed.

"This calls for a playoff," he said leaning her back on the pillows and pressing against her.

"Only if Jacks are wild."

"And Queens are willing?"

"Man, that's corny."

"It's the best I could do."

"Oh, I bet you can do better than that."

Later in the morning, Jack drove her to the campus to study and the discussion about Louie and Buck kicked up again. "I thought things over this morning, baby. If you hang around with Buck and Louie long enough," said Angie, "you're going to get sucked into something bad. It's inevitable."

"I won't let that happen." Jack had hoped to get through the rest of this good day without an argument. The previous night and morning had been better than ever.

"I know that's what you think right now, baby, but you could get caught in the middle of something. Someplace you don't want to be. Then what are you going to do? You've got to look at this situation and not rationalize an excuse just to work and depend on these bums."

"I won't let that happen." Jack said confidently. "I'd leave before I would ever get involved with something bad. The idea of jail or perjury doesn't appeal to me, not for any amount of money"

"I hope not," she said. "I don't want to be the girl who visits her lover in jail once a month."

"I'm just the photographer, and I'll stay that way," said Jack.

They arrived at the library. "I love you, baby," she said and got out of the car. "I'll try not to harass you about your business any more."

"Love you too. I'll give you a call tonight."

She walked away and Jack's eyes followed her attractive bottom wiggle as it disappeared around a hedge.

"No more harassment? That ain't gonna happen," he murmured to himself. He knew she cared for him too much to ignore her fears.

Chapter Twelve

Rollin' On the River

A few weeks went by and Acadia International Studios was rocking with various small-time artists and group recording sessions. Jack was picking up jobs here and there that paid the rent, but it was getting tougher to stay ahead of the bills. Louie included him on the sessions so that he would get a chance to meet these bands and offer photographic services for their publicity campaigns and possible albums. That was working, but it wasn't enough to make Jack feel comfortable with his finances. So he feared the inevitable was approaching. He might be forced to go back to a regular or part-time job to keep himself solvent. He'd been his own boss for nearly five months, and he liked it. The trouble with a real job was that it would take him away from the studio and there were certain to be conflicts between photo opportunities and another job.

Buck seemed to be around the studio less and less. He apparently was working on a deal that was still under wraps. But rumors were floating around the studio. Secrecy seemed to be an essential element of everything of any importance at Louie's studio. Randy had told Jack that Louie was somehow involved in helping Buck get started in his own business, just as he was assisting Jack. But, knowing Buck, Jack figured Buck's deal was going to be something substantial.

To Jack, Buck seemed to be a guy with a chameleon personality. He could be sophisticated and charming in one room and walk next door becoming a redneck, good 'o boy in the passage. Jack had watched him be polite to a newcomer and later disagreeable and threatening to another. Mona told Jack that he had a business degree from SMU. Buck was waiting for something for himself, a moment to strike. He guessed Buck was going to start his own record production label and start recording country western groups. That was about the only music Buck could tolerate. Jack only saw him a couple of times in the studio over a two-month period.

"Buck's up to something in Waco," Randy told Jack one day. "He's looking at buying a record company up there that makes 45's and albums. You know, a record pressing factory."

"You're kidding."

"And tape duplication too. I drove up there last week in a rent-a-van to take some cassette duplicating equipment. We put it in this empty store front just off Main Street near the City Hall."

"Waco, that's weird," Jack replied.

"Yeah, seemed kinda shady. You know how Buck operates. We put brown Kraft paper over all the front windows so's nobody can see inside. He had a desk and a phone in there. Nothing else but some big studio recorders and amps and some stuff I brought up. The equipment came out of a warehouse that Louie owns. Buck said it's worn out and worthless but they look good to a dumb ass like me. Buck said he was gonna shine 'em up and show to some Houston bankers. Raising capital or something."

"Sounds more like he's building a studio."

"I don't know about that, it don't look like a studio for making records. He's not saying much, but I can tell he's excited about the thing. You know Buck gets that intense thing going. Very serious you know; concentrated on what he's up too. I mean, he's charging ahead and I wouldn't want to be somebody in his way. I don't mind doing some work for him. He's paying me good for doin' this stuff. Next week I'm supposed to go to San Antonio to pick up some more recorders."

"Let me know if you need any help."

A couple of days later Buck came into the reception area of the studio where Jack was hanging out. He smiled when he saw Jack and motioned for him to come into

Studio A. Jack followed him in and Buck shut the door behind him. They had the control booth to themselves. Jack sat his coffee cup on the console.

"What have you been up to?" Buck asked. They sat down in a couple of chairs behind the console.

"I've been getting a few jobs here and there," said Jack. "Other than that, not much. I haven't seen you around these parts lately" He didn't let on that he knew anything about Buck's recent activities.

"Yeah," Buck said. "I've been really busy with a deal I'm working on. I'm meeting tonight with my investors, a couple of fellows out in Katy. A rich rice farmer out there. I'm setting up a big line of credit." Katy was just west of Houston about 15 miles.

"I want to fill you in on something," he said moving close. "I don't want anybody outside of here knowing, just our little group. I'm in the process of buying a record company up in Waco. It's not a studio like this but an old company that presses records, prints the jackets, the whole manufacturing process. I'll be adding a studio later."

"Very cool," said Jack

So, Randy's gossip was true. Jack held his expression and listened. He was learning to play these things close to his vest when he was around the studio.

Buck was almost whispering although he had the privacy of the sound booth with no one else was around, and the door was shut.

"Let me tell you, Jack, this is going to be a million-dollar deal." He was cock-sure of himself. "This old couple up there has had this business since 1947. They've pressed records for about every producer in Texas over the years and have a hell of a reputation in the business. They're independent operators and they're ready to retire. The old farts must be pushing eighty years old. Louie's done business with them since the fifties and they phoned him to see if he knew someone who might want to buy a regional plant. Louie doesn't want to take that on while he's building up the studio and his new acts. That's where I came in. We're putting a contract together right now."

"Man, that's great," Jack said. "So Louie's backing you.

"No, not with money." he said. "This is my deal. He's helping me make some music connections. I've got this old rice farmer in Katy. He's richer than Jesus and on the board of a bank out there. He's got an associate, an insurance man who's also loaded and they're getting the bank behind me for the initial money. That's about all I can tell you. I've got them on board and I think I'm close to finishing the negotiations with the Stallworths, this old couple, up in Waco. They're getting tired of working and just want to get out of the business with a good retirement deal. Nice folks."

"That sounds good," Jack said. "If you're that close to closing with these Stallworth people and you've got the money together, it sounds like you've just about got it done." Jack wondered how a convicted felon could pull this off with bankers. How did he win their trust?

Buck leaned back displaying a little boastful cowboy-shirted paunch he had been building and relaxed for a moment. He looked at Jack. "I got another tape duplicating shop up in Waco, right downtown, near the banks. I've collateralized it and some of Louie's old equipment there with Waco First Centennial. They think his stuff is mine, so I'm borrowing money on it. Then I'll haul it back to Louie."

"But Jack, I need your help, buddy," Buck said. "I've got an experienced bunch of people up there at the record plant. We've got a good old boy who's the production manager. I've got Shag Roberts lined up to be my general manager."

"I know Shag," Jack said. "I've worked with him a couple of times here and at a studio in San Antonio. He had a couple of acts he brought in to Louie, some Tejano groups out of the Valley. He's a good guy."

Shag Roberts was a long, tall, drugstore cowboy type and a successful small-time record producer and concert promoter based in San Antonio. A friendly type, who had had a couple of records chart near to Top Fifty. Shag also had produced a number of regional hits. But he'd never had a blockbuster that would raise him to the "A" level.

Buck leaned closer to Jack again. "The thing is, I've got this real Mex'can asshole who heads up the graphics department. I'm going to fire his ass once I get control. Maybe I'll just ride him out somewhere and shoot him. Don't get me wrong; most of the employees are Mex'cans. That's fine; I don't care if they're Eskimo's as long as they do their jobs. But, I didn't like this arrogant bastard from the moment I saw him. He's going, so I need your help Jack."

"OK, if I can."

"I'd like for you to come up to Waco next week and see the plant. I've got a new condo up there and you can stay in my place. I know it's hard making much money around here. I need you to take this job in Waco and run the graphics arts and printing department for me. I need you to manage the photography, album cover designs and printing staff. I need a smart, creative manager I can trust, and I think you're the guy, Jack."

That took Jack by surprise. Buck was talking fast and things were moving quickly. Buck Smith seldom indicated or gave a compliment. He leaned more toward intimidation to get people to do what he wanted.

"Thanks, that sounds interesting and I'd like to take a look at the place. You know, I'm doing all right here and Louie sort of depends on me to be here for his stuff. I don't want to drop out on him if I can keep from doing it."

"I can handle Louie," Buck said confidently. Jack started to worry that Buck might overplay his hand. He didn't want to get stuck between them and come out the worse. "Let me see. Maybe we'll both get with Louie and try to get you up to Waco and let you come back here to shoot for him."

"Maybe," Jack said. "I really don't want to lose my momentum with this outfit. Louie's been good to me."

"Aw, hell no," said Buck. "We can work it out. We'll make it work. We're gonna have some fun." Buck was showing confidence, more than Jack had ever seen. He was cocky at his prospects. Buck must have seen the hesitation in Jack's face. "Tell you what; we'll lease you a car after we get the company bought. That'll make it easy. I bet that old Mustang of yours is getting cranky. What we need to do is get you a place up in Waco to live. It's only a couple of hours run back to Houston. "

Getting a company car as part of the offer did not sound bad.

"I need for you to take this deal," said Buck. He could be intense when working somebody over to his side of a discussion. "Randy's been working for me. I may have something for him too."

"It sounds tempting," Jack said, not wanting to buy in too quickly, although in his heart he knew he probably go for it, providing he got Louie's blessing. Buck seemed to be pulling some of Louie's gang away with this deal.

"Tell you what, Jack. If you come up I'll get you a nice car leased and pay you $2,500 a month to boot. That's got to be more than you're making now. Plus, you can still do your free-lance stuff here and pick up whatever walks through the door in Waco. We've got a lot of business up there and you're going to meet plenty of producers who need a photographer."

That sealed it for Jack. That was a great fantastic base salary, plus a car, and a chance to widen his connections in the record business with producers. He'd never made more than twelve thousand a year in his life.

"How about it." said Buck? "You gonna come up to Waco on Tuesday? Take the day to tour the place and we'll have some steaks at the condo. You can meet the staff Tuesday and Wednesday morning and be back here by that afternoon."

"OK, Buck," Jack said. "I'll take a look at it. Thanks for the offer."

"Let's just keep this between ourselves for now," he said. "I'll talk with Louie before I leave and tell him about our deal. I don't think he'll have any problem with it. Like I said, he's been behind me all the way. He's going to get something out of this thing if we can get it to work. Do me a favor, don't mention what I'm gonna pay you to Randy."

"Sure," said Jack.

They shook hands, broke up the conversation and returned to the reception area where Louie, Mona, Randy and Hank were discussing James Brown. Louie quietly contended that James Brown ran the Washington D.C. drug mafia. But the singer was Randy's model for success and he found it hard to believe. Randy was working on Louie for some studio time to record a song he and Suze had composed. Randy had done a little recruiting. He has assembled a group of young musicians from Texas Southern University for a back-up band and was anxious to record. TSU was a black university in Houston with a reputation for turning out excellent jazz musicians. Louie agreed to give some free studio time. Jack was sure Randy would never sing a note for Louie until he was under contract, but Randy could care less about that.

After a few minutes, Buck asked Louie if he could talk with him in the back. Louie gave Jack a glance as he left the room and he had a feeling that Louie knew something was up. A few minutes later Mona's phone rang.

"Jack," she said. "Louie and Buck want to visit with you back in Louie's office."

"OK." Jack said. He went to the door and back down the hallway to Louie's office. He loved Louie's office. It was a mess as always. There were seven-inch reels of tape in boxes, stacked waist high in one corner. Demos, rejects, out-takes, all labeled with a Marks-a-Lot on the edge. Then there were scattered letters and contracts on every table along with trade publications and a few legal books.

He had a long velvet maroon couch along one wall. The carpet was a deep brown and three walls had floor to ceiling wallpaper that looked like a pine forest. The fourth wall was a mirror at a crazy angle which reflected the other three walls and Louie's desk at the far end of the room. As a visitor entered the room, they saw Louie in front of them at his desk. But as they stepped forward, the visitor would realize that wasn't Louie in front of them, but his reflected image. Louie was at the far end of the room to their left. This was disconcerting the first time and most people would nearly walk toward the mirror before realizing the trick. All the while Louie would watch from the other end of the room. He obviously enjoyed the startled confusion of the first time visitor as they entered.

But Jack had been in many times before and had learned to ignore the mirror before him. He sat down in the empty chair in front of Louie's desk, next to Buck. Louie's desk was on a four-inch raised platform so that Louie sat above his visitors. Behind him were more shelves and a table stacked with correspondence, reel-to reel tapes and cassettes. He had an expensive Kudelski-Nagra reel-to-reel tape recorder on one end of the large wooden desk.

"Hi Jack, thanks for comin' back here." Louie said. "Brudder Buck here says he wants you to come up to Waco an' help him with at Texas Star Records."

"Yeah, he told me about the deal this morning," Jack said. "What do you think?"

"I think it's a good thing for you," he said. "Gonna be good money, expand your horizons, you know." Jack couldn't help but be suspicious of the two, but it was a lot of money on the table for him.

"Well, I don't want to lose the connection we have Louie," Jack said. "What I want to try to do, if I go to work for Buck, is to come back here whenever you need me for sessions and whatever else you need."

"I think we can make that work," said Louie.

Buck said, "I told Jack that you didn't want to lose what you two have going. I'm OK with you doing both deals."

"Alright," Jack said. "Buck asked me to get up to Waco next week and check out the place. I'll do that."

Louie said, "We're pretty close to getting' dis Waco deal done. Buck tells me the old couple up der is tired of the negotiating and are ready to sell. We just got to make sure that da banks he's got lined up is on with us."

"In fact boys," said Buck, "I've got to get out to Katy to have dinner with my two backers. These old boys have more money than they can spend. See, they own a good chunk of the bank out there and I can't let them get nervous about the deal. The old farts smell blood in the water and think they are set to make a killing on this transaction."

"I'll call you Monday," Jack said as Buck left the office.

Jack sat there a moment and looked up at Louie who was watching him, as he scrutinized everyone around him. Jack knew that Louie seldom missed anything that was happening with those around him. What others were thinking; his radar was always on, watching expressions, reactions, thinking and planning ahead his every word and movement. Sometimes, he seemed psychic.

"How about it, ain't that Buck something else?" Louie asked Jack.

Jack paused and decided to be more open than usual. He had learned that openness was usually discouraged when you were around Louie or Buck, at least in public. By being candid, there was too much of a chance that you might step into an off-limits topic. There were cans of worms scattered around the building like landmines.

"I think you knew Buck was going to offer me a job before I did." Jack said with a slight smile.

Louie laughed out loud. A laugh Jack hadn't heard often.

"You right," he said. "Aw Jack, you catchin' on brudder. We talked about it last week. Der ain't none of dis shit goin' down that I ain't got a piece of. You jus' go on over to Waco wit' Buck an' everything gonna be alright, brother. I got you back."

"Glad to hear it," Jack said.

"Yup, I guarantee! Get your nose in dis trough, brother. You ain't gonna be der for ever, not with Buck."

Jack stood up to leave Louie to his office, and the piles of tapes and contracts scattered across his desk.

"Louie," Jack asked. "Tell me one thing. Why all the back room conversations, the intrigue? You or Buck could have just taken me aside and asked if I wanted a job. Hell, you know me. Why did Buck feel like he had to persuade or con me, you know, snake me into going up to Waco?

"That was Buck's doin's, Jack. Hope you know I didn't mean no disrespect to you. That's jus' him...is now and will ever be. He can't do nothin' straight to save his life. That's his way…you'll see."

"I guess so, but I don't understand him."

"Done worry 'bout understanding Buck! Nothin' to understand, Jack. I think he's pro'bly some kind of genius most of the time, but he's always Buck. You take care of you'self up der. But Buck…he's just got that larceny in his soul!"

Jack got over to Angie's apartment that afternoon after talking with Buck and Louie. He thought he could persuade her to go along with his temporary move. But he had to break the news to Angie. It wasn't going to be pretty and Louie's last words played in his mind like a tape loop, "larceny in his soul…larceny in his soul….larceny in his soul."

That was Buck.

Jack wasn't sure how to bring it all up to his girl. He hadn't neglected thinking of Angie when he was talking to Buck, but put their situation aside while he was in the studio. Now he would have to face his decision to go to Waco, and wondered if he could defend it to her satisfaction. Jack rang the bell at her apartment. She was surprised to see him at this time. Angie had been packing her books to study in the Rice library before an important night class. She was going to be there late into the night.

"I've got to tell you something important," said Jack. "Can you wait a moment?"

"OK." She could tell he had something serious on his mind. She braced herself, not knowing what to expect.

"What is it?"

"Angie, I've got a full-time job offer, a great gig. But, it looks like I'm going to have to move to Waco for a while to take advantage of it,' said Jack. "The offer is more than twice what I'm making now. It's either take it, or go back to some regular, full-time job like, and give up the photography. You know, money's getting tight for me. There's just not enough coming in every month."

"Slow down man, move to Waco?" Angie replied. She was taken by surprise and the idea shook her. "Why, what's in Waco?"

"Well, Buck Smith's buying a record pressing and manufacturing plant there. He's offered me a job. But I'll be back here as often as I'm up there. I'll still be working with Louie just like I am now. Buck wants me to manage the graphic arts and printing press people at the plant," said Jack.

"And what about us? Screw Buck Smith!" she said. "You're thinking about working for that jerk? I don't believe it!" He had reached to embrace her but she pulled back. "Don't go to work for Buck, not that crook…that sociopath!" She paused. "I want you here, baby. You can't do that."

"I'm going to be back every weekend and sometimes during the week," Jack said. He was talking fast. "We can stay the same. I don't want to let this get between us…it doesn't have to. I'm going to be here all the time." Jack was scrambling for words that would calm her, but it wasn't working. "We don't see each other everyday anyway."

She turned away from him and put her books on the table and her hands went to her hips. She stared at the wall with her back to him.

"I don't believe you, Jack."

"Listen."

"Why not just tell him no?" Angie was not shouting, but she was upset. "It's that simple. We'll figure something else out. Quit this shit with these record guys. Talk to Rudy. He's always got something going. He can help you make some money on the side." She would not face him.

"I need the work, the money, Angie. He's going to pay me $2,500 a month for the Waco job. I can make even more with Louie's business," said Jack. "Otherwise, I'll have to give this photography thing up. That's a lot of money and I'll get a company car. I've got to do something. This Waco job came along at just the right time."

"Not for me, baby," Angie said. She spun back around and went to him. Tears were beginning to run down her face to her chin. She swept them off. She reached out and took his hands, despite her anger.

"I was thinking that you and I were about to take our relationship to the next plateau. I think you know what I mean…a permanent commitment." She paused and squeezed his hands. "Oh hell. Jack, if you move out of town, I don't know if I can stand that."

"I'm sorry," Jack said. "But, can't we try? After all, this isn't a permanent move. I'm not going to stay in Waco long; no longer than I have to."

"We can try," she said. "I love you and I know you feel the same way." More tears ran down to her cheeks and she brushed them away with the back of her hands. "It's just such a surprise."

"I do love you, Angie. I don't want this job to kill what we have. But I've got to give this a try."

"OK, Jack," she said, but she didn't sound very

convinced. "If it's only temporary, I'll try. I've given you everything I have for the past year. I need you close. It's just the way I am. You know I need you backing me up, encouraging me to keep studying. I need you here close, everyday, not in some other damn city." She was working to regain her composure and Jack was fighting not to tear up. "But we can't let this deal get in the way of us," she whispered. "Don't let Buck and this damn job come between us. I don't care if you are broke. You can stay with me."

He held her and kissed her cheek. "I'm not going to sponge off you, I'll try this and we'll see if we can make it work." he said quietly. "I'll be around just about as much as I am now."

"Well, I've got to go," said Angie. "We'll talk more tomorrow. I've got to let this sink in for a while." Angie was obviously shaken by his news and his decision. A decision he had made before discussing it with her. She picked up her books and pulled a few Kleenex's out of a box. Angie walked out on the balcony of the apartment. Jack followed silently pulling the door shut behind him. They went down the steps and to her car.

She turned to kiss him and they embraced for a moment. Not the best hug he had ever had.

"You won't change your mind?" she said. He didn't answer immediately.

"I can't, I've got to see where it leads."

A quick kiss and she said, "I still love you, call me in the morning." She walked over to her car and opened the door. "I'm sorry; it's not fair for me to make demands. You've never make any on me. You have to do what you think is best, but I think you're making a big mistake. I wish you had talked with me before you made up your mind."

"I'm sorry Angie," Jack knew she was hurt.

"Adios, Jack"

"Love you," he said. "Be careful."

"You too."

She backed out and drove down the street leaving him standing there. Jack went to his car and sat in it for a minute before leaving for home.

Jack made the trip to Waco a couple of days later and the record plant was just like Buck had described it. The place was a little tired looking, but operational. Jack could see that it was an old production factory with old equipment. Pretty shabby except for the press room which was spotless. There was a small recording studio in an adjoining building. He told Buck it was a deal if the terms were still the same.

"You're damn right they're the same. Man, I'm happy to have you on board. It's twenty-five hundred a month; you'll get paid cash ever two weeks just like everybody else. Go on down to the car leasing place tomorrow in Houston and I'll set everything up for you. I'll give them a price range and you pick out what you like. The company pays for the car and the insurance but you've got to buy your own gas. You can retire that old Mustang."

"When do you want me on the job," said Jack.

"How about next Monday." said Buck. "I'll be here and can introduce you around. I took over this week but I'm flying back tonight. You can stay in my spare room 'til we get you moved. If I was you, I'd come up here by the weekend and start looking for an apartment. You know where mine is but I'll be back at home. Here's a key to the place. Make yourself at home. There's good scotch in the cabinet and a big color TV.

Jack made quick work of finding a place. It was a small, but workable studio apartment in a modern complex. It was fairly cheap, close to the condo Buck owned and not too far from work. He figured he could easily put fifteen hundred in the bank as savings each month. That was a big improvement over the three hundred a month he had been draining from his savings as he tried to get his photography business up to a sustainable level.

He went to Houston Auto Leasing and found that the price range for leasing that Buck had set up was more than generous. He set himself up with a new Pontiac Firebird, a brilliant white with blue racing stripes down the hood and a steel-blue leather interior. It had the new, RAM II 400 cid engine, quad headlights and a four-speed transmission. He had never driven anything so fast in his life.

A week later he moved his stuff to Waco with the help of Randy Sun and the studio van. The move went easy enough, but his good-by to Angie was hard on both of them. Jack kept rolling her words around in his head as he and Randy drove up to Waco.

"You're really going to leave me?" she had said.

"I'm not leaving you Angie," he replied. "I'll be back all the time. I don't think you'll have time to miss me. We'll both be busy, that will help. Maybe you can come up to visit."

"It's not the same, Jack," she said, "We'll never have it the same after you get up there. They're going to change you. I just know it. It's never going to be the same."

Part Two

Chapter Thirteen

Everyday People

"It isn't relaxed back there," said Jack. He was in the front office of Texas Sun records and only Shag and Wanda were listening.

"You got to remember Jack; you're the new gringo in town. We all are, said Shag. "They're watching us and their nervous, new owner and all."

"Well, I think I'm slowly working my way into managing the department."

He was the newcomer in a predominantly Hispanic shop, and their new boss. After the buyout, the staff didn't know what to expect. It was July, hot summer and the heat and humidity in Waco were enough to intensify everything. He had been on board two weeks. Most of the staff at Texas Sun had been working together for many years. They were practically all Hispanic and all good people who were cautiously friendly. He knew he was being tested and examined to see what kind of a boss he would be. The guy Buck had mentioned was the darkroom and layout specialist, Juan Vega. Buck fired him the day Jack arrived. In all honesty, Jack felt Juan was a petty jerk and hothead. It was for the best and now Buck wouldn't have to shoot him, as he had threatened. The rest of the staff saw it coming and didn't seem to miss him. Jack gave them respect and thanks for their work. And his sincere efforts were helping him gain their respect.

Amanda Garza was the supervisor of the three women who made up the graphic arts side. They did the illustrative and make-up work on the labels and album covers. When a job left their hands it was camera-ready and Jack did the darkroom camera work and prepress color separation, stripping and set-up before it went on the press. Jack found Amanda to be a sweetheart, about forty years old and she directed her small staff like a mother hen. They liked her and worked hard at their jobs.

Jesse Alvarado managed the pressroom. He ran a group of pressmen who burned the press plates for the big press. They made album covers and the 33 rpm and 45 rpm record labels that to be glued in the center of both sides of the platter. They were jokers who didn't hesitate to take advantage of Jack's lack of experience with their processes. He didn't mind and laughed along with them when he became the butt of some of their jokes.

Jack's high school Spanish got a daily workout, although almost all of the staff was fluent in English. But, as in most of Texas, a predominantly Hispanic staff tended to switch back to Spanish in personal conversation. He didn't mind although some Anglos would be offended by not understanding what the "Mex'cans" were talking about. Jack didn't care. When he did understand snatches of conversation, it was usually about family topics or other mundane gossip.

After a month or so, Jack thought he had been accepted since he had shown them he was not a company spy but just working a job like the rest of them. Jack began to learn more about their personal lives and interpersonal relationships. They were predominantly a satisfied group, happy to have a regular paycheck and a job in decent surroundings, considering that it was a record factory.

Jesse, the lead pressman was a natural leader and the other guys respected his knowledge and hard work and worked hard for him. It was a productive staff printing labels and record and cassette album covers. The days hummed by at work with little conflict or stress. Jack did not spend much time with Shag or Wanda during the days because he wanted to avoid having his staff reminded that he was part of the owner's team of Anglos.

Shag had pulled him aside on his first they there.

"Jackie," he said in a fatherly tone. "The one thing you got to remember about these folks is that jealousy runs in their veins. Just avoid hanging around the front office too much unless you got a reason. They're gonna be watchin' to see if you've got something special that they don't. I love these Mex'cans, but it's just the way they're built." Jack nodded in agreement. He wasn't going to argue about racial prejudices with Shag. He laughed to himself what Angie would have said if she heard Shag's words. Jack told himself he'd never share it with her. She'd just get further pissed with him.

Jack figured it was just a little redneck advice but he did try to avoid being the guy with some special privileges. The truth was that he did spend time with them when Buck was in town. It was early fall. Most weeks they had a Monday Night Football feast and party. The whiskey would flow after steaks. Buck had also acquired a call-girl girlfriend who flew up to Waco from Houston on occasion. She was a blond who seemed to be focused on trying to be classy. A clean miss by Jack's estimation. But, they were about the only friends Jack had in Waco.

Jesse and Amada no doubt realized the facts about Jack's inside connections, or some part of it, but did not make it an issue or subject of conversation at work. The months passed quickly. After working every day through the week, Jack would head back to Houston for most weekends. A few times, Jack returned briefly during the week for some studio work for Louie. He tried to connect with Angie most weekends, but he was not there as often as he had hoped.

He was losing touch with her and his other Houston friends. He felt it. It was lonely in Waco and he kept to his apartment most of the time.

A few weeks after Jack had moved into an apartment in Waco, Buck had acquired a roommate. A younger Katy buddy, Terry Cummins and strangely enough, a former boyfriend of Buck's daughter. She was starting college in Wharton Junior College. Terry was in the Air Force and was stationed in Waco as a recruiter. Buck gave him a room, rent-free and Terry was designated to "care take" the place when he was out of town. Jack thought that Buck just felt better having another guy in the house that he could trust. Terry had been a linebacker on the Katy Tigers football team and weight lifter. He had a tall, muscled-up build and didn't mind portraying a tough country boy attitude. He was smart with a quick, dry wit. He reminded Jack of a redneck Steve McQueen and obviously also had a wild side. Like Buck, he thought himself a lady-killer.

Buck had leased a condo in Waco the week the papers were signed, but had now moved to a bigger condo in the same complex. He said his wife didn't like the first when she visited, which was a rare event. It was fully furnished with three bedrooms, a good kitchen, den and fireplace. Buck had bought the biggest TV he could find for the den. Almost every Monday night after work, Jack would go by Buck's for dinner and Monday Night Football.

Both Jack and Buck liked large salads so Jack would set to work on a salad while Buck grilled the steaks and baked the potatoes. Shag and his girlfriend Wanda, Terry and Angelique Patron, would join them for the meal. Angelique was a nineteen year old budding singer from Monterrey. She was tall with Spanish blood and dishwater blond hair. She seemed to be striving for a Castilian trailer trash look. It didn't take long for Jack to realize that her taco shell was a little cracked. Still, who knows, he thought, it might work in Nashville. Angelique's mind was somewhere in a six-year old fantasy land most of the time and a little petulant when things did not go her way. Jack couldn't see any talent there, she sang flat, but Shag and Wanda had her under contract and were planning big things for her. She spoke broken English and lived in the extra room of their apartment. It looked to Jack like she was Wanda's pet singer. One that she could dress up and try to shape into a Tejano music star.

It wasn't that she was unattractive, but Jack didn't think she was a knockout either. By the end of the third quarter, a bottle or more of Jack Daniels would disappear and after the game Jack would return to his apartment. Jack wasn't much of a drinker but Buck and Shag made up for his part. Wanda would drive Shag and Angelique home. Jack soon came to realize that Buck was drinking too much in the evenings. He watched as Buck drank and his big talk and plans got more expansive with each drink.

From what Jack understood, Buck was supposed to make a second, big installment payment to the Stallworths for Texas Sun Records that month. Randy had told Jack that there were supposed to be four equal payments over one year to complete the purchase. Apparently, Buck put the first quarter down when the deal was signed and was then made President. Buck had insisted that he take over the helm from the Stallworths or the deal was dead. The Stallworths were tired and desperate because their auditor had finally told them the full truth about their twenty-eight year old business. It was virtually bankrupt, dead, but they hadn't seen it coming. They just knew the cash flow was drying up. Everything they had in reserve was depleted as they paid the bills but their customers were holding out on them. Not enough was coming in and the debts were building. It was time to get out with their home and some cash intact after all the years of work they had put in building the record business.

"I have them over a barrel of their own making," Buck boasted one night. They weren't about to pass up a $500,000 buy-out at their age. They had to let it go. I just slowly squeezed the spirit out of them." Jack could tell he was perversely delighted at the opportunity to drain them. Buck assured the couple that they would wind up very comfortable and secure in their retirement. They had the first $125,000 in the bank and put the company in Buck's hands.

Now it was time to come up with the second payment, which was another $125,000. Rumor had it was that one reason the Stallworths had to sell was that independent record producers owed them nearly a million dollars, some of them fairly big accounts. Many of the debtor accounts were successful and had plenty of cash. But the Stallworths had mellowed from the hard-nosed early days when they were building the company.

Buck bought at a discounted price because of the state of the company. He was paying practically nothing for the real assets, the land, buildings and equipment. He said the plan, after the initial down payment, was to make the following payments to the former owners by collecting from all of the debtor record companies that owed Texas Sun Records. He would come out free and clear on the business with a lot of cash left over. Then he said he had big plans to borrow much more and grow the company, and try to get some national business.

Buck wasn't afraid of using Louie's name and influence as well as other connections to first scare and then hammer the debtors. Buck spread rumors with regional record producers that organized crime in New York now had a piece of the new company. He hinted that they should settle rather than face the unknown. That worked with a lot of them. Money poured into the company daily as he made the small independents settle up.

He seemed to have had done well so far at collecting and dropped the accounts receivables substantially. Apparently his plan was working just the way he had laid it out. Shag's girlfriend Wanda told Jack that she had deposited nearly three-hundred grand into the bank over the first two months as Buck cleaned up the accounts. But his biggest debtor was Vaquero records, based in the Rio Grande border town of Eagle Pass. They were a major player in *Tejano* and *Norteno* music of Northern Mexico and South Texas. They sold records in all of the major Latino markets--Texas, Southern California, Florida and Chicago. The Gomez family in Eagle Pass had stiffed the Stallworths for years by bringing them more and more business, but paying less and less of the growing balance they owed. When Buck moved into the CEO's chair, a position he had forced on the Stallworths as part of the contract, they owed Texas Sun Records over $400,000.

Finally, Buck figured he had messed around long enough with Vaquero Record's owner, Juan Gomez. He had gotten nowhere despite numerous phone calls and empty promises. Now, he needed the money right away and he was insulted at them gaming him.

Jack was bent over his light table one Tuesday morning around nine, following the previous evening's party at Buck's. The game had been a stinker and Jack had checked out early, in the middle of the third quarter, when Buck had fallen asleep in his chair and Terry was talking to some gal on the phone.

The next day, Buck suddenly stuck his head in the layout room, adjacent to the darkroom. "Jack," he barked. "Drop what you're doing. We got to take a little road trip."

"I'll be back later," Jack said to the staff as he followed Buck back to the reception area.

"You got a tank of gas?" said Buck.

"Pretty near."

"Good, we've got to make a round trip to Eagle Pass today. I've got to hit the can. You better too, we've got some miles to make. Let's see how fast that Firebird of yours can roll!"

Within ten minutes they were on Interstate 35 heading almost dead south. Jack's head was spinning but he was figuring they were going to go nearly 700 miles before he got back to Waco. That was a long drive, even for Texans. Buck took the first leg through Austin and San Antonio. That was unusual, Buck never got behind the wheel when another driver was available.

Jack and Buck kept country music blasting most of the way but had to change the station several times. They stopped in San Antonio and La Pryor for gas before reaching Eagle Pass about two in the afternoon. Buck intended to confront Juan Amando Gomez, the old man and founder of the Vaquero Records. He wanted his money, all of it, today.

They entered Eagle Pass slowly and stopped to locate Vaquero Records on a street map. It was a dusty, small border town on the Western edge of big ranch country of mesquite and cactus. Piedras Negras, Mexico was just across the border.

As instructed, Jack parked the car along the curb and in front of the driveway where it could not be blocked in. Buck went into the office and Jack followed. The reception area was authentic South Texas ranch style. The walls were finished in varnished knotty pine paneling, with floor to ceiling award cases. There were several big buck deer heads on the wall and a full stuffed, snarling javalina in the corner. The furniture was Texas ranch sheik with heavy, tan cowhide cushions. Jack waited as the receptionist announced Buck. Two French doors opened and Gomez invited Buck in with a big smile. He motioned Jack in and indicated he should take a small chair just inside the door. Buck didn't introduce him and Gomez didn't bother to introduce himself either. They left him there and approached the desk.

The office was also decorated Texas a'la hacienda ranch style with a deep cowhide chairs and couches. On the walls were several bullfighter suits that were beautifully displayed, full length in showcases. There were also civic awards on the walls and a fancy Spanish saddle laden with silver buckles and studs.

They shook hands and Juan offered Buck one of two large, Mexican carved chairs near the desk. Gomez then sat behind a hand carved, mesquite desk facing Buck. Papers were strewn over the top. The receptionist, an attractive blond, entered with a tray with a coffee carafe, two china cups and some pan de polvo sweets. No one spoke. She poured a Styrofoam cup of coffee for Jack and also gave him a handful of the small, round cookies on a paper plate.

"Thanks honey," said Buck. She left the room, closing the doors behind her.

"Juan, I'll come to the point," said Buck. "I'm sure that you know you've owed Texas Sun Records a good deal of money for a long, long time. The Stallworths have retired. They're gone. I'm in charge now. I'm buying them out completely."

"I'm aware of that," said Gomez. "I congratulate you. How is our mutual friend Louie Thibodeaux?"

"I saw him last week, Juan. He's doing just fine. He has a great interest in my takeover at Texas Sun, as do others up North."

"I hope you are enjoying the coffee and sweets, Buck. I had heard he had a part of your purchase, as well as others."

"That's about the size of it, Juan, I own it and that's a big part of why I'm here today. I've come to pay my respects and collect the bill."

"It is not a good time for me to consider paying," said Gomez.

Any politeness was evaporating faster than the steam on their coffees.

"I refuse to believe that a man of your wealth and influence would flinch at paying this debt. I couldn't be that much to you."

"Not today. It does not fit my business agenda"

"Today is the day you will pay!" said Buck, suddenly turning up the intensity of the conversation. "Otherwise there will be business, personal consequences."

"I don't think so."

"I'll sue your goddam ass out of business to begin with," said Buck. "I'll goddam well ransom the masters, all your product at the plant, stop all production. You'll be dead in the water on those artists." Gomez had some hits working and he needed product in the stores. But Gomez wasn't giving in. He apparently decided to test Buck's will. See if he was bull or a milk cow.

"You say I owe a good deal of money. How much? I do not keep up with such figures."

"You owe me $467,928 dollars and twenty-one cents as of the end of last month. I want the cash or a check this goddam morning. I want my money. I'm not the goddam Stallworths. I'm not going to get fucked."

He paused and lowered his voice although Jack could hear the whispered words. "Look Juan, I also represent a very powerful group of investors in New York. Interests beyond my own. We intend to have the money immediately. You know who I'm talking about."

"I have friends also, Mr. Smith. If you are trying to scare me, I should remind you that it's a long way from New York to Eagle Pass. I have nothing to fear down here. I have my friends here, the police and judges on both sides of the border are compadres of mine. I'm not paying you a cent until it is convenient." said Gomez. He was only partially bluffing; Gomez was well connected in Texas and Northern Mexico. He had carefully nurtured the authorities and politicians on both sides of the borders for years.

"If I leave here today with less than half," said Buck. "I won't be back." He paused and looked around the room. "You've built yourself a pretty big empire here, Gomez. Your family has the company, this building and I understand a beautiful house on the edge of town and some ranches with fine Santa Gertrudis cattle. What I'm telling you is some fellows will be here from New York tomorrow to collect if I leave empty handed." Buck was bluffing but his intensity sold the idea to Gomez. "These are very serious people."

"Indeed?"

"You got a nice family," said Buck. "You're going to leave them an important name, a fortune, a heritage. Why take a risk losing it over a relatively insignificant debt. We can act like businessmen," said Buck. "As for your compadres, if you go away, they can always find someone else to launder their drug money. It's not like this is all of your fortune, Juan, but all of this debt is my fucking money.

"I do not like your language," said Gomez. Gomez paused for a moment to reconsider his options. This man was not a gelding. "You should shut your mouth with your insinuations. I will give you half today. That is all I can do." He reached in his desk drawer and pulled out a large checkbook. He scribbled across a check with a fountain pen, tore it out and tossed a business check for $250,000 across the table.

"You are a son-of-a-bitch, Mr. Smith. I will pay you this and the rest when I am good and ready. I would not come back to Eagle Pass, Mr. Buck. That is my most gracious advice. Certainly more than you are due. My people will be waiting for you next time."

"You're full of shit Gomez. You and your sons may be big stuff in this little ciudad, but you are a tick on the butt of my people. But ticks are an annoyance that must be dealt with. I expect the rest of the money in a month. Otherwise, Eagle Pass may be having some out of town visitors. They will not be as easy as me," said Buck. He leaned to the edge of the desk and scooped the check glanced at the figure and stuffed it into his coat side pocket.

"You have your check," said Gomez. "I am tired of talking and looking at you. Go away."

Buck was not ready to leave without making a final impression. His temper exploded and he suddenly lunged toward Gomez. Buck was flushed in a moment. The old man was caught off guard because he felt the meeting was concluded. The chair Buck was sitting in was kicked over backward. He leaned over the desk menacingly and put his finger in the face of Gomez. Buck was livid with anger, Gomez slid down in his chair.

Jack instinctively stood up but froze in place.

"Don't ever jerk me around again or I'll kill you, Juan!" Buck shouted, inches from his face. "I will break your dirty spic neck!" That was loud enough to be heard outside the office.

To emphasize his point, Buck snatched up the double light brass lamp on the desk and threw it against the wall, behind the old man. The crash destroyed a large photograph of the Gomez family in a gilded frame. He shoved the old man backward into his chair. Glass shattered, and the frame crashed to the floor. The door to Jack's left opened tentatively and the receptionist peeked in.

"I want all my money!" said Buck. "It better be in my hands in thirty days or you'll meet my friends."

She bravely slipped in as Buck turned and waved at Jack. He stormed past the girl and out of the building with Jack on his heels. He had given the elderly Gomez a shock with the sudden display of violence and insult.

"You drive," he said to Jack, throwing him the keys. "Haul ass. We better get the hell out of town. That old man might sic the cops on us for all I know."

Jack and Buck hit the road. Back at Vaquero Records, the old man sank in his chair and asked for some brandy but fainted before she could get him a drink. He looked gray and his secretary screamed for help. His son Antonio ran in from the warehouse and knelt beside his father. An ambulance was summoned and his family checked him into the hospital. Before noon the doctors told the family that he had suffered a mild heart attack. Gomez's youngest son Antonio, who handled A&R for the family business, went berserk and stormed across the border into Piedras Negras. He hit his favorite bar and rounded-up a couple of his Mexican thugs. He planned a trip to Waco for the next day. First he needed a few rounds of Tequila.

No one would have caught up with Buck and Jack that day. Jack used almost all of the four-hundred cubic inches to hold the Firebird at a steady 110 miles per hour on Highway 57, slowing only in La Pryor and then Batesville. He was focused on the road like an Indy driver. It was a road where you were more likely to get pulled over by a game warden than a highway patrolman. In Batesville, they stopped at corner grocery and gas station to pick up some ready-made sandwiches, pork rinds and a six-pack of Lone Star. This first third of the trip was through the South Texas brush country and big ranches. The highway was wide and there was virtually no traffic for the first one hundred miles. The road blended from Highway 57 into Interstate 35, slowing somewhat because of traffic and turned more northward, flying through San Antonio, Austin before arriving in Waco. They had made the trip of a little over 325 miles in less than five hours. Jack was so tired when he got back to the apartment; he took off his shoes and drank a half a beer before falling asleep on his couch. Driving fatigue and nerves from the trip and watching the rear view mirror had taken it all out of him. "I didn't sign up for this kind of shit," he mumbled to himself. After that thought, he was out until nine the next morning.

Chapter Fourteen

War

It was early afternoon the next day when Antonio Gomez and his compadres arrived at Texas Sun Records and stormed into the Texas Sun's Waco lobby. They had left Piedras Negras and crossed at the Rio Grande border into Eagle Pass early that morning, still drinking and vowing vengeance.

Jack was standing in front of the counter talking to Wanda when the trio arrived. Antonio Gomez was not that tall but had a boxer's build and quickness. His temper was over the top, probably a match for Buck's, and the veins in his neck were pulsing. He was ready to kill anyone who got in his way.

"Where's Buck Smith?" he shouted. "I'm Antonio de laVela Gomez and that bastard nearly killed my old man." One of his buddies stayed in the car and the other came in with him and stood near the front door. He had the look of a Mexican bruiser, built like a wrestler in a sweatshirt, red bandana across his forehead and an oversized black leather jacket, work jeans and rattlesnake skin boots.

"I'll let him know you're here," said Wanda. She rang up Buck in the adjoining office and calmly said, "Mr. Antonio Gomez is here to see you and he seems upset."

"Tony, Mr. Smith said for you to go right in," she said nonchalantly. His office is through that door to your left.

She was cool as a cucumber as she told him but the words barely got out of her mouth when Antonio lunged to the door and burst through it without turning the knob. Splinters flew into the room as the doorframe broke apart and the door twisted at a crazy angle. The top hinge came out and the door fell half way to the floor. Antonio kicked it aside and went around it, into the room.

Antonio's compadre stayed in the lobby near the front door and didn't move. Jack didn't think he spoke English anyway and seemed to be waiting and watching. They listened from the lobby as Antonio confronted Buck in his office, seemingly ready for a showdown.

"Morning Antonio," said Buck. "You bring me the other two hundred thousand your old man owes me?

"You son of a bitch!" screamed Antonio, "My father's in the hospital with a heart attack. You threatened to burn our place down. You ain't burning our record company down. I don't know who you think you're screwing with, we're Vaquero Records. We're the Gomez family of Eagle Pass, and we'll pay you when we get good and goddamned ready!"

He was getting himself even more worked up. "You don't talk to my Father like that you puke pissing *carbron*. I'm going back to Eagle Pass. I'll get my gun and come up here and blow your head off!" He moved up to the desk with his fists clenched, but Buck didn't move.

"That'll be just fine Antonio," replied Buck calmly. "Wish you hadn't of broken my door." He casually pulled open the lower right hand drawer of his desk and drew out a long-barreled chrome Colt .45 revolver."

"I've got mine…go get yours."

Antonio backed up a step. "You bastard, you probably killed my daddy, already. I'm going to see to it you pay!" he screamed.

"It's you who are going to pay me, you pussy! Get that straight!" Buck said as he stood up, gun in hand. He raised it to eye level, extended his arm and pointed it toward Antonio's nose, just a few feet in front of him. Buck was a big, intimidating figure when his blood was up.

"Fuck you and your old man," Buck said without raising his voice. He didn't need to. "You can go fetch my money now. Just get your scrawny, spic ass out of here before I personally pistol-whip your butt. You know, I don't mind going back to the penitentiary if I have to make a point."

Antonio turned to leave. He found Shag standing in the middle of the lobby between him and his protection man. Shag had a baseball bat, holding it full length and low below his waist with both hands.

"You can leave the same way you came in," said Shag.

Buck shouted at Antonio's back, before he and his buddy could go through the front door, "The next time I see you, you better have a check in your hand and not your tamale. You hear me, Tony?"

Jack walked to the front door as it shut behind them and watched as they got into a shiny black Buick Riviera and burned rubber out of the lot.

Buck came to his office door and surveyed the damage. "Wanda, send 'ol man Gomez at Vaquero a bill this afternoon for $75 to cover fixing this door. Like I said, screw them." They looked at each other and everyone laughed, relieving some of the tension that had filled the room from young Antonio's visit.

Jack followed Shag into Buck's office.

"You know Buck, that's one of those spoiled rich kids who's got a big temper. He's not going to forget being humiliated," Jack said.

"Yeah," said Buck, "but he's got no real balls, or he wouldn't have come in here with the threats of what he was going to do. He would have just done it. You know, had us all gunned down some night by some of his *pachuco* gang compadres. Now, with his buddy seeing what happened, running away, he can't hire it out or he'll look weak to his friends. He'll just give them some excuse for letting me get away with insulting him. He's a punk. Now go on, I've got to call Louie"

Jack left hoping that Buck was right. Too many nights he would leave Buck's apartment alone after a party or watching a football game with the gang, and look around while he got in his car. It left him wondering about his future in Waco.

The following weekend Jack was in Houston and spending some time with Angie. He found her unhappy with the way things were going, "I don't want to nag you, Jack," Angie said late that Saturday night. "I just don't like this. I'm lonely. I wish you would move back and give up that job." She was upset and felt left out of his life. "When are you coming home, baby?"

He's just following his dream she told herself, just as she was pursuing her studies at Rice. But it wasn't easy. Angie was staying busy with her work. She wondered if she was just someone who needed a lot of attention. Would that day come?

Jack was telling himself that after the trip to Eagle Pass and the run-ins with the Mexican Mafia, that he had better to figure a way out. There was no doubt he was losing Angie.

Chapter Fifteen

Honky-Tonk Woman

The band was just a rhythm section of Mombo, Lee and Mel from Blackplanque and a black keyboardist Jack didn't know. Jack had been summoned from Waco and arrived late in the afternoon.

Jack sat on a stool at the far end of the Studio A sound booth between a couple of 8-track AG-440 Ampex recorders and Shingles was sitting behind the mixing console in the center chair, where all the knobs, switches and slide controls lined up under 24 VU meters for the different microphones and instrument input lines. At the far end of the room was the new AF-1000, 16-track recorder, Louie's pride and joy. To the left of Shingles sat Louie, where he could shout in instructions his ear as the tracks were laid down. Louie liked to keep the studio monitors scorching loud. After most sessions, Jack would go home with his ears ringing, still hearing a high-pitched tone as he lay in bed.

Moonie took the third chair on the right. Louie and Moonie looked at each other for a moment, Louie smiled and Moonie gave him a brief, positive nod. No words were exchanged. Louie turned to his right and said, "Shingles, I think Moonie here likes your taste in the ladies."

"I do my best bringing in only the most talented for our guests," replied Shingles

Moonie had gone back into Louie's office about thirty minutes earlier after he and Louie had returned from dinner. A few minutes after Moonie came up the hallway from the back offices and sat down at the board, a young woman entered the booth. Apparently she had been back in the offices.

She stopped at the end of the console, which came up about chest high on her. The console area was built on a raised platform in the booth. Anyone standing beside the deck had to look up at the producers and engineer. She looked down the line of chairs at Moonie, Shingles and Louie and then lay her head down on the console on her folded hands. She shut her eyes for a minute.

She looked about twenty, or maybe a weary eighteen. Well built, she wore tight, faded bell-bottom jeans with a paisley panel along the outer inseams beneath her knees. A gypsy cut, tie-died blouse and a few rings and bracelets on her arms, completed her. Her long, brunette hair was in a ponytail that was pulled to the back, but behind her right ear rather than square in the center of her head.

Jack thought she was Shingle's girlfriend since she had first smiled at him when she came in the room. But this first guess was quickly proven wrong.

Louie got up and slid down behind Shingles and Moonie tapping the chick on the shoulder as he walked past her and out the door, then turned toward the back rooms.

"Come on, honey," said Louie.

She opened her eyes and straightened from her brief rest and winked at Moonie. She was cute, even with a partially chipped front tooth.

"See 'ya, Moonie" she directed a smile toward him and followed Louie out.

"Next time," Moonie replied and looked away.

A few minutes later, Louie came back in the producer's booth refolding a wad of bills and stuffing it into his front pants pocket.

"I 'tol you Moonie," he said. "You're gonna like dis Acadia studio. How do you like my place and the special features?"

"Marvelous…just marvelous."

"That's great," said Louie. He clapped his hands together. "I love it when everybody's satisfied. Let's do some recordin'."

Hidalgo Martin stood alone in the middle the Studio A in front of the microphone. He had been reading over the charts and lyrics of a couple of dozen songs. The lights were turned down low in the room and his lips were just in front of the nylon mesh breath baffle. He had been in this place many times before. Louie had many hours of tape from the previous years when he had been Hidalgo's first producer. They had a real success run previously, and were planning for another round. This time he would have Moonie behind him as well. Eleven years earlier Louie had discovered him singing at the Veteran's Hall in Hebbronville, far down in the Texas Valley, east of Laredo. It led to a gold record single and a gold album. Hidalgo had been a brief nationwide rock 'n roller sensation back then.

Hidalgo's father was a ranch hand near Realitos. A true vaquero, who cowboyed on some of the big ranches in the area and loved the unique Tex-Mex/Hispanic music in South Texas. Early in his teens, Hidalgo was fronting a band playing traditional *rancheras* and *cumbias* for local dances. They also mixed in some of the rock and roll classics from the Fifties to keep the crowd going, and a few traditional Mexican ballads. Sometimes he sang in English and sometimes translated the rock songs into Spanish for the audience. Hidalgo was smart, clever and worked to please his audience.

His parents had made sure that Hidalgo learned English in school and both his parents spoke English and Spanish in the home. In that predominantly Hispanic area of Texas, many of the older generations spoke very little or broken English. Most of the Anglos who lived on the ranches spoke Spanish. Louie was taken by his expressive tenor voice and open stage presence. He was a natural entertainer, about five feet, ten with a short Mexican-Afro of curly black hair. Beneath it was a face that expressed joy, enthusiasm and a friendly manner as he sang. He played a fifties Fender Jaguar which seldom left his side.

Louie met with Hidalgo and his father Juan the next they after that show. Everyone called Juan, "Gallo" or Rooster, because he was short, stocky and more than a little bow-legged from years in the saddle. After sharing a few *cervesas* under a spreading live oak tree in the front yard of their wooden house, the contract were signed. It was a beautiful South Texas winter they and the sun shown down on them. Gallo even found Hidalgo's first guitar that was up on rafters of the work shed and showed it to Louie.

A month later Louie had Hidalgo in a studio in San Antonio and they cut, *Long Days Ahead*, a soulful tune, which had a touch of R&B, and the second verse in Spanish. It was a song about a breakup of lovers and the man's long search for peace after she left him behind. Not too original but the chorus was one of those catchy, sing-a-long melodies.

"It's got the hook," Louie was said to have announced to the group in the control booth, after the first take. He added some strings and a horn arrangement to the last verse then chorus and declared that it was going to be a "monster." As one last stroke, he changed Hidalgo's last name, Ramirez, to Martin, like Tony Martin, although there was no conceivable resemblance. Hidalgo, trusted Louie completely, and never hesitated to follow his suggestion. Louie told him he just felt Martin would play better with the plans he had in mind. Louie was being careful not to let the "Mexican thing" overpower the predominantly Anglo market he was after with this song.

Hidalgo didn't mind, but his father was annoyed at his son losing the family surname. Calling in favors, Louie had carefully greased the tracks with a number of major DJ's and station managers in South Texas and it was added to the play list. He then broadened the distribution into Louisiana, Houston and Dallas. Hidalgo hit the road on a Texas and Louisiana tour of promotional concerts and radio station interviews. Louie had learned how to power up for a regional hit. It was aided by the fact that it was a great song and performance by Hidalgo.

Louie pushed hard and it became a regional hit in a month. Louie took it to Saturn who leased it for national distribution. Saturn believed in Louie's talent for picking hits. The song had potential and they put a big promotional effort behind it.

Long Days Ahead, Hidalgo's single, hit the Hot 100 charts at 84 with a bullet the first week out. By the second week it was 48, third week 12. Before the end of the month it was number two in the country, and stayed in the top five for three weeks. A new agent came through on the heels of the release and got him booked on Ed Sullivan and Dinah Shore's variety show.

It was 1960, a time when a young Hispanic pop crooner was close to a novelty act. But Hidalgo came through on television with his fresh and personable act. He captured conservative, Middle America with his clean-cut, wholesome smile. He was accepted by the audience and Ed Sullivan invited him back three weeks later where he revived an old song, *To Each His Own,* with a soulful touch, including one verse in Spanish. Louie knew the value of a formula in pop music and wasn't about to let anyone mess with a winning formula. Already a favorite song from earlier years, the post WWII audience ate it up. Within two months it reached the top, number one. Life magazine came to South Texas to do a feature article with Hidalgo and talk about his boyhood in South Texas. He charmed them and they featured pictures of his home and parents back in South Texas.

Louie had him back in the studio two weeks later and they finished the album, including the new song he did on the Sullivan show and made plans to put it out immediately. *Long Days Ahead* had drifted back down to 25 after ten weeks, but Hidalgo's appearances on afternoon TV teen dance shows like *Shake It* and *Laguna Beach Party* swept the album into gold. Hidalgo Martin was hot and a grand tour was planned for the next three months where he would be in a caravan of stars hitting 63 cities in ninety days.

It was too good to be true and put Louie into the limelight as a producer who had the magic touch. Acts began coming to him to produce their songs and he brought back Blue Vaughn who had another big hit. She went gold with a song that Louie had owned the rights to since 1957, *Step Over My Broken Heart*. It made it to number one on the rock & roll charts and stayed in the top fifty for two months. Louie rushed out an album that nearly went gold as well, with a third hit from Hidalgo and Blue on the charts, Louie was on a roll. He had taken Hidalgo from the ranchland and into pop music and broken Blue Vaughn's music out of the race stations and into the more lucrative rock and roll world.

Louie set up permanent residence in Houston and recorded his acts in San Antonio, Nashville and Biloxi Mississippi, where he and a Mombo had a small recording facility. He was feeling more comfortable in a big city with a big airport.

Louie was now a nationally known producer, and money from record sales, royalties and his share of the performances was coming in like gulf waves into his bank account. But then Hidalgo blew up. On the road, his plane landed in Abilene and the airport police decided to search his bags since he looked a little offbeat. They found two joints of marijuana hidden in a packet of guitar strings inside his music kit bag. It might as well been a multiple homicide. Dope just wasn't seen in this conservative West Texas town.

"Hell's bells," Louie commented. "That boy would have been better off if he'd been caught bangin' the mayor's daughter on Main Street."

The event made headlines across the country and the local DA had the most exciting trial of his career. Although Louie hired top-fight attorneys, Hidalgo Martin was sentenced to five years in the state prison. A musician bringing dope into a conservative community like Abilene didn't stand a chance and the Anglo jury intended to make that point to the world. It was tragic for his career and a huge financial blow to everyone involved. Louie stuck by him and managed to get Hidalgo paroled after three years but his music career was ruined. Hidalgo played around Texas, but under the terms of his probation, he was barred from working at any place that sold liquor such as nightclubs and bars. He played social clubs, wedding receptions, and halls, just like in the old days and managed to make a modest living. He still had a little money coming in from record sales. The years went by and he and Louie waited for the parole to end. Louie promised him that the two of them would be back in the big time one they.

Now Louie and Moonie had a scheme to send Hidalgo back to the top and make themselves even richer. Moonie had been preparing to leave Saturn Records for some time, but did not want to go empty-handed. If he was going to leave and join a new record company, he wanted to have a big hit early and establish himself as a king maker. Hidalgo's latest contract with Vaquero Records in the Valley had expired without a hit.

This session would be the first step. Louie and Moonie signed Hidalgo to a new recording and personal services contract which would tie up any recording or performance work he might do. The recording began, and went on for the next three days. Moonie returned to New York satisfied that there was a gold record somewhere on the tape. Louie would work in the studio with Shingles and his arranger editing and polishing up the sound. He added backup vocals, strings and other instruments as needed. Lee Lewis came in several times to add guitar flavors and Mombo rerecorded some of the bass work. It took him a month, but he needed the time to get it right. Whether or not his producing techniques were outdated, he knew how to make a hit. Louie figured that there were several potential monsters on the finished album. He and Moonie had selected the songs carefully from hundreds of tapes. All were new songs, fresh material. All of it was the work of writers they had under contract.

He picked out the one he felt would be the first "monster", and a backup that Moonie might need to select the first release. He packed his bags and the tapes and set out for New York. He got into Manhattan and met with

Moonie in the producer's apartment where they listened to the finished album and Moonie agreed on what would be their first hit song with the new Hidalgo. Neither had any doubt of success. In their minds, it was a great song and even more important, they knew the *fix* would be in. Saturn Records, where Moonie had established his A & R career was never a part of the Hidalgo's return although Moonie was still under contract with them at the time.

Moonie probably owed Louie more than anyone because of the deals they had been involved in. Louie had always cut him in for a share of the spoils. This time they were co-producers. He was also listed as co-writer of several songs on the album which would give a cut of the royalties.

Unlike their first encounter many years earlier, Moonie took him at his word that they had a hit on their hands. The deal was done. Lawrence "Moonie" Levine was leaving Saturn Records to join Southern Cross Records in Nashville as their Vice President of Artists and Recording. He felt country music was going to be the next national wave and he wanted it to ride that horse into Nashville from New York. Although he was still taking a paycheck from Saturn, Hidalgo's record deal would go with him. It could be a double win for Louie and Moonie if they played it right, and they did.

Louie brought in his "New York Jew lawyers." They went to work putting together additional music contacts and Moonie quietly hired one of the top agents in Nashville.

Moonie announced that he was leaving Saturn and took the act and songs with him to Nashville as he left. The Saturn executives never knew of Louie's visit to New York or the plan that he and Moonie had put together. The two presented Hidalgo and the prospective hit to Southern Cross records like a prize bull in a fat stock show.

Southern Cross loved the record and Hidalgo. They sensed a new market angle, a void to be filled. Hidalgo's legal problems were behind him and the PR department went to work creating a new born again, guy next-door image for him. He was back with all of the American virtues. Moonie and Louie set Hidalgo up for a promotional party at the company offices and invited the country music press. They had him coached on his on-camera appearance and how to answer reporter's questions. Louie threatened him with annihilation if he got near any liquor or drugs. Hidalgo didn't argue. He hated jail and didn't want to go back. Southern Cross released the record nationwide with major sales and public relations push. Louie and Moonie also called in favors from his wide range of contacts as insurance. Promoters contacted radio stations and pushed the record onto playlists any way they could. They weren't going to let this one slip away. The favors owed to Louie by so many in the entertainment industry were called in as Louie worked the phones from his office. Hidalgo Martin was rocketing to the top again.

Chapter Sixteen

Time has Come Today

Hidalgo was drawing big crowds on his first of three trial shows in South Dakota, Oklahoma and Kentucky. His record had been out two weeks and was moving up the charts with a red bullet. His original South Texas band was backing him up on the road, but they were in a little over their heads playing to big crowds. As his record neared the top of the charts, he did five small club gigs as a test of his popularity in Denver, Phoenix, Albuquerque, Nashville and Atlanta. Moonie had his marketing machine working overtime and drove the song into power rotations in the biggest Top 40 markets. Gold was just around the corner. The test show venues proved his broad popularity to everyone's satisfaction. Louie brought him back home, paid off the compadres who had been with him on the road and then fired them.

Hidalgo had a hard time sitting there when Louie dropped the ax on his backup band, but Louie took the heat for the decision. They were Hidalgo's hometown buddies, sons and brothers of families he had known all of his life. It scared him a little breaking these ties. Louie tried to assure the band they were welcome to get back in the studio with him when they formed a new act. He said he'd be their producer and help them get a booking agent.

"You brudder here, Hidalgo, wouldn't be going where he's going without you behind him all the years." They seemed to feel good about that and it made Hidalgo feel a little less like he was abandoning them. "When you boys get some songs together, jus' come on back to see me and we'll get you your own hits."

Louie called in Blackplanque for a production meeting the next day. They came into Studio B and sat down on various chairs and amps. Louie stood before them.

"Glad you could make it boys, I got somthin' to tell y'all." He paused. Jack was in the control room looking at some proofs and could overhear the conversation. "We got yo'r new album out didn't we. I've done took it to New York but still can't get nobody to buy it. We all worked hard on it. Put all we had into it, but fellas, don't none of us think there's a hit on it. It's my fault. Don't be blamin' yourselves."

"Aw Louie, we know you tried," said Mombo.

"I'm your producer, ain't I? So what I want to tell ya'll is I'm releasing you guys from your contract. All of you. You all need a fresh start. I mean it. Don't mean you should break up your band. I ain't sayin' dat. You got steady work down at da Basement Blues Club, but I just don't think our deal is workin' out and I don't wan' to waste any more of your time. I love you guys. Some of us been together a lotta years. We've tried different kinda shit but I think we all know it ain't workin'."

The group was taken off guard, like a Gulf wave had swept their feet out from under them. The Blackplanque band was taken aback by this sudden decision. They knew their original material was working. They had gone through that many times during practice. They just didn't have a plan to improve things. It took a moment for them to recover and Louie paused to give them a moment to think. Jack watched. The previous week, he had witnessed the frustration coming out of Travis in the Basement Blues' office. He had seen Travis' martyrdom to his craft. Standing crazily on that desk like Jesus; something coming from deep inside him. The attempt to sell their live album in New York had tanked. They were back to zero. It was the truth, and the band members exchanged glances. They knew it wasn't working on vinyl, and they weren't having much fun anymore.

"I don't know what you want to do next, got no idea," said Louie. "If you want to leave and carry on somewhere's else, I wouldn't blame you. You guys are great. Lots of talent."

"I don't think we'd know what we'd want next either, Louie" said Travis. "But we know you're speaking the truth."

"You got your gig downtown," said Louie. "I can get you guys some studio work. Maybe you just woodshed for a while and find out what you wanta do. Now dis ain't in the contract, but I got a closing-out check for a thousand bucks for each of you."

That was a surprise and a little relief. "And, I got an offer for each of you. Everyone. I wanna give you a new start. Fellas, I've fell into a damn goldmine and I think you can get a piece. A new gig. You can take it or leave it. That won't madder to me and it don't change nothin'. Whatever each of you wanna to do is fine. Here's the deal, a road job. We need to form a new stage band for Hidalgo Martin. A real, professional back-up band. He's got a gold record comin' and a 75-city tour scheduled over da next three months. We got us a brand new, big 'ol bus and its going coast-to-coast. Big gigs and big money. He's hot as a firecracker."

"Yeah," I know too well what a hit he is and we ain't," said Travis. "Just wish it was the reverse."

"Your day is comin'. But for now, I'd like for you guys, his tour band," said Louie.

"But, we ain't gonna be touring as Blackplanque?" said Lee. Mombo was squinting at Louie trying to see inside his head. Mel and Jacob looked skeptical. Jack knew Jacob had lived through a national tour a few years before, when he played organ with Triage, a New Jersey band. Jacob had told Jack he hated the road.

Travis said, "I don't know Louie, I kind of just got used to Houston."

"Think about dis," said Louie. "It could give you guys some fine exposure. You gonna be associating in LA, Nashville, Vegas, and New York with some the best musicians, the biggest acts goin'. I think it would do you guys some good."

"What's the pay?" said Mel "Going on the road can be such a drag. I'd have to leave me wife behind. Strange shit can happen when you're gone for three months. I'd need to get home now and again, wouldn't I?"

"The pay?" said Louie. "How about two thousand a week for twelve weeks. Plus pay for the month or so that you gonna be rehearsing."

That got their attention. It was a small fortune. They could make last year's wages in only three months.

"And, That's jus' the start," said Louie. "If dis works, and I think it will, der gonna be a second national tour and den we'll take Hidalgo to Europe for a month. Maybe Japan. Fellows, dis is gonna be a monster year for him and he needs the best musicians with him that I can find. Dis year's got to set the pace for a lot of hits and a long career for him. I owe this to you for them years we done struck out together. You can be a part of that if you want."

"Two thousand a week?" said Travis. "What about expenses, hotels, food and that kind of other shit."

"All your hotels are paid for by the tour and you get twenty-five dollars a day for food and other crap. Dis is a good deal if you want it. I hope each of you decides to do it, but it's up to you. I want' you to know that there's a whole lot of money behind dis. The record company ain't holdin' nothin' back on this project. Hidalgo's goin' big!"

"Wow!" said Mombo. "That boy's hit the big time. He's gonna be set for life. A real star."

"Yeah, but, no hard feelin's or any that shit if you turn dis down," said Louie. "I hope you guys to stay with me on this. And I'm askin' for Hidalgo for a big commitment too. I talked with him last night and he really wants you to go on the road with him. He'd like for you would stand behind him on those big stages and TV shows."

"Thanks for bein' honest, Louie," said "Mombo. "That's good money. I think Blackplanque's done. I'm sorry fella's. We tried but it ain't workin in the studio. I don't know about the rest of you guys, but I'm gonna go home and talk to Dee Dee about the Hidalgo gig. I think you can count me in, Louie."

"Another ting," said Louie. "You can forget about that fruitcake Jocko Dove. Buck and me went over to see him last night to talk some bidness. I threw him some deals for the future. He seen the light and tore up your personal agent contracts. You ain't workin' under him no more less you sign back up wit' him."

"I like that!" said Mombo. "Never understood what was wrong with that boy."

"Anyways," said Louie. "You sign on with dis deal with Hidalgo and I'll be your agent for the first tour and only take five percent, not fifteen like Jocko. We'll also come up with sometin for' each of you as a personal recording and services contract so we can think about recording you all in the future as single artists."

"I'm gonna take a pass, Louie," said Jacob. "I'm sorry to be leaving you guys. You're as good as I've ever played with. You know, I've been playing for a few years. Seen some success, too. We've got the chemistry when we play on stage, but we've never put the studio thing together. It's been a pleasure, but I think I'll skip your offer Louie. It's tempting, but I think I'll stay in town. I wish you all the best."

"OK, Jacob" said Louie. "I'm sorry but you got my respect. I'm gonna take you up on that offer. You play with' a lot a soul."

I'll be around if you need a keyboard man in the studio. I got an idea of trying something new here, in Houston. Something solo, work on my playing."

"You got it"

Lee was the next one up to speak. "Travis and me are a team," he said. "We made that pack a long time ago. I'd kinda like to see the road, maybe up my playing. You play around the best and you get better. We've worked with Hidalgo; he's a straight up guy. If Travis agrees, we'll make the tour. I'm tired of playing in that basement. Are there going to be some practices? I've saw one of those Las Vegas shows on my honeymoon and it ain't no off the cuff jam when you get into that game."

"Great," said Louie. "Naw, it ain't."

"Sure," said Travis. "I could use the money and the experience. My girl's off in school the next three years learning nursing." He turned to Lee, "Let's do it partner. I mean, if it's alright with your wife, Marylou." Everybody laughed as he admitted that they might need a final approval from Lee's wife. So it looked like Travis, Lee, and Mombo were in.

Mel hadn't responded to the offer. "Louie, I'm gonna need to talk this over with me wife," he said. "I don't want to commit to you and then have things go to shit at home. She keeps herself busy on her job, so I think we can make it work. You can you put me down for a tentative OK can't you?"

"Yeah, Mel," said Louie. "Dis is important so I got to be sure. Let me know in a couple a days. You boys are gonna meet some important music people along the way, could help us get you your break. You never know."

"Our new production company gonna set ya'll up with a wardrobe woman in LA, and a show writer and a choreographer to help stage the performances for big venues," said Louie. "Me and Moonie have hired us a famous show producer to come on board to put the tour on the road."

"We ain't gonna have to dress up like the Osmond Brothers are we?" said Mombo. "I don't look good in gold satin."

Louie and the others laughed. "I can't see you as a chorus boy."

There was some excitement building among the group. The biggest crowd they had played before was 3,000 people in a football stadium rock event. This was a major musical artist tour.

"Then it's mostly settled," said Louie. "We'll get dis thing together over the next few days."

Louie gave them all his congratulations and wished them good luck with their decisions and walked back into the control booth after passing out their checks. Jack had watched it all. He was pleased for them.

Louie saw Jack and walked into the booth. "Dem boys gonna come back home slicker than a skink's dick," he said laughing. "Dey gonna get the Hollywood glow out der on the road. Just hope they learn somthing while they at it. I may get some hits out of dem yet."

A couple of days later Mel called back to say he was in. The foursome flew out a week later to California where they would join with Hidalgo and the other artists and roadies to start practice and build a show.

Chapter Seventeen

No Sugar Tonight

Randy Sun had helped Jack move to Waco and they borrowed the company van, an ancient Ford Econoline to make the move in one trip. Jack was not sure whether it was Louie's or Bucks but he really appreciated the help. When Randy approached Jack for a favor, Jack was ready to help. Randy needed some publicity photos.

"Say, Jack," he asked. "Suze needs something to help her get a better job than the joint she's at now. The tips are lousy out at that dump. She could be making a lot more. I need some shots of her dancing and doing her act. And, we need some shots of both of us in the studio like we was recording our songs. Wonder if you'd mind helping us out."

"Sure," he replied. Jack felt like doing anything he could to help Randy and Suze. They didn't have a pot to piss in and were still living in the shack behind the studio. But Randy had his dream.

"That would be great, man," said Randy. "She's working right now in a club down on Old Spanish Trail not far from the Astrodome. If you could come there Tuesday or Wednesday night, there wouldn't be too much of a crowd and we could get some shots. I need some black and whites; eight by tens with her name and phone number on the bottom, real professional like."

"Sure, I can shoot some and get that done for you," said Jack. "It doesn't cost too much for the pictures, they're like fifteen dollars for a box of a hundred and they will even put the information at the bottom. Film's cheap and my labor's free for ya'll. You know, I'm in Waco all this week but I could do them Friday or Saturday night."

"Thanks, Jack. I can give you the cash, but it might be a little while 'til I can pay you for shooting the pictures."

"Well, it's not going to take much, maybe twenty-five dollars for film and photos," he said.

"Oh, I can do that in about a week or ten days. Buck owes me for something I did for them and I'll have some cash."

Jack didn't mind carrying him. He'd do the job for expenses. Randy had done him many favors. He had turned Jack on to another Black producer who used to work for Doug Knight. It turned out that this producer was recording a number of Black soul bands at Louie's studio. Louie had a connection with a guy and had underwritten the cost of setting up a remote studio in a van. He could take the van to locations like churches, nightclubs or concerts for recording and had recorded Blackplanque in

Baton Rouge for their live album. He was also doing some pictures for a large Black church choir album down on Alameda Street.

Jack met Randy that Saturday night about nine at the nightclub, which turned out to be a pretty seedy strip joint, *Bodacious*, way out OST. He parked close to the door. There were only a few cars in the lot. Jack saw the beat-up old Ford van parked so he went in to meet him. Randy talking to the bartender but Suze was nowhere in sight. There was a skinny, dishwater blonde dancing to the music, which was a raucous soul song. She was awkwardly spinning and dipping and occasionally slipping off another bit of clothing. Pretty sad, Jack thought. She was a long way from making it to Broadway. About a dozen black dudes, who seemed unmoved by her performance, sat at nearby tables. Jack wondered if they expected the entertainment to improve or figured they were getting their money's worth for a few beers.

"Hey, brother," said Randy. "Suze is gonna be out a little later if you want to get set up. I really appreciate this, brother. Hope you don't feel a little strange here with all the brothers."

"Say, can you get my friend a beer." Randy said to the bartender. He was having a beer himself, which surprised Jack. He was not a drinker and Jack had only seen him take a hit off a joint once, during a soul band's recording session. He thought at the time the Randy was only participating in order to be a part of that scene.

Jack had been in Randy and Suze's house a few times, and there was no hint of drugs or liquor around. "I don't do that shit!" he had told Jack. "It just drags you down. I got to be up, up all the time. Booze and pot, all that crap just makes you think you're a loser and that's not what I am. We be winnin' all the time, movin' up. Suze and me are gonna' make it to the top if we work hard."

"I think you're right Randy." Jack said. "Why do that stuff if you don't need it? We've both seen a lot of folks who let that habit ruin their talent, their lives."

"You know, some folks just can't seem to leave it alone. It's their lives and if they screw it up it's their fault. But Suze and me decided a long time ago we were going to' leave it alone," he said. "If others want to do it, it's their business. I've seen dope and what it does to folks like in Watts. They's back in slavery as far as I'm concerned. My people in LA, we just had to get out and try to leave it behind. But we still got a lot of friends and relatives back there. Thank God we're in Texas. I love it here. It's a fresh start and we are on our way."

Jack took his camera and walked the perimeter of the stage. The stage lights restricted his work and helped as much as they hindered. There were posts and tables next to the stage to contend with.

Suze came out after the blond left and danced on the stage for a couple of songs. She wasn't that bad, but certainly not that good.

After the music stopped, Jack had her pose against the pole and other places around the stage and he took some stills. He shot some full length and then had her come down and took some head and shoulder portraits as well. Jack set up a pair of flashes on lighting stands in one corner of the room with the stage in the background where another dancer was performing. Suze would be sharp and well lit with the out of focus stage and dancer in the background as a backdrop. As Jack had figured, he had all he needed in about thirty minutes. Both Suze and Randy seemed pleased with the attention and offered another beer but Jack passed. Strip clubs always made Jack depressed. The dancers usually weren't talented and it seemed to him that they could have just stood there and taken their clothes off slowly with a lot less trouble and embarrassment. But, he thought, somebody out there must dig it. Most of the ladies seemed to obviously be having a tough life to be doing this for a living. There had to be something better for them out there somewhere. But who knows why they were there. Maybe many of them felt this was just a way station on the way to stardom, like Suze.

Besides, this was a pretty grimy place and Jack didn't feel that comfortable hanging out all night in a black strip club on the edge of town, even with Randy. He knew he was a lover, not a fighter. Randy walked with him back to the car. In the back of Jack's mind he half expected to walk back outside to find the Trans Am gone.

"Man, I really appreciate your help. I know they're gonna be just great. It's gonna make Suze look fine so she can get a gig in a better joint. I can't thank you enough."

"Anytime man, I'm glad I got a chance to help." So Jack said his good-byes and promised to let them see the finished proof sheets as soon as he got them finished.

Jack went off to Waco that Sunday night and developed the film that Monday at work. The proofs look pretty good so he mailed them off to the studio in Pasadena. Jack wouldn't be back in Houston until the next weekend. So, it gave him an excuse to call Pasadena and let Mona know to be expecting them in a day or two.

"Hi Jack," she answered with her usual perkiness. "Where you at?"

"I'm in beautiful downtown Waco, as usual," he said. "I wanted to call and tell you to expect a package of pictures in a couple of days, for Randy. If you wouldn't mind giving them to him, I'd appreciate it."

"OK, we been missin' you"

"Same here," Jack said. "What's been going on? Have I been missing any good sessions?

"Let me see, last week we had Hidalgo Martin in for a session with Don Slidell and Augustine Davila. Doin' one of them multiple-star albums of a bunch of songs from Louie's catalogs. Just more fodder to make Louie richer. Then Moncreif Pier, this Black New Orleans saxophone player, came in for an album session with his band. Kinda jazzy stuff, New Orleans's style. We had a couple of rinky-dink boy-rock bands that were here, just studio rental time."

Jack would have liked to have been at the Hidalgo session. Don Slidell was an Austin country artist who had quite a catalog and following in Central Texas. Augustine was a Cajun fiddler, raised in Louisiana who had had a big hit with Louie a few years earlier. Jack felt like the trio would have come forth with some solid album material from the session and maybe a regional hit at the least. It would have been a typical Louie session with several of the songs he owned mixed in for the royalties from potential album. If they sprung a regional or national hit record, you could be sure that Louie would stick one of his songs on the back of the single.

"That sounds like they've been keeping you busy."

"Yup," she said. "And how are things going up there with Buck running the show?"

It was an inquisitive question, like she was taking his temperature. "Fine," Jack replied. "I'm plugging away, sorta boring at this point, but I keep getting a regular paycheck. I sure don't have any plans to do anything different for a while. Just saving my money. I don't think I want this to be my career destination until I retire."

"Well, I had just heard some rumors there might be some trouble, maybe not. I was just wondering how you were."

"I'm just as handsome as ever and broken hearted at not seeing you every day," he teased. "I'm going to leave about noon on Friday so I'll drop by AI when I get to town."

"I know it's tough on you, not gazin' on my fine self every day, cutie. But, look, Jack, I've got to be going, Louie just came up from the back and he looks like he's on his way out."

"OK, give him my best."

Jack drove back to Houston from Waco almost every weekend. Occasionally, he also made quick runs during the week to shoot a session at Louie's. He didn't make any effort to make friends in Waco. It felt more like a temporary station and the apartment felt more like a motel room. He just did the work during the week and looked forward to getting back to Houston as often as possible. The company car was a savior for his old 1965 Mustang. He parked it behind the garage at his brother's house. Jack figured that the only original part still on it was the left rear window.   He had a hundred and twenty thousand mostly city miles on it and its end was near.

Jack was anxious to get back to friends in Houston and maintain his relationship with Angie. He and Angie had been dating for about a year and Jack missed her companionship and the intimacy of their relationship. But, inevitably, their affair began to deteriorate as the weeks went by. He could sense that the extended separation was wearing on their love. The closeness they shared of days and nights together was fading. At first Jack would stay with her or later with his ex-roommates, on their couch for Friday and Saturday nights.

Weeks built into months, her studies became even more intense and often stood between them when he was in Houston. His job in Waco just made things worse. She had picked up a campus job at the library and was often there, or working on her thesis. Angie would finish her academic work during the next semester and she wasn't yet sure what her next move would be. From the beginning they understood that they would be together as a pair, but not demand that one or the other sacrifice their own goals or career for the other. This had worked amazingly well as long as Jack was in Houston, with her. But increasingly, she was building her own life while he was away, and they both sensed that the best of their love was in the past.

Eventually, and inevitably, she told Jack that she had met a young engineer who worked for Exxon and was also taking graduate courses at Rice. Some guy named Mark. Over a few weeks the new relationship had changed from getting a ride home, to dinner, and into a new boyfriend status. Now there was new factor in Angie's future, other than Jack or a possible doctorate run. Jack felt like they were in a sad bad spiral and so did she as their lives seemed to be diverging, despite their affection for one another.

Jack wasn't surprised and didn't blame her. He was the one who left her behind. Jack still had deep feelings for her but he couldn't deny that they had moved toward the status of ex-lovers, but friends. There was affection between them but the romance was gone. It did not make her happy either and made him decide that he probably did the wrong thing. She was a special girl and deserved a companion and a lover who would be close by. She had told him what her needs were. Now he knew how much she meant it. Their lives were obviously on different roads now, and Jack had made choices that had taken him to far away from her, away from her side.

Jack called Rudy and asked him to meet him Thursday night at eight, outside of Basement Blues club. Good to his word, Rudy was standing under the awning of the club when Jack pulled up. It was drizzling and wet. The first cold front of winter had moved into Houston. Jack parked at the curb and reached over to open the door for his friend.

"Damn Jack," said Rudy. "Where in the hell did you steal this set of wheels? You're moving uptown my friend."

"Well I didn't steal or buy them. It's enough just to feed it gas. It came with the job in Waco."

"No shit! This is a nice ride," said Rudy. "Bet Angie digs it."

"I don't know to tell you the truth. She seemed to like the look of it at first. I haven't seen very much of her lately, maybe you heard."

"Well, she sort of hinted last time I asked, that you two had cooled it. So there's a new guy on the scene."

"It's mostly my fault, moving out of town and all. It's not really what I wanted, but it's going downhill. Once I left, the tide started changing."

As the engine idled, Rudy and he visited about Angie. The heater felt good, but Rudy felt bad that his sister's and Jack's relationship was fading.

"That's life ain't it, Jack," Rudy said. "Guess you and me ain't ever gonna be kin. You know everybody I know is just trying to find their own peace. I think she was with you longer than anybody so far. She's never flirted around with a lot of guys. But, I doubt if you're the first guy she's loved or screwed. I don't know, this is the Sixties man. She's not like some of these gals that are into free love and shit. Everybody's got to find a thing to be happy with, doing what you like and feeling good about it."

"I would have changed things if I had known where this was headed."

"Regrets just come when you look at the past," said Rudy. "You have a right to do what you need too."

"Rudy, I had it all for a moment. I thought she was all I would ever need. But she's gone."

"Yeah, you both had it all, man. She loves you, I know she does. You're a righteous dude. But if it ain't meant to be, you can't force it. She's got a mind of her own and some big goals. You know she wants to teach at some college someday."

"Yeah," Jack said. "That could take her anywhere from here to Spain. She really wants to study in Europe. We're just not ready. I know I'm not."

"Angie got the brains in my family," said Rudy. "Only her and one of my cousins got a degree. I went a couple of years to a junior college, but it wasn't my thing. I ain't got that kind of a brain. I need to be out in the action."

"I know what you mean."

"It's gonna be all right, man," he sympathized. "You're both good folks, but I just don't think it was meant to be. Like I said, you got to find your destiny. The thing that will make you happy. Maybe she ain't it.

"You're some philosopher, Rudy," said Jack.

"Sometimes dreams don't fit with reality," said Rudy.

"No...they don't."

"Maybe there's a compromise, you lose a little of your dream, you gain a little reality and you try to be happy with it. Hell, the world ain't perfect," said Rudy, "and the people ain't either.

"It's not easy, man."

Chapter Eighteen

Bad Moon Rising

Jack had never met JD Beaumont, but Louie had often talked about him. JD had been a rock and roll icon in South Louisiana since the mid-fifties when a very bold Baton Rouge AM station, KLAA, set him up as the disc jockey of the seven to midnight show. The station manager was bold because JD was black and bold because he was promoting rock and roll and rhythm and blues programming to white kids. There were successful "race" stations in the south, but they played to a black audience, with Negro disc jockeys.

A Black disc jockey on a "white" station would not necessarily play well when a good part of the Protestant South felt that the devil had embodied in the Little Richard, Elvis and Jerry Lee Lewis. Their rock 'n roll hit the airwaves and conservative parents went over the top, producing many fiery sermons and organized record burnings in conservative American communities. But JD had a little advantage. He didn't sound any more like a southern Negro than just about any soulful Anglo born in the bayou country. The radio station kept the public wraps on him as long as possible and he became very popular before anyone guessed he wasn't a native, white, *good old boy.* By then the popularity of his show kept the advertisers coming despite his color.

And so he continued on the air for the next fifteen years without slowing down. JD had kept his reputation cleaner than clean, supported school and civic events and was raising a family in Baton Rouge. He was close to breaking into a second generation of fans. He was always careful to not push too hard against the old Southern Christian traditions and adamantly avoided politics. Although, he would have had a fair chance of winning if he had ever run for mayor.

He and Louie had teamed up in the early days and it was JD who brought Venus Blue to Louie's attention when she was just sixteen. She had a curious voice with sort of voice with a little girl's hoarseness. As Piedmont had told Jack, she was a black Brenda Lee. They had produced a gold record with her in the late fifties using KLAA studios and Louie continued to make pilgrimages over to JD's country every spring, for auditions. JD would always have some fine talent lined up for them to review in a side room of the city civic center.

Later, the chosen ones might drop by Louie's motel room where he and JD would further investigate their talents, and possibly sign contracts. Louie was well known in the community as a star-maker and they drew singers and band from all over Louisiana when they held auditions every spring.

Over the years they had prospered together and only a few knew that they co-owned a record store in Lake Charles. It had often been the springboard for their regional hits as JD and other friendly DJs in Lafayette, Lake Charles and New Orleans would push the pair's songs onto local playlists.

It was this knowledge of Louie and JD's history that came to Jack's mind when he arrived at the studio one they to shoot a session for Louie

It had been cancelled.

"What happened to the session?" Jack asked. Mona filled him in as he poured a cup coffee and took a seat in the reception room.

"You know JD Beaumont, the DJ?" she said. "He's an old, old friend of Louie's. They've been doin' deals since the fifties. Last night he was in a terrible car accident in Baton Rouge. Damn near killed himself from what we hear. So Louie took off like a scalded dog to see what he could do for JD and his family. They're real close."

"Louie got a call about two in the morning from Willie," said Mona, "That's JD's brother-in-law. Raynon,

JD's wife, told Willie to call Louie. JD crashed his car going down the highway near his home last year. It seems that JD was all alone and on the way home from his show. It was one of those terrible Louisiana rains and he slid off a curve. He hit some kind of a guardrail and flipped over a few times. He came to rest upside down, but he still had on his seat belt, thank goodness. Somebody saw it happen and got him out, but he's bad hurt. Raynon said his back is broken or crushed or something. Anyway he's in intensive care in Baton Rouge.

"Oh man," Jack said. "I bet Louie's upset."

"Oh, yeah, beside himself. He whipped on his clothes and filled a suitcase and was out of the house in a minute," Lynette said. Lynette was Louie's girlfriend who had moved down from New York to be with him a few months earlier. Jack had heard a lot about her but never had seen her in the studio.

"Anyway, he phoned me this morning and he was there. He said Raynon was taking it pretty well and Louie was trying to keep their kids entertained until her Mom can get there from Shreveport. They've got two little girls and a boy. I don't think there's a man in the world that's closer to Louie."

"How old are the kids?" Jack asked

"Oh, probably about five to eight years old for the girls and the boy's ten I think. Something like that. They just worship their dad, and Louie. He's like a rich great uncle to them. They love him. Louie's spent a number of Christmas's with them. He brings them toys like he was the real Santa Claus. They're real close."

"I guess he'll be there for a while."

"I imagine. I don't think we'll see any more of him for a few days, 'til things settle down."

"Well, tell Louie to give them my best."

"OK, Louie asked to have you call him tomorrow, not today, tomorrow. It sounded important. Here's his telephone number at the motel." She handed Jack a memo note with the number and the name of hotel in Baton Rouge.

"Thanks, I will." Jack finished his coffee and they visited a few more minutes about random subjects before he left to go back to Waco.

Jack phoned Louie a couple of times the next they and finally caught up with him about eleven that night in his hotel room. He sounded exhausted.

"I tell you brother," he said. "We jus' done appreciate what we've got. You know what I mean? Poor old JD's layin' in that bed and his family's 'roun him and he ain't movin' a lick. The doctor's say he ain't gonna die from dis, but he's really messed up with a broken back."

"I'm really sorry Louie," Jack said. "I know you two are like brothers."

"You bet, he's my number one brudder," said Louie. "I'm as close and trustin' of him as I was of my own Pappy. I got to do somethin' for JD right now! Got to do somethin' for him and his family." He paused. "Listen up, I want you to pack your camera shit and come over here. Get some sleep and get up and drive over here tomorrow. We got to take some pictures of JD and maybe his family. He's gonna need some money, some help from his fans."

"OK," Jack said. "I'll let them know at the record plant that I'll be out a couple of days helping you."

"Yeah, done worry about your expenses. I'll get you some money to cover your trip. I'll book you a room here. Just come to Our Lady of the Lake Hospital and find his room. Hang around if I'm not der 'til we can get together."

"I'll be there as soon as I can tomorrow."

"Thanks, Jack. I won't forget dis." He hung up. Louie sounded exhausted and at the end of his rope. Jack had never heard that kind of emotion or anguish coming from Louie. It sounded like JD and his family had some tough days ahead, even if he recovered from his injuries. He wondered what all Louie might have in mind.

Jack packed his gear that night and got a few hours' sleep. At five in the morning, still well before daylight, he was up. He made a pot of coffee and filled his thermos and grabbed a deep, coffee cup. It was early winter and the days were shorter, even in Texas. He figured it would be about seven hours over to Baton Rouge, no matter what highway route he took. Jack wound up going down Interstate 45 to Houston and caught Interstate10, although it seemed like a lot of extra miles for the privilege of wither highways. The Firebird ran like a rocket down the interstates and as he kept an eye out for the Texas Highway Patrol radar. He worked his way quickly through the traffic. He stopped early for a quick lunch in Lake Charles and got into Baton Rouge a little before two.

Louie was in the hospital room with JD's son. They both looked a little better than he had pictured, but still lacking rest. Louie was very jumpy. JD hadn't awakened from his accident and Louie said they had him heavily sedated to give his body some time to recover. No one knew if he would be paralyzed upon waking up, but his prospects were pretty grim.

Jack got his camera and flash set up but Louie wanted to wait until the family could all be assembled for photographs. Jack was hoping that JD might be awake by then as the doctors were beginning to reduce his dosages.

Later that day JD came out of his coma and was able to look around the room. The doctors examined him and found he could move his head slightly as well as the fingers on his left hand. So, they took that as a good sign. He didn't seem to be able to talk but understood a little bit of what was going on around him. Raynon and the kids arrived after their evening meal and Jack took some shots of them gathered around JD and some of Raynon and Louie next to his bedside. JD could roll his eye around the room and could seemingly focus on his loved ones and friends.

Jack took the film down to the local Baton Rouge Advocate daily newspaper and found a staff photographer who agreed to develop and print out a proof sheet if the newspaper could also use the shots in the next day's paper. He talked to the City Editor and by dropping Louie's name, persuaded him to give JD some extra coverage. While he was in the lab Jack got with a city reporter and brought her up to date on the story and JD's condition. JD was a big name in the city and the accident had created quite a stir on all of the local radio station's airwaves. She worked it into a nice piece for the morning edition including some false quotes he threw her way from Raynon and Louie about how much JD loved his fans and how they knew his friends and fans would be praying for his recovery. The next morning a feature story and Jack's pictures of JD were at the bottom of the page one and Louie was brimming with excitement when he saw he coverage.

'Dis is gonna help dem a lot," Louie said. "Can't help but lift der spirits. You done great, Jack! It makes me feel good. It puts that a positive light was shining on dem. Let me see what we can do next."

By mid-morning, Louie talked to KLAA management and who called up their bank and offered to donate $5,000 to start a JD Beaumont Recovery Trust Fund. Louie kicked in another $5,000. The bank seized on the PR opportunity immediately and the station offered to broadcast free promotional spots for JD's fund. The commercials would mention dropping by the bank to contribute. It was settled and set up. There was another feature in the paper the next day, updating JD's story and mentioning the fund. Now Louie was on a roll. Jack left the next they for Waco to get back to work at the record plant.

Chapter Nineteen

Sweet Little Sixteen

Louie began to put the JD Beaumont Trust Concert Fair together to raise money for JD and his family. He had lined up about a dozen of his acts including Hidalgo Martin and Venus Blue who would headline the event. Hidalgo's backup band, the Blackplanque boys, would serve as the stage band for the concert. He had called in favors to fill out a backup vocal group, horns and strings for the acts. It was fall, so there was no way to know whether the temperature would be in the thirties and raining or a sunny seventy degree day. Winter days in Louisiana were a toss-up. The most they could do was plan and hope the weather gods smiled on their efforts.

Louie called on his studio arranger, Leonard Strange to be the musical director. Leonard assembled the artist's music and charts for the songs they intended to perform and got them to the band with extra musicians and backup singers.

Louisiana State University had agreed to lease them the stadium for the day. The Governor and Louie had persuaded the university president and worked it out through the bank for police support for traffic and crowd control. Louie seemed to have a pipeline into Louisiana's political structure that greased the rails. He dispensed up-front VIP passes by the dozens for friends and families of the VIP's, who would be in attendance. The Mayor volunteered to lead off the concert with a tribute and award from the city to JD Beaumont for his civic contributions and an "Icon" award as a city hero.

Everything was falling into place but Louie had needed a promoter to help coordinate the event. It was getting much too hectic to keep up with and Louie wasn't really into the kind of detail management that was being required. Mona was overwhelmed by the detail. As it happened Jocko Dove dropped in on him that week.

"I want to apologize for my behavior a couple of months ago Louie. I've been sober for two months now. I'm trying to keep it together. And, I've picked up some new acts. You might be interested in some of them. One' a guitar player and he's incredible. He's teamed up with this chick who writes her own stuff. I swear, she could be the next Carol King. They are dynamite!"

Louie listened. "That's good Jocko. I hope you can keep your shit together. Is this pair playing anywhere?" said Louie.

"A nightclub out near River Oaks on West Gray. It's kind of one of those supper clubs with a bar where people go after dinner. Very elegant. I'd love for you to hear them."

"Maybe I can do that brudder," said Louie. "So you been holdin' it together, Jocko?"

"Yeah, I swear I have. I'm so happy the Blackplanque boys are succeeding in backing up Hidalgo. I still think they have the talent to be big someday. I believe in them to this day."

"Say Jocko," said Louie, skipping to a new subject, "You used to be in the concert promotion bidness didn't ya? Weren't you with Magnus Productions?"

Jocko brightened up at the memory. "Yeah, Louie. I hope to shout! Mostly good times. I was with them for thirteen years. I helped build the company to tell you the truth. You could call Albert Goldman, he owns it. Ask him. I was a key player with them until I started drinking. That's something I did to myself. I ruined it. He had to let me go and I've always felt bad about that."

"Exactly what did you do for dem?"

"I'd go into cities and work with the municipal authorities to rent their coliseum or ballpark, whatever to set up for concert tours. All over the US. You know, rent the place, handle publicity, set prices for tickets and set up the ticket sales. I'd manage the sound system. Then for the concerts, I'd secure the money from the tickets and the souvenir or record and t-shirt sales. Pay everybody off and head for the next town."

"Tell me Jocko, you still remember how to do all that shit? The whole shindig?"

"Well, it's been over six years but I guess most of it stuck with me. I produced over fifteen hundred concerts in my day with them," said Jocko.

"That's a shitload all right! You know Jocko, you can't never assume you know somebody's talents...what dey know how to do. You got to spend some time with' dem. You do that and you find most people are just amazin'."

"Thanks, Louie."

"I got a job for you man," said Louie. "If you think you can handle it. It ain't gonna pay that much 'cause it's charity work. But I'd count it as a personal favor. Maybe we could take a look at some of you' acts after we get dis out of the way."

"Sure, what do you think I could do for you?"

"I'm workin' on throwing dis big concert in Baton Rouge for JD Beaumont."

"I know about him," said Jocko. "Such a tragedy. I know you've done a lot of business with him. He's one hell of a DJ in Louisiana isn't he? A legend even. How big a crowd are you expecting?"

"Hell, I don't know. It's gonna be free, so's we can get everybody in. JD and I have been buddies for over twenty years. His family gonna need a lot of money and we're hopin' for big donations and souvenir sales, contributions. They's special to me, and all of South Louisiana. If all his friends and fans show up we might have thirty or forty thousand. Shit, I don't know. I think we already got the LSU football stadium rented for the day."

"Heavens!" said Jocko. "Louie, that's very big."

"The question is…can you stand the boogie. Gonna be a lot of pressure on you if you get into dis thing. Don't you go tellin' me you can get it done and den go off crazy drunk. Dey gonna be depending on you. We ain't in it for the money dis time aroun'."

"If it's like you expect, you going need some organization for the ticket distribution, souvenirs and concessions. Health permits, insurance and all. The wheels in his head were turning quickly, remembering all the ways he made money for Magnus and promoted hundreds of concerts. "You got much overhead to cover?"

"Not much. We do have to lease the stadium, but the Governor stepped in and negotiated us a good price. We're gonna give him some stage time seein' how he's up for reelection next year. Der's insurance. Dem muderfukers won't give us no breaks. Den der's a little security and some set up costs to build the stage and fences and clean up afterwards. We got the radio station and da bank behind us."

"Then we ought to raise a lot of money, Louie. Sounds like you got a lot of it put together. I can go over the plan and plug the holes. I definitely want in. I've done this lots of times. I'll get us set up with the t-shirt and souvenir vendors. We'll make it work."

"OK," said Louie. "You got it. I'm gonna put you in touch with all the cats over there. The Governor's office, ad mayor, university, bank and hospital. You got to call me twice a day from now on. That's the rule. And no drinkin'. If I catch or hear you drinkin,' I'll send some boys up der and whip your ass! I'm dead serious about that, Jocko. Now, I got a motel in Baton Rouge Dat's our headquarters. I've used it for auditions for years and years and de is donatin' all the rooms we need for a little publicity during the show. I'll let dem know that you the man with the plan. Get'cha a room der."

"You bet. I'll give it all I've got. Let me a little business arranged, and I'm off to Baton Rouge."

"Here's a couple of hundred to help you along," said Louie, reaching into his pocket and pulling a couple of bills from a money clip. "You understand that from here out, you is a volunteer."

"Right on."

So Louie gave Jocko Dove a chance to coordinate the concert they for the event and redeem himself to Louie. Redemption could mean connections and major money for Jocko. He also would ticket handler, booking the concession and souvenir providers and the contribution collectors for the concert. Louie didn't want any part of the stage announcing or to be the front man. Local schools lined up nearly 400 volunteers to work the booths and collections. Security was lined up by Jocko to protect the money that they would raise. The bank personnel would work with the volunteers for counting the cash and the police would be on hand for protection.

Louie contacted his mobile recording crew and had them co-ordinate the sound systems and record the entire concert. He figured that he could probably get a live album out of it and make a few bucks for himself and JD.

The day came and over 35,000 fans streamed into the stadium where the stage was set on the twenty-yard line. It was like a winter festival and although it was cool, it was a dry, sunny day. Jack was there early as official photographer and parked in the VIP lot next to the stadium. It was going to be a long day and he didn't expect to finish until long after midnight. The act's busses and a few limos began pulling in around noon. Louie had a VIP tent set up behind the stage with plenty of food and drinks and few private areas for the stars. Police and troopers would be around the perimeter for security but not inside the tent.

The infield was strewn with concession stands and vendors selling t-shirts and posters for the event. All of the profit after the concert expenses were paid would go to JD. Louie was playing it straight and had co-funded the expenses of putting the concert together with the bank. They would be paid back through the profits and would have clerks and security on-site to handle the money and transport it back to the bank. All would go into the trust that would then pay off the concert expenses.

Outside the stadium, Louie had set up tents along with booths to sell his act's albums and posters. He had some autograph stands set up for Hidalgo and Venus and they had agreed to stay for at least an hour meeting the fans.

The crowd was just assembling following the four o'clock opening. The concert opened up with the Blackplanque band playing a half a dozen of their favorite rock and roll classic covers. They mixed in a couple of originals which seemed to go over well enough with the crowd. Louie hadn't opened the gates until the music was kicked-off. The crowd brought blankets and folding lawn chairs and strollers. It was promoted as a free family event that would help the JD Trust Fund. JD's generations of fans showed up for a party. All ages from infants to grandparents filled the football field and stadium. No food or drinks were allowed in. He was depending on concession stands and donations to help carry the day.

Following Blackplanque, Sixto Hernandez did a set and then Alphonse Jones, the jazz saxophone player from New Orleans did his thing with his band. A country band that Buck was producing played next and the pair Jocko was promoting followed them. Evening came and Venus Blue took the stage for a set of rhythm and blues. The donation buckets were circulated between each act then brought back to the banker's tent. Blackplanque came on and did a couple of rock classics and a rock and roll medley which was made up of about twenty old classics strung together into a twenty-two minute event.

Then it was time for Hidalgo who was introduced by the Governor. He also had a humanitarian award ready to present to JD Beaumont on behalf of a 'grateful state." Surprising the crowd, JD along with his family, was wheeled on stage to accept the award. He was in a special wheelchair that held him upright and kept his head and neck rigid. The crowd loved it and many shed a tear as they gave him a standing ovation that lasted several minutes. The Governor brought a reluctant Louie on stage and shook his hand as the man behind the event. The Mayor of Baton Rouge spoke a few words next and then joined the Governor and Louie in asking for generous donations to the crowd for the trust fund. They asked that the crowd empty their pockets for this good man.

Buckets were taken throughout the crowd by high school volunteers, like an old Southern tent revival, and delivered to Jocko and the bankers who poured them, under police guard, into big carts. The tally was growing and kept the bank employees busy.

Night had fallen and it was getting dark. Spotlights and special stage lighting came on and the Governor introduced Hidalgo with a flourish.

The band began playing the Vegas show prelude and as the instrumental reached a peak, Hidalgo and he hit the stage running. The band cranked up his current hit. An up-tempo song, with a beat that bordered on rock and roll. It brought the crowd to their feet again and the dancing began.

His enthusiasm and stage presence was magical. He transitioned into his Las Vegas act with the boys from Blackplanque backing him like never before. The Vegas act featured special lighting and fireworks. Near the end of the show, he paused to say a few words about JD Beaumont and how much he loved him for playing his records in the early days.

He asked the crowd to be generous on the way out and empty their pockets of change and even their folding money for JD for all the years of entertainment and civic service he had put into Louisiana over the years. He promised that when JD returned to the air, he'd be in the studio on behalf of his fans. "I'll be in there myself for that first show," said Hidalgo. The crowd cheered and cried some more.

He went back into his act and played another thirty minutes. At the end the stage was lit in soft, romantic blue shades and he did a haunting version of *To Each His Own* as volunteers made their way with buckets through the crowd one last time.

"It couldn't be going any better." That's what Louie was thinking as the artists filled the stage to sing a couple of rocking gospels tunes to wind up the evening. Everyone was amazed. It was a huge success with over thirty thousand people crowded into and around the football stadium. It seemed like half of Louisiana was there. Inevitably, at the end of the show, a spontaneous jam session would start and go on to midnight. Louie was thrilled by it all and he had never felt better in his life. It was a good night, but Louie was tired. Near the bandstand, Jack was even more tired and looking forward to the finale.

But first there came an end that Jack would never forget.

"Mr. Thibodeaux?" she hesitated. "Mr. Thibodeaux, can I talk to you for a moment?" Hidalgo had just left the stage.

Louie turned around to see a nervous young white girl, about sixteen, trying to get his attention. She was cute as a button and had on a yellow *Let's Help JD* t-shirt and jeans. It had already been a long day, the crowds and tension was just about to get to Louie.

"Evenin' darlin'," he said. "What can I do for you?" She was cute

"I'm kind of embarrassed," she said. "My names Melinda Hughes and I'm working over there at the souvenir booth. My daddy's chairman of First Southern Louisiana Bank. I think you've been working with him on this deal. I just feel terrible about this but I had to tell somebody."

"Sure, yo' daddy's a great guy! Well don't be feelin' bad. What's got you so upset?" he put his hand on her shoulder and he could see she was shaking.

"Like I said, I'm working over there and we're selling everything, the banners and t-shirts and the key rings. Money's just pouring in but our manager, the man who's running things; I think he's stealing from the register."

"What?" said Louie. "Who you talkin' about?"

"It's Mr. Dove, they call him Jocko. I noticed him earlier and didn't think much of it, but I keep seeing him doing it. Sometimes when they hand him the money he slips it in the cash bags, but then I see him put some into his pants' pocket when nobody's looking. I just feel terrible telling you this. I mean, it's just bad."

"You told anyone else? Anybody else seen him?"

"No, I'm the only one working behind the sales team. I unload boxes, so I got a different view of what's going on."

"Oh my Lord!" said Louie. "You don't know how much I appreciate dis. Don't you worry darlin', you done the right thing. I'll get a couple of our security guys watchin' him and we'll straight'n things out."

"Oh, thank you. I just don't understand how anybody could steal from a crippled man."

"Me nether," said Louie. "Thank God we got's some honest people like you mixed in with the bad ones. Honey-- Melinda when the show winds up you just march over to the right edge of the stage and I'll bring you backstage, into the star's tent and you can visit with the stars. You like dat?"

"Oh, yes! That would be wonderful, thank you Mr. Thibodeaux."

"Thank you honey," said Louie. He took the opportunity to give her a long hug. "Thank you. I'm lookin' forward to talkin' with you later."

She hurried back to her job and Louie looked around and saw Jack. He waved him over.

"Jack," he said. "I need Buck and maybe Terry over here right now. We got a situation. I bet they're over by the beer garden. Tell them to get der asses over here lickeddy-split." Jack took off on his mission. He could see that Louie was serious about something and mad as hell at something. He found them just where Louie predicted and the three of them returned in a few minutes.

"Thanks, Jack," said Louie. "You don't want to be here for the rest of dis.

"OK," Louie," said Jack as he went off toward the backstage.

Louie turned to Buck and Terry.

"We got us a discipline situation here if you boys are up to it. I hope you ain't been drinkin' much beer; 'cause I don't want nobody to fuk did thing up."

"No Louie," said Buck. "Maybe a couple apiece. What's up?"

"What's up is Jocko Dove. That little bastard is stealin' cash from the concert. I gave that little shit a chance to do somethin' good and he's done his usual thing. A little lady over der at the souvenir tent told me she seen him pocketing some of the proceeds. It's that white tent toward the back."

"Don't surprise me a bit, Louie," said Buck. "That little pervert liable to pull anything. Sumbitch, I'll stomp his head like a snail's."

"No, not yet. I want you two to go over der and watch him a while. If my tip is right, get Big Adolph and take care of Jocko. Adolph's at the rear, guarding the back door to the star's tent. Grab one of the uniform cops and give him that duty."

Big Adolph was a young monster they had met in college. Louie contacted now and then when he needed a persuader. Guarding a concert door pushed his intellectual abilities to the limit. Adolph was diagnosed as a borderline psychopath who had developed a loyalty to Louie in prison for some unknown reason. He saw Louie as an 'older brother' who had kept him out of trouble since his release on probation. Louie worked with him in college to help him control his temper. He still had a strong sadistic streak that he just managed to keep under wraps. Louie got him a job at a brickyard in "D'Hannis, Texas, after his release. So far he hadn't committed any of the assaults, rapes or muggings that landed him in the jug.

"How much taking care do you want," said Buck with a slight smile on his lips. He knew Louie was seething.

"Jus' sumthin' he's gonna remember for the rest of his life. Nothin' permanent if you know what I mean. Be creative. Sumthin' a fella like Big Adolph gonna enjoy.

But not here. Take him somewhere an' scare the shit outta him, you know. Get the money and bring it back to the kitty."

"We can do that, Louie," said Terry. "We'll make you proud."

"Be careful; don't get in trouble with the law. Don't make a scene outta dis, here or out wherever."

"Finesse is the word Louie. We'll get back to you later," said Buck. "You won't have that little turd bothering you anymore.

They turned and left and Louie went back to his meeting and greeting.

Chapter Twenty

Roadhouse Blues

Buck and Terry circled around in back of the souvenir tent and stationed themselves behind some Port-a-Cans to watch Jocko. Buck spotted Jack and waved him over.

"Go get your car and get ready for a little ride. You're in the VIP parking area aren't you?"

"Yeah," said Jack.

"Just watch for us to come out the gate. Warm it up. When I give you the high sign, just follow us in your car. Got it."

"Sure." Jack wasn't sure what was happening, but he could see that Buck was dead serious in his request. He knew Buck was acting on Louie's wishes. He went outside the gates and started the Firebird, which was parked about a hundred feet away from the exit.

Buck went back to where he had left Terry. Sure enough they saw Jocko slipping cash from the register into his right pocket whenever the crew was otherwise busy with customers. The booth was almost sold out and they saw Jocko pull one of the volunteers aside and tell him something. Jocko went out the tent's side exit and seemed to be heading for the parking lot. Buck and Terry followed at a distance as he made his way into the parking lot behind the stadium. They closed the gap and watched him casually open the trunk of his Buick. Buck and Terry rushed in from behind and grabbed his arms.

"What are you up to, Jerk-o?" said Buck. Jocko looked around and was shocked to see Buck and Terry to either side, who grabbed his arms.

"Just thought I'd sit out here a little bit and rest." said Jocko.

"Why don't you just get in the back with me," said Buck. He opened the back door and shoved Jocko across the seat. He turned and waved at Jack who was idling close by. Buck got in beside Jocko. "Give Terry you keys. Terry, go get Big Adolph and bring him out here. We're going for a little ride." Buck reached down and squeezed Jocko's right thigh. He heard a crunch. "What have you got there, Jocko, that ain't muscle?"

Buck saw Jocko wilt under his eyes. He made no attempt to get away. He didn't want to agitate Buck any further. He knew Buck's history and something about him had always scared the be-jesus out of Jocko.

"Let's just sit here quietly until they get back. We got something in store for you Jocko. I can't believe you've been stealing from Louie and his cripple." Buck looked Jocko in the eyes. Jocko thought he saw a sinister look came over Buck's face.

"You ain't ever going to do this again," said Buck.

Jocko looked down at the floor and began pulling cash from his right pocket. He began to shake. Apparently he had sewn a long pocket down the inside of his pants legs which was stuffed with money. He kept digging and soon the floor around his feet was six inches deep in cash.

"There's more under the front seat," Jocko said, deciding to come completely clean. I'll give it all back, Buck," said Jocko. "I'm just in desperate trouble with some fellows. I just needed some cash. I was going to pay it back…with interest."

He looked out the window and saw Terry and Big Adolph hurriedly returning. One look at Big Adolph and he almost fainted. It was obvious Big Adolph wasn't being brought along for conversation. Terry got in the front seat and Big Adolph twisted around to Jocko.

"I don't like queers," Big Adolph said. "Specially thievin' queers!" Adolph threw a short right hand jab against Jocko's ear that both deafened him and made his eyes pinch together in pain. He let out a short yelp. Nobody had ever hit him harder. "You just wait 'til we get to where we're goin'."

They pulled out of the parking lots and onto the highway. Buck turned around to make sure Jack was tailing them. He was. Buck knew the area and directed Terry to a highway going north out of town. Jocko held his head in his hands and didn't say a word. He wasn't shaking anymore, it hurt too much. Eventually they came to a beer joint and parking lot, on a farm to market road.

"Pull around back, Terry," said Buck. They circled around back to the dark alley behind the beer joint. Jack parked on one side of the front lot and walked down the side of the building to the group. A little sliver of moonlight came through the clouds.

"You're going to love this place, Jocko," said Buck.

Buck looked over toward Jack.

"Jack", Buck said. You go over there where they've got those empty beer boxes. I want you to search Jocko's car, front to back. Look under the sets and all. Put all the money you find in one of them boxes and stash it in your trunk."

"OK, Buck." He went over to the sedan and opened the doors and scooping the cash into a box. There was enough cash inside that that he had to stuff down the cash to shut the carton lid. Jack put the obvious together and figured Jocko Dove was a thief who had been caught red handed by Louie and the boys. It looked like Buck and the boys were going to have it out with him before they called the cops.

Jack had noticed that the front lot was full of choppers when he pulled in. There were probably thirty bikes parked at all angles near the front door. The sign said "Pirate's Stash" and it looked like the favorite biker hangout in the parish.

"Get his attention Adolph," said Buck. Big Adolph pushed Jocko hard up against the car and threw a right punch into Jocko's stomach. Jocko bent over and nearly fainted, the air whooshing out his lungs. He went to his knees and rolled over. Big Adolph kicked him in the crotch. Jocko threw up on the oyster shell covered ground and moaned. His face getting cut up from sharp edges as he nosed into the ground. "Don't you ever steal from nobody again?"

Jack looked up from his work gathering cash. He saw Big Adolph reach down and pull Jocko to his feet and Terry grabbed him, holding Jocko's arms behind his back. Big Adolph delivered a flurry of slaps to the sides of his head and Terry dropped him again. The group waited, giving Jock time to get his breath back.

"Oh, shit," Jack said to himself. This was something he didn't want to witness, but it was way too late now. A slap from Big Adolph could break his neck. It now seemed obvious to Jack, that Buck's German throwback was going beat Jocko to death.

"Stand up Jocko." demanded Buck. Jocko eventually managed to get to his feet. Either side of his head was bruised and black as the night. "Take off your clothes Jocko," said Buck.

"What," said Jocko? Jack heard the command but couldn't fathom what Buck had in mind.

Adolph cuffed him again, not as hard as the prior slaps and punches. Jocko's head was cut and bleeding and his shirt was dirty and torn.

"You heard me, take every stitch off," said Buck

"What are you going to do to me?" said Jocko. He was wobbly. For some reason Terry found this funny and began laughing at him.

"Just what you deserve," said Buck. "That's all. Give me your belt, Terry. Terry stripped off his military like web belt and handed it to Buck.

Jocko slowly stripped. "Ever stitch, Jocko," said Buck. "Throw his clothes in that dumpster Terry. You got all the money, Jack?

"Yeah, Buck."

"Take it and put it in your trunk. Meet us out front with the motor running."

Jack turned, put the money away and hurriedly started his Firebird. He drove over near the joint's front door and stopped, pointing toward the exit to the highway.

Buck grabbed Jocko's arm and marched him around the building to the choppers. The broken shells of the parking lot hurt Jocko's feet. He was beyond yelping. He hobbled, bent over, with Buck holding him up as they went. Buck picked out the chopper nearest the door.

"Bend over that seat Jocko," said Buck, pointing to the chopper. It was a nasty black and chrome. The owner had painted *Bandido BathAss* in yellow on the tank. The Bandidos motorcycle gang was big in Texas and throughout the South. They were a southern version of the *Hell's Angels* on the West Coast and said to be heavily into drug pushing, prostitution and strip joints.

"Don't do this Buck, please," said Jocko. "Let me go."

"You done lost my sympathy and your pleading privileges."

Jack watched in his rear view mirror. Buck turned Jocko around and Adolph bent him over the seat in the middle of the bike.

"Grab your ankles," said Buck. He knelt and tied Jocko's wrists and ankles together beneath the bike with the belt. Jocko's bare rear end faced the door of the bar, fifteen feet away. "You're gonna make some biker a sweet gift Jocko. Hog tied like that, you're just liable to get branded." The group laughed at the finale.

"Please, don't leave me this way!" squealed Jocko. Jack felt sick.

Big Adolph laughed and turned back toward Jack's car.

"Let's go boys," said Buck. They walked over to Jack and Adolph thudded into the front passenger side. Buck and Terry got back into the back.

"He could wind up marrying one of those bikers," joked Terry.

"Yup," said Buck. "Or at least a quick love affair. Jack sped out of the lot, spraying oyster shells, and onto the highway heading back to Baton Rouge. He found himself speeding, near ninety, and decided to slow down and be careful. He really didn't want any of the local sheriffs to stop him with this group and a box of cash in the truck. He just wanted to get back to the concert and get as far away from the trio as soon as he could.

"Let's stop up at that little liquor store I saw at the edge of town and get us a bottle of Johnny Walker," said Buck. "I'm buying. We, gentlemen deserve a drink." He reached over the seat and put a firm hand on Jack's shoulder. "Forget about that little faggot, Jack. Just forget about this whole affair. If anybody asks, we were all with each other drinking beer at the concert. I know I was."

"Damn straight," said Terry.

"By the way Adolph," said Buck, "I'll tell Louie you done real good."

Big Adolph smiled, "Thanks Buck. I really appreciate that."

Jack kept a neutral smile on his face, but his thoughts were swirling. What if Jocko died and there was an investigation. He might go to the police or wind up in a hospital. But, Jocko couldn't tell the truth or he'd be admitting to theft. It would probably work out. Perjury wasn't in Jack's plan for his future, and nobody would want Buck, Louie, or Big Adolph as an enemy.

Chapter Twenty-One

Love the One You're With

The Hidalgo Live tour had been extended an extra month and everybody was making money. They had been on the road nearly full-time for three months and he had another hit climbing the charts. They were filling coliseums, music halls and coming to Las Vegas for a big casino show. Jack, who was bored and lonely in Waco, was surprised by a call from Louie.

"Mornin' Jack, how you doin'?" said Louie.

"Good, Louie, real good." he said. "Everything's just kind of percolating along. Nothing new."

"Say, I was talkin' to Buck last night and asked him a favor and he agreed with me. I need for ya to fly out to Las Vegas wit' me on Friday. We're going to the Silver Slipper Casino an' Hotel out der, my friend. Think you'd like to do that?"

"Oh, yeah, Vegas? I'm in." The Silver Slipper was one of the largest of the new venues.

"See, Hidalgo an' the boys are playin' in the big room der. Packin' in two thousand peeps a night, fourteen shows a week. Man, we are makin' money. So I need you to get out der with me to take pictures of Hidalgo and me, and the old Blackplanque boys. He's ridin' hot on two monster hits, couldn't be any better if I finagled for it."

"Yeah, right." Jack couldn't help but laugh. "When do you need me in Houston?"

"Meet me here at the studio about 10 o'clock Friday morning. Mona's gonna get dour tickets and make the arrangements. Done need to bring no money, it's all on the production company an' 'course I'll pay you 'bout five-hundred dollars a day for your time. We all makin' money dis time aroun'."

"Man, thanks a lot!" Jack said.

"It ain't nothin, like I said it's on the company.'

Glad I can do it."

"OK, I'll be there at ten," said Jack. "How long are we going to be in Vegas?

"I figure we'll come back home 'bout Tuesday or Wednesday, that alright?

"You bet!" That could be two grand or more.

Jack met him there Friday.

He actually arrived at the studio about nine-thirty, which gave him some coffee and visiting time with Mona and Hank. He was pumped.

"Louie's got some big plans for Hidalgo," Mona had said. "He' already got some people working on a tour for Europe, Australia and Japan. It just keeps getting bigger. I think this is the first time Louie's had an international artist and hit. Louie and Moonie just got to keep the hits coming for Hidalgo"

"That's fantastic," Jack said. This will be Louie's biggest thing ever, I guess."

"Things are looking good. He's planning to do some improvements around here too. Gonna fancy the place up. New paint, furniture, fixtures, and not so bare bones in the other rooms. Louie gave me a budget and said he didn't care what I did as long as it didn't come out lookin' like the ladies' restroom at the Beverly Hilton."

"So, he's been in there?

"Hell, I don't know, but he's got a vivid imagination 'bout such things."

Louie came in and said good morning. He said, "Grab your shit and throw it in the trunk out der. We'll get out of here soon as I can swallow a cup of coffee."

Jack went out and found the trunk open and transferred his suitcase and camera case into it. He shut the trunk. He went back in and Louie was looking at paint samples Mona had brought in.

"We're gonna fix dis place up so it looks real nice," he said. "Mona's gonna be the decorator. If she need's help, we can call in Queenie." Louie laughed; he was also in a great mood.

"Matter of fact Mona, see if you can get that boy in late next week to begin rewiring the board in Studio B. He still ain't got the whole rig workin' right.

Let me know if he's gonna be able to come in for a few days"

He finished his coffee and they were on the road.

After the plane took off from Hobby Airport, Louie filled him in on his plans. They were in first class and comfortable. He was in a good mood, looser than Jack had ever seen him and brimming with confidence.

"I got dis idea," he said. "The road been so good for Travis and the boys. That Mel Mobly, the Englishman and Travis have got together and written some new songs. Dey sent me a tape wit jus' acoustic guitar playin' and a little rhythm. Dey's into a whole new thing. I couldn't believe it! See, Hidalgo's kinda country, you know, kinda a country ballad guy with a popular music flavor. You know, you hang around Cajuns long enough and all your cookin' starts to taste like fillet. You live in South Texas for years and it'll taste like chili powder. Big talent rubs off, it challenges a person. It's getting' to dem without even tryin'. So everybody likes him, a country-crossover singer. Makes for big record sales 'round the world."

"So's he's rubbin' off on da boys, playin' dat shit day after day. De's from hard rock into country, but takin's some of it with dem. I got to talk with dem while we're in Vegas. I want you to take each of the boys and try to shoot some individual pictures of dem. Be thinkin' 'bout album covers, publicity shots, everything. If you can't get it done over the weekend, jus' stay der until you get some real, good stuff. I don't care if you got to follow dem when de leaves Vegas. The company's payin'."

"You want the best stuff I've ever done."

"That's exactly it, Jack. We need top quality stuff. I got a feelin' dis new ting gonna be big. Country music been around and makin' big money for fifty years but it's always been a southern ting based in Nashville and the Grand Old Opry. Hidalgo's takin' it out der further. Kinda like Eddy Arnold. I mean Elvis and that gang came from country and blues. They took it beyond. But, I want you to take your time and get some good stuff on each one of dem. Portraits, album cover stuff. Some pictures of dem havin' fun backstage, casual shit. You know?"

"I see what you mean," Jack said. "A complete portfolio on everybody.

"I got to find me some more acts like Hidalgo that can breakout into these new areas before somebody else does."

Jack sat back and pondered the plan. Louie was right. Anybody that could remake an old popular product and introduce it to a new market in a new package stood a good chance of making a lot of money. You just needed to keep the essence that made it true to itself, keep the best qualities and wrap it up in a new box.

Hidalgo was basically singing classic popular music with a touch of country and a great Latin personality. Boom! He was new and fresh but still familiar to the ear. Louie would make sure it had the hook. He had the ear for it. Hidalgo's success was based on good, American music that had a popular sound. He was a hit.

So, how could Louie and the guys from Blackplanque pull off another success? Jack wasn't sure. He hadn't heard their new stuff. There was a world of competition in the music marketplace for something new and exciting that would catch on with the public. Another home run like Hidalgo Martin was a long shot, but when you're hot, you're hot. Especially in show business.

Jack's thoughts turned to his work over the next few days and how he might stage some of the shots in the desert. He reached under his seat in the plane and pulled out his camera bag. He opened it and for the tenth time inventoried what he had brought with him. He had the normal 50mm f1.4 lens on the camera and a 105mm f2.5 short telephoto and his 24mm f2.8 with him. All Nikkor lenses for his Nikon F.

Louie watched as he fussed over the equipment.

"Say, Jack," said Louie. "I love you love dem Nikon cameras. De's Japanese ain't dey.

"Yeah, but there the best," said Jack. Even the National Geographic shoots them, as well as almost every newsman on the planet. They're built like bricks and as sharp as it gets for a 35.

"That sounds good. Now last week I was watchin' dis fashion photographer fella in New York, in the big park. He had dis little fat camera, looked like a silver box with a big ole lens. He told me it was a Hasselblood, a German camera. De any good?"

"Oh yeah, Louie. That's the Rolls Royce of cameras. It shoots a larger format, bigger film. You get more detail and contrast that way. Beautiful shots that you can put on billboards. It's like working with diamonds. Nikons are good, but Hasselblads are as good as it gets."

"Could you tell the difference on something like a poster?"

"Oh yeah. There's a difference."

"How come you ain't got one?

"Cause I got about two thousand in this rig. A Hasselblad with lenses equivalent to these would run you about three times that once."

"No shit!"

"I'm afraid so."

"About as much as a car." Louie thought it over for a minute. "I'll tell you what. They got dem Hasselblads in Las Vegas?"

"Oh, yeah, I'm sure they do. If it's expensive, you can find it in Las Vegas. That place attracts big spenders."

"When we get der, I'll get you some cash and I want you to go get a camera like that and all dem lenses. Don't forget the film, too. Will about six grand cover you?

"Yeah."

"You sure. I don't want to skimp on dis. We need the best pictures we can get. You can't be the best if you ain't got the best."

"That ought to do it. It will cover a good light meter and plenty of film." Jack was dumbfounded although he knew it would be a charge back to the production company. Bottom line that meant Hidalgo would pay for it out of his cut. That was the way it was in the music business.

"You just pay us back something someday when you feel like it. Bring me the receipt." Louie smiled at Jack and gave him a wink."

They landed in Las Vegas and the hotel had a limo waiting for them at the airport. The airport was smaller than Jack had imagined. It was his first trip to the city.

They arrived at the hotel and walked into the front lobby, which was a circus of slot machines and gamblers. Louie and Jack got the VIP treatment, and were personally checked in and escorted to their rooms by the hotel manager. Louie said he was going to take a nap to get ready for the evening and told Jack to come by his room about eight-forty-five. Jack's room was very large and gaudy, a small suite with a great view of the strip. He immediately wished Angie was with him to share the trip.

He tried to call Angie early that morning, but no one was at the apartment. Jack had tried for a couple of days to reach her and had finally called Rudy.

"I bet she went home for a couple of days, Jack," he said. My Mom's sister died down in Victoria and she wanted to go to the funeral. She was real close to her when she was a girl.   I'm surprised she didn't let you know.   I thought she'd be back by now."

Oh," said Jack. "We've been missing each other's call for a couple of days. Just too them busy I guess."

"At least you know she's all right."

"You, bet, I'll talk to you later brother."

"Right on, *cachatone.*"

Jack and Angie had tentatively planned to get together Friday night. Now that was off, he was in Vegas. Jack decided he'd try again to phone from the airport but had no success. He wound up catching up with her late Sunday afternoon after getting to Las Vegas. She was not happy and the conversation was brief. He apologized but she was less than excited by what he thought was his good fortune. She was angry with him for breaking their date. It led to some contentious words, and they ended up in an argument and both hung up mad. It had been too long since they had spent time together. She hadn't told him of her plans either, but somehow it wound up his fault. She wasn't his girlfriend anymore it seemed, and he was no longer "special". Jack tried to put it out of his mind for the rest of the trip. He wasn't entirely successful at that. There was a knock at the door and a complimentary basket of fruit and a bottle of champaign arrived. The note attached said "Enjoy, Your friend, Moonie."

Jack could see that they obviously were getting way above average treatment. The Silver Slipper had an old San Francisco theme and the lobby and rooms all reflected the San Francisco gold rush movie set look. It was kind of wild in Jack's eyes, looking at the fields of gambling tables, miles of slots, bars and restaurants. Lots of noise, color and very isolated from the outside world.

Jack was restless and excited. He left his room immediately after exploring it. Jack went back down and out on the street. He visited several other casinos during the afternoon. When he returned to the Silver Slipper, he went to security and picked up a badge that would allow him free access to the backstage and dressing room areas of the theater. Jack wasn't a gambler but did manage to drop about twenty dollars on the quarter slots. Jack didn't know what he was doing and knew it. The slots seemed to be the easiest way to lose money. It seemed a lot less complicated and less stressful than trying to play Blackjack or rolling dice.

Jack had put on his tan suede sports coat and starched khaki trousers because he wasn't sure if jeans would work for the show. At 8:45 he took the elevator up to Louie's room. Louie was ready for dinner and had on a western cut dark maroon suit that had gold stitching on every seam and then some. He wore a bright emerald green silk open-collared shirt and a gold chain with a small peace sign. Shiny patent maroon slippers completed the outfit. He was quite a site and would have really stood out anywhere but Vegas or Hollywood. Louie wasn't one to be overlooked, that was for sure.

At the theater, they were led down the aisle of the huge dinner theatre to a table on the second row, center left. It was a booth-like table facing the stage thirty feet in front of them. Louie and Jack slid into the curved bench set for six. It was high-backed with stuffed cushions cover in red vinyl, simulated leather

"My name's Louie," Louie said to the hostess. "We really appreciate the attention honey, dis here is Jack. You from here?"

"Oh, I'm from Kansas City, Mr. Thibodeaux. We're very pleased to have you and Mr. Clifford here tonight. They told us you'd be with us tonight. You just tell me what I can do to make the night more enjoyable. Just ask and it's yours."

"Thank you honey. I'll do dat when da need arises. But that's Louie and Jack, ok? I'll do that as the needs arise." She smiled and left with their drink orders.

"Moonie's here with his gal," said Louie, turning to Jack. "Der probably be here in a few minutes. I called and he was finishin' up bangin' her in the room so he said dey might be a little late." Louie laughed and shook his head. "When I called his room I'm afraid I done broke up his rhythm. Ol' Moonie never missed an opportunity to get laid or make some dough."

The hostess returned a few minutes later accompanied by two young women, a tall black girl with a showgirl build and a shorter auburn haired beauty queen in a glittery mini dress. Both were incredible young women who looked like they just came off a LA movie set. She introduced them.

"This is Ruby," the hostess said to Louie, referring to the Afro-American girl. "Mr. Levine wanted you to meet her this evening. He felt you might like some company. And Mr. Clifford, this is Angel. Mr. Levine wanted you two have a special friend this evening to show you the town after the show. You all enjoy the night."

"Thank you for the introductions" said Louie. "You ladies jus' slide on in." said Louie. Ruby sat on Louie's side of the seat and moved in close to his side. Angel smiled at Jack and said, "It's a pleasure to have you in Las Vegas" as she slid up next to Jack.

"We hear ya'll are from Houston," said Angel. "I was born in Dallas, myself. Ruby's from New Orleans." She had a familiar North Texas, sort of Dallas accent. Angel had long dark red hair pulled into a ponytail at the back with a tie-dyed scarf. She was a knockout, built like a brick outhouse.

"You from New Orleans, honey?" said Louie. "That's too much. I was just borned 'bout seventy-five miles east o' der. I'm Cajun down to the bone."

"Why Louie," said Ruby. "I love the way you put that. I'm jus' 'bout pure Creole myself. We're gonna all get along jus fine." She had that *high-color* look that Jack knew drove Louie crazy. These girls were no accident.

The conversation went from there to talk about our hometowns and favorite places. Louie laced in stories of his good times in New Orleans. Angel quietly took Jack's hand beneath the table and rested it on her bare leg, holding it in both of her hands. Her disposition was just too sweet. During the show he discovered she had a relaxed, casual way of speaking with an easy laugh. She didn't seem to have a phony bone in her body Jack found it hard to believe that she was also a call girl. She might have made a fine actress.

After the first round of drinks, Moonie and his girlfriend, Alicia hurriedly sat down and Moonie ordered a bottle of French champagne to kick off the evening. Both he and Louie were intent on celebrating the evening and their star.

"Hope you're enjoying the evening with these lovely, young ladies," said Moonie.

"Des both lovely," said Louie.

"You're all beautiful. It's going to be a great night, thanks."

Moonie leaned over and whispered in Jack's ear. "That little redhead of yours has got some pair of boobs. You gonna get a hand full there." He pulled back and winked.

Jack blushed. He looked at her and saw that she had seen the blush on his face. Angel smiled. She was beautiful and looked to him like a college cheerleader, not a Vegas prostitute. He never expected a hooker as part of the deal. It was a first for him.

The show began after they finished their meals. Hidalgo's act was excellent and the crowd fell in love with him.

It knocked Jack out also. This was a Hidalgo that Jack had never seen during the recording sessions. He was dynamite on stage, another man. Hidalgo showed poise and a casual charm on the stage and sang his repertoire of songs along with stories and jokes about his childhood in South Texas. He and the band were obviously well rehearsed and wove an entertaining spell over the audience. The backup band, Jack's buddies, was solid, as Jack expected them to be. He congratulated himself on his ability to spot talent, even in a basement blues club. He'd have to remind Louie of that. During the show, each of the band members got some sort of a solo or individual performance that showcased their talents.

Lee brought out a classical Spanish guitar and preformed an intricate acoustical introduction to Hank William's *I'm So Lonesome I could Cry*, done with a Latin flavor and beat that transformed it. Only he and Hidalgo were on stage in two blue spotlights. Lee, who was offstage, joined them, singing harmony on the last chorus. It was exceptional and bought a good number of the audience to tears.

After the show, the couples broke up. Louie left soundly drunk and kept his arm around Ruby as she guided him to the elevators. Moonie sent his girlfriend back to their room and went off into the casino to gamble.

Chapter Twenty-Two

Bluebird

"What would you like to do, Jack?" Angel said, as they walked through the casino lobby. The sounds of the gambling and noisy slot machines filled the casino. Lights flashed and he could hear occasional shouts from the tables. He wasn't in Pasadena anymore. She walked along with him, holding tightly to his upper arm.

"Let's get some coffee," he said. They walked over to one of the bar areas near the poker tables where it was a little quieter.

The couple sat down and ordered. She suggested Irish coffee and Jack thought that was a great idea. He had enjoyed a couple of drinks and champagne during dinner and was a little high and very nervous. He didn't really want to lose his buzz.

"I'm kinda new to having a beautiful girl like you offered for the night," said Jack. "I hope you don't mind me saying that. That was too blunt."

"I can understand that, Jack. Just relax, honey. I bet you and I are about the same age. I like that. I'm really just sort of a regular gal. You know, this escort business isn't my whole life. I'm a dental assistant by day."

"You're kidding," he said. "So you're just moonlighting for a little extra dough?"

"I moonlight, as you put it, for a lot extra dough. You're a smart guy right? College, I bet. I made eight thousand last year on my day job. I earned almost fifty from my dates."

"Holy shit! You're not afraid of getting arrested?"

"No, there's not much reason to be scared of that. They know me here in the casino and hotel. I take care of the valet and the floor bosses and they help me market my services. They know I work alone and take care of our customers. It's what's called a symbiotic relationship. Everybody's happy. But I do keep my attorney's card on me at all times if something gets screwed up."

"I see."

"And it's tax free, Jack. But I'm only going to do this for two years. I made a vow. Just two more months and I retire. Then I want to go to college and major in psychology. I want to do social work, poor single women, their kids."

"That's pretty noble. You're not just feeding me some bull are you?"

"Nope, that's my plan. I think I'll work on redeeming my soul."

"But, you've been paid for tonight, right?" said Jack. She nodded and gave him another lovely smile. "Well, I don't have a lot of experience with girls in your line of work. I mean, I have a girlfriend back in Houston, and I'm pretty committed to her, I think. We've always tried to be honest with each other -- about other people you know."

"You, you're telling me you don't want to spend the night with me?" she laughed. "You been getting too much lately? Now, you tell me the truth."

"It's not that. Not getting that much, especially lately." He laughed as well.

"I don't need to know about that. Not really."

"No, not that you aren't very inviting. I don't want to hurt your feelings. Angel, you're the best looking girl I've seen in Vegas. I'm serious."

"Thanks," she said. "I think I understand what you're saying and I respect that. You didn't exactly ask for me did you?"

"No, you were a complete surprise."

"Who are your friends?" she asked.

"Louie and Moonie Levine are big time record producers. Hidalgo Martin's one of their acts."

"You don't seem like a producer," she said. "I bet you're a musician?"

"No," he said. "I'm a free-lance photographer. I work for them some of the time."

"That's cool. Do you do pictures for Hidalgo?

"Yes, and others around the music business in Texas.

"That sounds exciting. Wow, I can't drink anymore. I think I'm already over my professional quota. What's next? Seems like you have ruled out sex for tonight.

"Yeah, so you want to call it a night?" said Jack. "I can't drink anymore and I don't gamble."

"Neither do I. I don't have that kind of brain, all I do is lose. Sometimes my clients want to gamble and give me money to gamble with them. It's so sad, I always lose it no matter how hard I try."

"Well, I guess we'll say good night, Angel. I hope you make it to school."

"Oh, I will, I'm going to go to Boulder, Colorado. It's beautiful, near Denver and at the foot of the Rockies. Alright, Jack." She stood up and put her purse over her shoulder. It was bright red with a long gold chain strap. "It's been a pleasure to meet you and I wish you well with your gal." She reached out and shook his hand. "Good night lover."

"Don't call me that," Jack said smiling. "You're much too tempting."

"Last chance to change your mind," she said.

"Bye-bye Angel."

She turned to walk away but Jack took a couple of quick steps and gently caught her wrist. She had stirred his curiosity.

"Wait a minute Angel," he said. She turned. "I'd like to talk some more. Maybe about your plan, this dream of yours. Just forget about this call girl and client routine. I'd just like to talk. You know what I mean?"

She hesitated and considered the proposition. "OK. I like you, Jack. This is a little unusual, well beyond accepted protocol, but we'll give it a try". She smiled and said quietly. "It's been a while since I really talked to a regular young guy. Where do you want to go?"

"Someplace quieter than here," he said. "How about my suite?"

"All right, you sure you just want to talk? Not that I'm against doing whatever you want. I'm yours for the night if you like."

"No, remember, I'm no longer your client. Drop it. I really mean it. Just pretend we're friends or something. I'll make you a deal, if you get bored or I get weird, you can leave. You don't have to stay past this point unless you really want to. I'll understand."

"What the heck," she said. "You seem like a normal guy and believe me; I don't meet many like you."

"Come on." He took her hand and they went to the elevators. Inside the room she sat on the couch and he took a chair.

"Are you hungry or thirsty? I've got a load of fruit over there and some champaign in the refrigerator from Moonie."

"Not hungry," she said. "I'll call to have them bring some more coffee. I've got to watch my figure anyway. Nice room." She was not much over five feet-four and about one hundred and five pounds, Jack guessed.

She untied the scarf around her ponytail, and her long auburn hair dropped down over her shoulders, flowing over the tanned breasts that rose out of her mini-dress top. Jack looked her over again. Nice legs ending in high heels. She reminded him of the Clairol "Summer Girl" on TV that was always lying on a surfboard, on the beach. But she was no blonde.

"You're very hard to resist," Jack said. "Just beautiful." She looked at him inquisitively. "Tell you what I want. You'll probably think I'm crazy, but I want to know more about you. I'm curious, it's just my nature. Tell me the truth and I'll tell you about myself, the truth. It's the journalist in me I guess, tell me your story and I'll tell you mine."

"Okay, why not, but drop the flattery, it makes me uncomfortable."

"Let's see, do you have many friends in Las Vegas, a boyfriend, girlfriend, some relative?"

"No, Jack, none of the above except for one other girl. We've become friends, sort of. She actually is a dental assistant. I'm not, I actually only made sixty-thousand last year. She doesn't know my profession, but we've done a few things together, movies, shopping, you know. She thinks I'm a greeter at the casino. And no boyfriend, I decided to give real relationships up while I was out here. Just focused on making money and saving for a future. I didn't think that would be fair to him or me."

She paused a moment and kicked off her shoes. He followed and draped his sports coat over a nearby chair.

"I'm twenty-four and I was born in Amarillo." That was a year older than Jack.

"So far, so good."

"Oh, and also, my real name's Maggie, Maggie Allen. I'm single as you might have guessed."

"Hi Maggie, I'm Jack Alvin Clifford. They stood up and they shook hands again laughing.

"You're a very smart girl, Maggie. I hope you're serious about going to college?"

"Yeah, I figure I'll leave Vegas around Christmas. Try to get started in the spring or first summer session. I'll have a hundred thousand dollars saved by then. No IRS you know. Can you believe that? I've got it all in gold and cash in a safety deposit box. I'm going to cash in a little at a time after I start school. But I did indulge myself last month, a little gift to myself."

"What was that?"

"Now I'm embarrassed, a yellow corvette convertible. It's wonderful."

"Too much. But you should go to college. I hope you can do that," said Jack. "You'll be free to do anything you want after you leave this town. This gig can't be very much fun, and there's a lot of risk doing this."

"And you care?"

"Yeah, why shouldn't I? I think you've got a great future, once you get out of here. Everybody deserves a chance at their dream.

"Yeah, I hope so. Women in my line of work seem to have an early expiration date. I'm getting out way before that time. That alarm clock will ring someday. So much for me, tell me about you."

"I'm in love, but I'm afraid my days with her are numbered."

"And what's her name?"

"Angie Trevino, she's a student at Rice University, super smart and motivated. She knows where she's going and she knows I'm unsettled. I think our paths are parting little by little. It's just not working anymore. By the way, I'm twenty-two."

"So, I'm finally the older woman who nearly robbed the cradle," she laughed.

"Better than robbing graves."

"Some of my dates are almost there."

"Just looking at you must have brought them back to life."

"No comment. But it sounds like we're both approaching a change of direction. I'm sorry about your Spanish lover. Jack, it sounds like you love her and she's leaving you. Maybe she still loves you too. Humans are so hopeless at managing their affairs. I imagine it's not fun for you, but things are always changing you know. Maybe it will work out for the best. It might be, you know."

"That's a little too optimistic to suit me at the moment."

"Anyway" said Maggie, "I've got a goal and a way to get there. I hope you done\'t think I'm gloating."

"Well, my future with her is bleak, unless something dramatic happens."

"Jack, will it break your heart when she leaves?

"I think it's already broken. I'm just holding on, clinging to some fantasy. Makes me think all love is just a delusion. It's more like a depression at this point. I wish you were a psychologist, maybe you could help me know what I really want."

"It's too bad that I'm not. Maybe that's what I'll do, get my doctorate someday." The coffee arrived and she poured each of them a cup. Maggie and Jack both preferred it black.

She took his hand and led him to the king size bed in the other room. They sat side by side sipping from their cups. Neither one's feet reached the floor.

"Where do you live?" Jack asked.

"I've got a little apartment on the West side. I hate it. I don't spend any more time there than I have to. Just bathe, sleep and change clothes. It's so lonely. My only real indulgence is my Corvette. I like to take the top down and drive it out in the desert whenever I get the chance."

"That's cool. As for me, I just commute between Houston and Waco. But, tell me more about your plan. I need some optimistic inspiration"

"I've been in Vegas nearly two years and the end is in sight. I'm not a dumb chick. I just act that way sometimes when I'm on a date. It makes guys feel more comfortable. Truth is I don't do dope, and only drink a little when I'm on a date. I'm getting into being a vegetarian."

"How about you? What else going on with you?" she said. "Outside of your love life."

"Oh hell, I'm a little lonely and depressed at the thought of going back to Waco. I should be living in Houston, that's my real home. My regular job with the record company in Waco is a little shaky, so I'm happy to do this for Louie. Actually, Houston's even becoming a bummer. I think I'm tired of that scene, uninspired"

The two talked well into the night, lounging on the cushy bedspread, and shared more with each other than either would have expected. It was easy, comfortable and they fell into sync without any particular effort. Finally, they just wore out. It was a little past three.

"This hasn't been like most of my dates, that's for sure," said Maggie. "Thank God. Most of them are just sad or screwed up. Mostly older than you, of course. Usually they're looking for excitement' cause they're away from mommy. Or they want to fall in love with me. Hell, they don't even know me, and they think I'm going to love them more than somebody they've been with, and raised kids with, and provided for, maybe twenty years or so. What the hell are they thinking? Do men need those fantasies so bad?"

"Some do, that's obvious. Maybe it's a good thing if you go into some kind of counseling profession. I think you've done your internship."

"Yeah, on my back. Sometimes I'm so ashamed. Other times I'm proud. Crap, I'm as crazy as my clients." She looked over to him and into his eyes for understanding. "What if I stay tonight?" Maggie said. It doesn't sound like either of us want to be alone," Jack said. "Can I?"

Jack paused before he answered. He was getting sleepy.

"I'll even stay on my side of the bed," Maggie said. "But, I think you're just being true to a memory."

"OK, hell, why not. It's way too big for one anyway. I really dig you Maggie, the real you. I hope you've enjoyed tonight, the show and the conversation."

"The conversation has been the highlight," she said. "But that was a great show. I haven't had much time for honesty in a couple of years. I really like you Jack. I'd like to think I can trust you." Maggie stood up and gave him a quick, chaste hug and then turned around.

"Jack please unzip this thing." She raised her arms above her head. Jack unzipped the back of her dress and she shimmied causing it to drop to the floor. He gazed at her back as she stepped away from him. It was nicely tanned but no bikini line. She bent and picked it up, walked over and draped it over a chair. He caught himself holding his breath as he watched.

She went over to the other side of the room, slipped off her pantyhose and hung them over a chair while he took off his shirt and khaki's. He kicked his shoes and socks off by the end table. She was way too hot.

She turned and said, "That feels better." She wore a skimpy black bra and panties that covered very little. Maggie looked at him and gave him a quick smile. She was too beautiful for him to turn his eyes away. She walked around to the far side of the bed and turned back the cover. She slipped under the covers and Jack was surprised when her bra appeared in her right hand and she threw it over to the nearby chair.

Jack turned out the bedside light and the room went dark. He turned back the covers on his side and got under the sheet and blanket. He lay on his side facing her back in the blackness.

"What brought you here, Maggie? I don't mean to my bed, I mean to this town."

""It's classic," she said. "I grew up on the north side of Dallas. We were what is called affluent. My Daddy was an oilman in Dallas. Big surprise, eh. It killed him about three years ago. He loved the business but it busted him."

"I'm sorry."

"I was pretty spoiled and thinking about SMU, like my friends, but my second year in high school, Daddy hit the last of three dry wells in a row. They were in proven fields and he didn't think losing was possible, so he had put up most all of his proven reserves as collateral. He lost it all, almost overnight; we were broke. He broke the news to Momma at a Junior League fundraiser just before

Christmas. Just pulled her behind the tent and told her. It broke both their hearts and his spirit. He was humiliated and I think he figured that we lost all respect for him that right. But we didn't. We loved him. Momma didn't care as long as we were still a family. But that wasn't enough. Within months, we had moved into an apartment and Momma went back to teaching school. Daddy hated that. He'd always wanted to put mom up on top of a big, soft magic carpet."

"I know what you mean, Maggie."

"Anyway, Momma quit the Junior League and lost most of her friends as well. That's Dallas for you. A few of Daddy's business contacts helped him get into brokering leases so he could begin to make a modest living again. I wanted to go to college but SMU was out – way too expensive. So I got a job at Whataburger after graduating. It wasn't long until I was thinking about a new future and that wasn't it. I said to myself, 'you can do better than flipping' patties.' Does that sound too vain?"

"It sounds like reality, I guess."

She paused. "I know better than acting too proud."

"Anyway, that day I decided that I had to get out of Dallas. I told Momma and Daddy I was leaving for the West. I got in my Corvair and headed west on I40. I got this far and actually did get a hostess job at the front door of this casino. I don't think Daddy ever was disappointed in me. Never had a clue that I lost my virginity in the country club pool house when I was sixteen. I always was adventurous. Thank God he hasn't seen me the last two years. He'd die. Oh my Lord, that's a terrible expression. I'm sorry. I know he doesn't know, because nobody sad or disappointed in Heaven, and I know that's where he is. He loved us so much. I miss him."

"I believe you're right, Maggie. There's no disappointment up there."

"You have the right," said Jack.

"Momma's still in Dallas and she's doing alright. I get back to see her every season. Four times a year at the least. I promised them that. She's all I've got now. Dammit! That sounds so melancholy. But I'll be closer in Boulder and she can come up to visit."

"That's nice."

"So, I've come from the Dallas Cotillion beauty queen's society to here."

Maggie rolled over in the bed so that she was facing Jack. There was still considerable space between them on the king sized bed.

"Jack, maybe we can be friends, real friends" said Maggie softly. She seemed tentative in saying that. I mean neither of us have an agenda at this point."

"That's true. There's no promises or commitments between us, are there?"

"You'll probably leave soon," said Maggie. "Why don't we trade phone numbers and call each other now and then, after you get back to Houston . We'll be telephone pen pals. How's that sound? Just honest talk, with no strings. We'll just share our thoughts, problems, get advice. I don't know. I could use a friend who can be really honest with me."

"That's a fine idea," said Jack. "You know, it's hard for a person to have a completely honest relationship with a member of the opposite sex. At least at our age."

"Yeah, there always that sexual thing there, no matter what."

"What in the heck am I doing," Jack thought without the words leaving his lips. Ten inches from him was a warm, beautiful, girl. Bought and paid for. But now he knew her, and she knew him. I must be getting real screwed up, he thought. I should have that kind of open and intimate relationship with Angie.

"Maggie, that sounds like an interesting proposition." Jack said. "I think we should give it a try. I promise to phone you when I get home."

"Thanks, Jack. That makes me feel so good and I'm already looking forward to visiting with you. Call me at least every month, or I'll call you."

He thought could feel her warmth nearby. She was quiet.

"I like you Jack," she said, almost in a whisper.

"I like you too, Maggie"

"Maybe we should say good night," she said

"OK, 'nite."

"Sleep tight."

They both lay still. Her breath rhythmically warmed his upper arm, beckoning him to move closer. Then, she moved a little and her warm right leg gently crossed and settled over his. Her hand reached out and her fingers found his cheek and touched his lips. A soft touch. Something Jack had not felt lately.

Chapter Twenty-Three

Just Like a Woman

Five days later, Jack was back in Houston visiting his brother and sister-in-law. Jack also had not spoken Maggie since that first night. After breakfast, they had decided to leave their relationship to the telephone. He had not seen her for the rest of his stay in Las Vegas. He was looking forward to the first telephone visit.

He gave Angie a call early in the morning. He hadn't talked to her in a week and was weary from the trip. Angie answered the phone and it sounded to him like he had awakened her.

"Good morning," he said brightly.

"Oh, Jack, how are you? Are you back in town? My roommate said you called again from somewhere like LA or Vegas."

"I got back from Vegas last night late. I tried and tried to call you before I left. I'm sorry but it happened real fast. Louie flew me to Las Vegas for some photography. I was there for five days taking pictures of the artists. "

"So you and Louie went to Las Vegas without me. How was it?" said Angie. She sounded dubious.

"Pretty crazy. I wish you had been with me. He wanted me to take a portfolio of pictures of Hidalgo and also the boys that back him up. He even bought me some better cameras, Hasselblad's. I also photographed the old Blackplanque band guys. They have really gotten great. Very professional. They put on a great show."

"So you got to see them on stage out there."

"Yeah, they were playing the Silver Slipper Hotel for about ten days. They packed the place every show."

"That's great."

"What have you been up to?" said Jack.

"I went up to the University of Texas for a few days to do some research in their library," said Angie. "That's why you couldn't reach me. First my Aunt Maria, died and Mom and I went to the funeral. It's been a busy week."

"Oh, I guess so."

"Jack, I went up to Austin with my new friend," she said matter-of-factly. "That guy I told you about. He'd never been to Austin or UT," said Angie. "You should know. I'm thinking about going for my Doctorate up there, if I stay with school. It's very pretty, all of the hills and rivers."

"Yes it is. What are you doing tonight, I'd like to come by," said Jack.

"Yeah, that would be good. We need to talk, Jack. All of this time away from each other, since you moved to

Waco, has given me time to think. I've got to make some decisions. Not just me, we do! You know Jack; I've always been a one man kind of girl. I don't fool around with different guys at the same time. Never have."

"And now there's me and him on your mind?" said Jack.

'That's about the size of it," she said. "He says he's falling in love with me."

"And I'm already in love with you. I have been since we met. We've been together now about fourteen months," said Jack. "I don't want to end this."

"But you're not here Jack, you're gone, on your job, your career." said Angie. "We're just not together. You know how I feel about that damn job. How you being in Waco most of the time affects me too. I don't know anymore…we need to talk."

"I'll be there at seven," said Jack. "Dress up. We can go get something to eat, I'll take you to someplace nice."

"OK, I'll see you at seven."

Jack hung up. He felt guilty. It was about eight and he hadn't anything for breakfast. He went over to his refrigerator and opened a can of Coke and a slice of bread. I've got the whole day to get through before we can solve this, he thought.   Jack knew he was going to be upset and anxious the entire day.   Things weren't right anymore.   He didn't like confronting this kind of change in his life.   He had serious doubts about his earlier choices; living in Waco and leaving Angie behind. All of it.   He loved her, but he loved the work as well. And now there was her new friend who complicated Jack's feelings. Maggie and that night in Las Vegas kept invading his thoughts.

Army wives put up with separation, he thought. Lots of men have jobs that caused them to leave their women behind. Traveling salesmen, corporate executives and more, all had to leave loved ones.   But, she wasn't his wife and they were still young and free to make choices. Maybe that was the difference.

Maybe they should get married and put all of this separation behind them.

He was at her apartment at seven sharp.   He had decided to take her to a quiet French restaurant on Richmond on the edge of the Montrose area.   Jack had plenty of money after the Las Vegas trip and felt like spending some.   She deserved something nice after too many days on a student food budget.

Angie's roommate, Cherise answered the door.

"Hi Jack," she said, "Come on in. Angie's finishing up dressing in the bedroom." She smiled and then dropped her eyes, avoiding any further eye contact. She turned and walked toward the kitchen.

"Come on back," Angie called from the bedroom. "I'm almost finished." He went back to the room. It seemed much smaller with Cherise's single bed pushed up against the back wall. The room was too small for two. Angie was putting her makeup back into a shoebox.

"Hi," she said. She came to him and gave him a peck on the cheek, avoiding his lips. She turned to put the shoebox on the closet shelf. Jack couldn't help but notice a couple of men's shirts hanging there along with her clothes and a pair of men's shoes on the closet floor. His heart sunk further. He wondered if this was going to be the 'good-bye' dinner. Some kind of a perverse celebration of what they once had, that was now lost.

She turned and smiled at him. "I missed you," she said. "You look good, is that a new shirt?"

"Yeah, I picked up a few things in Las Vegas. Thought I'd better clean up my act while I was associating with those Hollywood types. They dress in expensive clothes, but they don't take them to the laundry often enough."

"Really?" she said. "Yuck. Well, I'm glad you're back. I worry about you."

They drove to the restaurant making small talk about the past week. It was French and expensive, romantic and made for intimacy. Three candles lit their table. The conversation stayed light during dinner, superficial, and he told her of some of his adventures in Las Vegas. He left out Maggie and Ruby. They skipped over the real cause for the evening.

"All of that stuff on your trip just confirms what I've told you before," said Angie. "You're associating with successful and glamorous creeps. Think about where it's leading you. Do you really want a life like that?

He left the question hanging as they left the restaurant and got back into the car. It was a short trip back to her place and they pulled into a dark parking place in the apartment lot.

"Here we are," he said turning off the key. "I think it's time to talk about us. I know you're unhappy with me. I don't enjoy that, but what can I say? I have my work, you have your school. Has that much changed? Have you and I changed that much?" There was a long pause. Jack was without any more words.

"Time...distance," she said. "Jack, I haven't had much of your attention these past months. I need all of you. You're just not there for me anymore and I'm not there for you. It breaks my heart, but it's the truth."

"What can I do," he answered. "I'm caught right now between my work and Waco and you. It's not going to be like this forever, I promise. I want to be back with you. It's my own fault, I left you here."

"But you're not ready to quit your Waco job, are you," she said

"No," he said. "I don't think I can leave it yet. I'm sorry Angie."

"Then, there it is."

They got out of the car and walked silently up the stairs to the apartment door. She got her key out of the purse and turned to him. He looked into her face and saw tears forming in her once bright eyes.

"He's asked me to marry him," Angie said. "To be with him forever. He's ready and I think I may love him too. Is that possible? He's a good man, just like you. But I still care so much for you. I guess I always will."

"I do love you, Angie,"

"I know."

She stepped toward him and looked in his eyes. They embraced and kissed briefly. She pulled her face back and they looked at each other again. It wasn't enough.

"Jack," she said tenderly and kissed him again. This time not holding anything back as they kissed fully and held each other tight. Her tears moistened his cheeks as well. He kissed her neck and held her tightly. She pushed away slowly and stepped back, and held both his hands.

"Tell me," she said. "Just tell me! Do you want me to turn him down? If you say so, I'll tell him no."

"Angie...I could never tell you lies or mislead you. Even as much as I want you to be with me. I do love you. But I just don't know what's ahead. I don't know what's next."

"Just say it! Say no or something. Please." She was sobbing. "I really thought we had a chance."

"There's no forever I can promise you right now. Maybe someday."

"Say no. Say, don't marry him."

He was silent. She looked down and shook the keys in her hand for a few seconds.

"I'm so sorry." she said and looked up into his eyes again. "I feel like I'm missing something. We're still in love."

"It's the future we might have had…together."

"Maybe so."

"I'm so sorry it's like this," Jack said. "Bye, bye, Angie."

"Adios Jack, vaya con dios," she said. She looked into his eyes and blinked like she was taking a photograph. Tears glistened on her chin. She turned and disappeared behind the door.

Jack turned and went down to the car. The Firebird was dark and quiet inside and the streets were empty. He turned the key and the twin exhausts rumbled under the carport. He pulled out onto the street. A block down the street, he pulled up to a stoplight. Tears filled his eyes and he gripped the wheel tightly. He sat there waiting for the light to change. And a tear escaped and trickled down his cheek. He looked to the left and saw a couple sitting in the car next to him. They hadn't noticed him crying next to them.

Jack wiped his eyes with his shirt cuffs. I'm glad they didn't notice me, he thought to himself. Things were bad enough already.

Chapter Twenty-Four

We Gotta Get Out of This Place

Jack wasn't too surprised when Buck called and asked him to come to his office. It was a Friday, and Jack hadn't seen Buck for a couple of weeks. After six months, Jack had settled into the manager's job at the plant, but had become a drag, since his private world had gone to hell. But, he knew it was good money until the next thing came along. The plant seemed to be running smoothly for the most part and Buck always seemed to have one deal or another keeping it running. Things were not going badly for him financially; his savings had been growing rapidly. He had cleared over twenty-five hundred from the Las Vegas trip. His staff did their job quietly and competently and Jack's main function was directing which jobs needed to be done first or set priorities as records came in for graphic production. Every now and then Jack took a mid-week day or two off to go down to Houston for a studio job with Louie.

It was the end of the week and he saw Buck was at the plant on a Friday, which was unusual. Buck more often came in on Monday morning and stayed through Wednesday.

Jack was laying out a color separation on goldenrod paper, aligning the magenta and cyan color separations when Buck called. He had no idea what Buck wanted. He hoped it wasn't another lightning trip to Eagle Pass. And he didn't want anything to do with another incident like the one after the concert. Shag and Wanda were huddled behind the office's front counter going over some paperwork and didn't look up as Buck and Jack came through the outer office.

"Morning," Buck said after Jack sat down. Buck stood up and shut the office door and returned behind the desk and sat down. Most of the time he would have asked Jack to do it, but he seemed nervous and distracted. "I think we are just this close to landing a big deal where we'll be pressing some of the new Rolling Stone albums," said Buck. "I was talking this morning with their label and we ought to know soon. It's going to be a big contract and might carry us into arranging financing for all new record presses." So that was it, he was just pumped up at the prospects and wanted to share the good news with Jack.

But, it struck Jack as odd, because he was well aware that the Stones were pressing their latest albums on the new plastic materials, not the old black vinyl that Texas Sun used. The old vinyl records were much thicker and did not have the flexibility or sound quality of the new records. They reminded Jack of his parent's old, brittle'78's. Jack had seen in the trade magazines that many of the top bands were now requiring in their contracts that only the highest specs and newest technology be used so that their "sound" would not be degraded by second-rate record pressing. It had become an issue in the industry as artists were gaining more control over their music. He decided not to ask any questions about this fact for the moment and Buck continued on.

"Jack, I've got to be honest with you. We're having some money problems right now. Cash is tight like in any buyout transition. The Stallworths are bitchin' about their next installment payment. We're a little behind. But, I wanted to let you know that I talked to Louie this morning. He's helping out. I think he may take a part ownership in the plant pretty soon." said Buck. "I was talking with Shag this last night and we've discovered that some of the paychecks we wrote last week didn't clear the bank. We're gonna have some real upset people around here, but we'll make it good this afternoon. I'm having some cash flown in from Houston this afternoon to pay off anybody who had a problem."

"Damn," Jack said. "How many bounced?"

"I don't know exactly, maybe a dozen or so. I need you to go out to the airport this afternoon at 2:30 and meet Southwest Flight 31 from Dallas. There will be a package in the pilot's bag marked for Texas Sun Records. Bring it back to Shag as fast as you can. It's the payroll to cover the last payroll, about $45,000. Try not to lose it."

"Don't worry about that," Jack said. "I'll get it back as fast as I can. I usually only have about ten dollars on me."

"I know," he said, ignoring the joke. "You know how important it is."

"Sure, Buck."

Today was Friday, payday again. Jack figured many of the employees would not even be aware that last week's paychecks were bouncing all over Waco. Most of the employees at Sunset Records were relatively poor Hispanics who lived paycheck to paycheck. They worked on the press production line or printing or packaging machines and didn't make very much. Pressing and packaging the records was a skill that was not very transferable to other companies. The problem would be that most of them cashed their paychecks at local food markets, check cashing services and a few Waco banks.

Not many had checking accounts to deposit their checks into or any savings to fall back on in difficult situations.

"Buck," Jack said. "Most of your folks here are going to have a problem when they try to cash this week's check, if last weeks bounced. The shit's gonna hit the fan when they go in for their money and find out they owe for last week's."

"I know," he said. "I feel bad about that, but most of them will figure out something. We're giving them cash today to make up for the last check. At least the ones we know about. This week's checks will be good. We'll tell them it's an advance on wages and balance things out later. But, I'm going to have to furlough almost all of them today for about 10 days to two weeks; until we get this financial situation fixed. A little Christmas vacation for them. Then we'll get back in gear and bring them back. Shag's gonna meet with them late this afternoon and explain things."

"I'll need to call my bank and see if my check cleared before I write any more checks,"

"Yeah," Buck said. "I'm really sorry for the inconvenience, Jack. Why don't you just take a little time off and relax. Leave some numbers where I can reach you and I'll call in a week or two to come back up here."

The longer this conversation went on the more uncomfortable Jack felt. Buck wasn't one to admit to any fault. A couple of days earlier Jack had gone into the local photographic supply shop to buy some film, paper and chemicals and had been asked by the clerk to inquire about Texas Sun's past due account. That was unusual. He said they hadn't received payments for the past two months on the account. Jack came back and asked Wanda to look into it, and hadn't thought anymore about it. He had also overheard Shag talking to Wanda saying that they were having trouble getting raw vinyl from suppliers because Buck hadn't sent them any checks for previous shipments. They were running out of black vinyl and paper for the album covers and labels. Something was up.

"Just wanted to let you know about the situation," said Buck. "We're going to have it cleared up within a week. I have some new backers coming on board and we'll get past this. Louie and some guys in Dallas so don't worry about it."

"Do you think we'll lose some of the people because of the layoff?" Jack asked.

"Naw," said Buck. "What else are they going to do for a couple of weeks? Most of them need a good siesta. They're just gonna have to tighten their belts or hit up relatives until we can bring them back. That money's going to be here soon. Check on your bank account and if there's a problem get with Shag. He'll have some cash to take care of you. I've got an eleven o'clock flight back to Houston this morning, so I'll see you next week. If you're in town next week, come over to the apartment and we'll do our usual Monday Night Football dinner. OK?

"I'll do my part. See you Monday, night."

Jack left and went back to the graphics department. No wonder Buck seemed a little hyped up. But he wondered about the Rolling Stones deal. It sounded too good to be true and not likely to happen with the production equipment they had in the building. Would new backers and a contract mean a renovation or was it just more bullshit? Louie would know.

Jack walked across the street to the 7/11 after meeting with Buck, and made a call to his bank. Sure enough, his paycheck had been returned and Jack had two insufficient checks as a result. He asked them to take two thousand out of his savings to cover everything. A new cold front was blowing in and dropping the temperatures rapidly. It was going to be cold by dark. He was a little shaken by the morning and wondered if Buck was going to float him along until he got the business stabilized. Jack had savings, but things were building in an ominous direction.

None of the employees there or in the print shop or graphics department had any idea that they were about to lose their incomes for some time. They worked eagerly along after lunch, happy to be getting closer to the 4:30 quitting time. Then the word came through the departments that the entire staff were to have a 4:30 meeting. Most of their conversation centered on having to stay late after punching out. Many of the employees had buses or other rides to catch, and a long meeting could jeopardize them getting home on time or missing a ride.

It was the second week of December and getting colder as northern fronts began to regularly make their way through the state. Christmas was just around the corner and a layoff wouldn't help lighting up anyone's Christmas tree.

Jack left the record plant on time to meet the Southwest flight and sure enough they had a fat package at the counter. He picked it up and slipped it under his coat and made for the car. It hit him suddenly on the way out. He really didn't know where this cash came from, legitimate or not. There was a moderate number of passenger's lobby of the small airport and he got into the car, slipping the cash envelope under the seat. He couldn't help looking around him as he locked the doors. Now I'm a bagman, he thought. First the concert aftermath, then the beating of Jocko, and now meeting a plane for an envelope of cash. It was just getting worse and worse, working for Buck. He re-locked the doors and fired up the car. There was nothing or no one to see and no one seemed to be following him as he drove back into town. Christ! He thought to himself, I'm getting as paranoid as the rest of them. But, it's not every day I've got forty-five thousand dollars under my rear end. So this was business as usual for Buck. But, it was an uneventful drive back to Texas Sun and Jack delivered the money safely to Shag and Wanda.

About three-thirty, Shag opened the door and gave Jack a quick wave to come into Buck's office and Jack told him about his bounced checks. He could tell that some of Shag's usual self-confidence was not there. Most of the time he reminded Jack of Tennessee Ernie Ford; a cool country gentleman. Today he just looked shaken and a little scared.

"This isn't good Jack," he said. "When I break the news to these Mexicans that their checks bounced last week, they're gonna be upset, real pissed. Even if we give them back the money at the meeting to make up for the bad checks, wait 'til they go back to where they cashed them. Then I've got to give them this week's checks, another check, not cash. There's going to be some pissed off and confused folks. You think they are going to trust another piece of paper from Buck and me? You know, a lot of these people have worked here for years, for the Stallworths. They're loyal to the company and now we're screwing them. You know, these folks have an emotional nature; they can get real mad, real quick. And they won't forget this. Some may be back next week, and not to work."

Shag was nervous and upset at the task Buck had left him. Buck surely wasn't bothered by ruining his employees' Christmas or leaving Shag to take the blame. Shag was by nature an easy going, "take things in stride" guy, but this was something he was not looking forward to in the least. Shag liked to keep that cowboy-cool image going all the time. But, he was scared of the fallout down the road if they lost experienced staff.

"Now, I've got to tell them that they are furloughed or laid off for ten days or so," Shag said. "To call back after Christmas and see when we are going to reopen, if they still have jobs. These are passionate, jealous people. It's cotton-picking' Christmas time for Christ's sake. A lot of them don't have anything else. This is going to be bad."

"Here Jack," he reached in his pocket and counted out thirty $100 bills. "I don't know what Buck said to you, but I think this is more than your paycheck. I want to make sure you're good for at least a couple of weeks. I think we're in for a long ride before Buck can get these folks and our suppliers paid off. It's a lot of money we owe. He says he's got big money backers coming in but I'm not sure who they are."

Jack was surprised with how big his payoff was.

"Thanks Shag," he said. Jack looked into his eyes and saw a worried man. "Do you think he can keep us up and running?"

"I don't know. It's a lot worse than he's letting on. I only have enough cash to pay off these folks for last week's checks and a little extra for a couple of critical bills, like electricity. He said that more was wired into the bank to cover the next payroll. They are going to have to take checks for this week's pay. We're going to have a lot of upset people. I hope they come back."

"Well, I'll be here," Jack, said. "What about all that money he collected from our customers? Buck told me he had brought in over seven-hundred thousand dollars in the last six months, and business has been good all that time."

"No shit, but it's his flights, his call girl and he's leased six cars just for his family in Katy. You and me got one too." That was true, I had a new Firebird 400 and Shag was driving a Ford LTD. "You've seen that new gold Eldorado convertible his wife drove up here last week. For god's sake, she parked it right in front of the door. You know the employees checked that out. None of them have Cadillac's! I don't know where all the money's going, but it sure ain't paying the company bills. Not for months."

"And the Rolling Stones"

"What about them?"

"Uh, oh never mind, it was just something Buck said about a record pressing contract."

"Just more Buck crap, Jackie. Right now we couldn't press pancakes for IHOP. You better go back to work," said Shag. "If anybody asks you what's going on over the next few days, just play dumb. I'd take off at 4:30 if I were you. Oh, when you get back to the pressroom, ask Jesse to come in. Buck wanted me to give Jesse some cash privately, like you," said Shag. "We have some other print jobs to get out next week for Buck. He wants to make sure he'll stick around a few more days."

"OK."

"Alright, I'll let him know you're in here."

Jack left and decided to go straight to the bank after work. He wondered how Jesse was going to react to a secret payoff when none of his *compadres* in the pressroom were going to get special treatment. He had a young family, three kids and was exceptionally bright and capable. Jesse had a natural integrity and work ethic that could get him a good or better job somewhere else. Jack bet he might stay around, but begin looking for another job.

Jack went back into his office outside the darkroom and considered the multiple bombshells of the fall. He didn't feel good about his prospects in Waco. He didn't feel good about the future of Texas Sun Records either. He'd blown it with Angie. Jack decided he'd better start saving the money he had.

Four-thirty came and the employees gathered outside the main building for the meeting. Shag stood up in the back of one of the pick-up trucks in the yard so everyone could see and hear him. A chilly wind was blowing in. It was as cold and at the moment as heartless as Buck Smith. Jack had decided to stick around near the back of the crowd so that it wouldn't look like he knew more than anyone else. Paychecks were always for the prior week's work, not the current week, as in most businesses. Shag began to talk slowly, in English and broken Spanish, sentence by sentence. The employees could sense that he was unhappy from his tone of voice. He spoke slowly and carefully, like he had a stick of dynamite tied to his chest. He apologized repeatedly for the inconvenience that the company was causing in their lives. It was all just an accounting mistake. For most of the audience, it was closer to a disaster. There was a murmur in the crowd as some people repeated his words in more perfect Spanish to those who spoke no English. He didn't take any questions and finished up with an optimistic lie concerning the company's future.

That was what most of the crowd focused on, not yet considering the trouble they were going to have cashing this week's checks.

Then, he then explained to everyone that there was going to be a one week layoff or furlough. Next week only a few folks would be needed to maintain the plant. Everyone else would get an advance in cash today. He named the employees that would need to be there on Monday and gave the others a handout of instructions in English and Spanish, and the phone number to call after Christmas to see when they should return to work. Most of the workers were in shock at the sudden turn of events and the prospects of losing a week or more of paychecks. He and Wanda quickly passed out envelopes with each employee's names on the outside. Inside was cash for their bad paychecks covering the prior two-week's period. They also each got a new paycheck covering the prior week. As it turned later, not some, but all employee paychecks from the first week had bounced, and some to vendors as well. Jack wondered how many of them were going to find it impossible to cash the new paycheck in Waco.

The gathering broke up and Shag and Wanda went back to the office. The employees ambled off to their cars and the bus stops saying little to each other. A few of the women choked up a little, fearing for the future of their families and bad prospects for Christmas gifts. A number crossed themselves as they turned to go home.

Jack went home and spent the weekend laying low in Waco, watching TV, playing his guitar and pondering his situation. He decided that with the cash Shag had given him, he would stay around another week or two and see what happened next. Jack was considering what he would do if things in Waco, and Texas Sun Records went completely down the drain. He could move back to Houston and in with his old roommate and pick up with the studio and other contacts again. Maybe find a new girl there. His love affair and life with Angie was over. But,

Buck said he had new backers, more money coming in. If anyone could pull this out of the fire, Buck was probably the guy. It sounded like he had more money stashed or available from wherever or whomever he had gotten the forty-five thousand. Then again, he was a serial liar. Shag had confirmed that. The man had no apparent morals or regrets for his actions. Jack decided it would cost him nothing to stick around and see what the hell might happen next.

It had been a month since Las Vegas and Jack had been good to his word after he returned to Waco. He had called Maggie the morning after he and Angie broke up.

She answered. "Hi Maggie, it's Jack."

"Good Morning Jack, you woke me up. I had a late night, but I'm glad you called. You know, you must be a good guy, Jack. I didn't know if all that talk we had was just bull. I'm glad you called. How are you, honey?"

"I've been better," he said. He went over the previous week's events and the final meeting with Angie.

"That's rough," she said. "I'm so sorry. It's going to take some time to heal, you know, to get straight."

"I know," he answered. "It's just that life continues to go downhill right now. Thanks for listening to me whine. I wish you were here. How are you doing?

"Well, I had a date last night."

"Was it a hit or a miss."

"I don't think back on the details, Jack. When they're over I just put the money in the bank vault, the memory in a box and throw away the key, like it never happened. But I do have a thousand dollars in my glove compartment that wasn't there this time yesterday. You think I'm too hard…I mean too cold?"

"I don't know Maggie. It's you not me. You have to live with yourself. I mean your life. Please don't think I'm preaching. Your work there is almost over isn't it? I'm sure it's made you harder in a way, but Maggie, you've got a good and kind heart. I've seen it."

"I guess, but I've had it under wraps for a while."

"When you get to Colorado and it's going to come out again like a flower in spring. You've just had it covered by the icy snow the last two years." Jack told her about vacationing in Colorado when he was a kid and how much he loved trout fishing and the cold rocky streams. "It's one of the most beautiful places you can imagine, Maggie."

"I know, and I love it when you call me Maggie," she said. "I don't think I ever told you that. "Out here it's

Angel. With you now, my new friend, I'm Maggie. It feels good."

They made small talk for a while and then he said good-by so that she could get some breakfast. He felt better.

Monday came and after work, Jack went over to Buck's for the usual Monday Night Football feast. Buck, Terry, Angelique, Shag and his girlfriend Wanda and were there. They had steaks, baked potatoes and a salad and the scotch was flowing even more than usual. Nobody mentioned the business disaster of the last week. Terry had left early to make the honky-tonk bar circuit. Shag and Wanda sat closely on the couch and we watched the game. It was the Dallas Cowboys versus Washington, and a tight one. There was still no talk about Texas Sun. Everyone pretended that all was well.

By the end of the third quarter Buck was loaded and coaxed Angelique onto his lap in the recliner from which he inevitably watched the game. Jack had seldom seen her drink, but after Buck had pumped her up during dinner with promises for a big recording and movie career in her future, she was drinking steadily, like the rest. Buck was drunker than usual and began bragging large about his plans for Texas Sun to Angela. He talked and groped and she squirmed. It just made Jack feel ill as he watched Buck fabricate until he apparently did not know his fantasies from reality.

"Man, with this new backing, I think I'll buy some property out on the edge of town on the Brazos river," Buck said. "Got to get a realtor next week. Remind me Shag. It can be a company retreat house and we'll put in a few private cabins. We'll put the new studio out there. I want a big ranch house and a Mexican cook. Jack, we'll have a cabin for you and Terry to live in on the property, rent-free. Then we'll add a couple of bunkhouses for bands that come in to record. A beautiful place, where they can work and relax by the river. Hell, go cat fishing. I can see this natural, creative place where they can make music. Acts will be booking a studio like that as fast as they can, once the word gets around."

All of the time as Buck kept spinning out his plans, his hands kept wandering back to Angelique's bottom or breasts and she continuously squirmed and evaded. Buck began whispering occasionally in her ear and she would smile but shake her head no. Wanda glanced over occasionally from the couch and frowned. Their drinking kept up and he eventually coerced Angelique into sharing his glass of scotch. The bottle was beside the chair on a table so he could reach it easily. The game was well into the fourth quarter both on the TV and in the lounger. Her protests became less apparent and she was beginning to nod.

Eventually, he announced, "Well guys, me and Angie are going to watch the rest of the game in the back." Apparently he had misplaced her name during the evening. The word Angie brought a little pain to Jack. The drunken son of a bitch doesn't even remember her name, thought Jack. Buck swung the footrest of the chair down and managed to stand up, lifting her from his lap and into his arms. He was a little unstable so he sat her down and put his arm around her. She giggled as he guided her back toward the bedrooms, both of them helping the other walk.

They disappeared and Jack heard the door slam shut. No big surprise.

"Dammit!" said Wanda. "Dammit, dammit. Dammit! He's been trackin' at her like a cat after a mouse for all this time and never made a move 'til tonight. I knew this was going to happen. I knew the day would come, that old hard-dicked bastard."

"Aw, Wanda," said Shag. "It was bound to happen sometime. She wern't gonna stay a starlet pure forever. You know that's the truth. Shag had drunk his share of scotch as well. Some guy was gonna get it. She's a big girl"

"You better hope her Momma in Monterey doesn't find out," she warned.   "She's just nineteen and's been protected all her life. You said you were gonna take care of her like a daughter up here. You swore that to her. Momma's gonna come up here with a knife if she gets wind of this and cut your gizzard out!"

"She ain't gonna find out nothin'," he replied.

"I'm going home" said Jack. "I'm finished! You two turn out the lights, I do believe the party's over. The fat lady has sung."

"Good night, Jacky," said Shag. "Be seeing you."

"Night, sugar," said Wanda. "Please don't grow up to be a turd like Buck."

"Yes mam."

Jack decided he wouldn't; he wasn't coming back. Not to Buck's apartment and not to Texas Sun. It was over.

Chapter Twenty-Five

Mr. Fantasy

The next they he began to move back to Houston. Jack didn't have any reason for staying in Waco. He had stayed the first week after the check bouncing episode and went into the graphics office everyday but had very little to do. He experimented with some photo techniques in the darkroom for future reference. He only had one album cover to layout and finish, and it was completed by Wednesday.

He went back into the pressroom a few times to visit with Jesse. Jesse was printing some cassette covers that Buck needed for a batch of the duplicated tapes. They were for a Tejano album by some obscure production company. Shag and Wanda were manning the office. The rest of the pressroom was gone, only Jesse was at work. The plant foreman was the only person in the record pressing side and he was doing maintenance only.

It was very quiet. On Friday Jack came in and visited with Shag about work.

"I've got nothing to do," he told Shag.

"Aw, Jack, you might as well go home and give me a call in a couple of weeks. Give me a number where I can get hold of you if you go to Houston."

"Sure," said Jack. ""Let me know if you need anything."

"I doubt I will," said Shag. "I talked with Buck this morning and he said just to shut down and lock the office and the gate tonight. It's gonna be at least a week or ten days before we can think about getting up and running again. The materials vendors, both the vinyl and paper ain't gonna ship us a thing until we get paid back up. Then it's gonna be cash on delivery for a long time. We got them scared."

"Yeah, Buck going to need some big money to get the plant up and running again. And he's going to need to recover the workers as well. A lot of them may not be available after what happened. There will need to be a lot of new training and breaking people in."

"I don't even want to think about that," said Shag. We're gonna be hanging around waiting for news and trying to answer customer's questions about our future."

"Well," said Jack. "I can't see any reason for hanging around Waco. I'm going back to Houston and try to make a few bucks until we see what happens."

"I'm sorry Jack," said Shag. "I guess we're all in this together at this point."

"Yeah," said Jack. "You all take it easy."

"Bye Jack," said Wanda.

"I'll be calling you," said Shag.

Jack went back to his apartment and packed up most of his clothes and a good bunch of other essentials into the Firebird. Neither Shag nor Buck had said anything about returning it to the lease company. As far as Jack knew, it was still leased, although he was wondering if Buck was behind the payments on the car as well. Jack took his cameras and the Hasselblads out of the office and put them in the car. He got on the road to Houston. He planned to dump his clothes and the cameras at his brother's house and sleep on their couch until the smoke cleared. His parents would be in town and it would be good to see them. He decided not to leave any of his valuables in the car while in Houston in case it was towed away by the leasing company. He figured they would not have any way of knowing where he was staying in Houston, but they'd chase him and the car down eventually.

He went by the Waco Post Office and put in notice to have his mail forwarded to his temporary Houston address. If the leasing company notified him about wanting the car back, he would turn it in. He still had the Mustang parked in Houston. Jack also cut off his phone and paid off the utilities. His rent was paid until the end of January in Waco, so he wasn't under any pressure to move the leftover furniture out of the apartment. His stay in Waco was history. He would need to make plans about moving the rest soon. But, he wasn't really excited about moving back to Houston. The question was, back to what?

Angie had disappeared over the horizon. He had talked with her once and she told him she was making wedding plans and she wanted him to get together with her and her soon to be husband sometime after the wedding. To continue to be friends. That was before the plant had closed.

Now he was at loose ends, at a point to start over.

Jack got back to Houston and settled in temporarily at his brother and sister-in-law's house. They welcomed him back to Houston and he told them he wouldn't be there long, just long enough to get resituated in an apartment. He had saved over ten thousand dollars which could support him for months.

Chapter Twenty-Six

Only the Strong Survive

Louie picked up the phone and dialed the out of town number Mona had passed to him. It was late January and he figured the time was right. He had the pieces and players in the game set on the right squares. It wasn't chess, but he figured he'd make his play. A woman answered on the second ring.

"Texas Sun Records, this is Faye. How may I help you?"

"Morning, Faye," said Louie. "My names Louie Thibodeaux, I believe I've talked with you before. I wonder if Mr. Stallworth might be in the office?"

"Yes sir, he is. Of course I remember you, but it's been a few years. It's good to hear your voice. Let me see if he's available. We've been pretty busy around here the past couple of days, since Mr. and Mrs. Stallworth took over again."

There was a long pause and Jim Stallworth came on the line.

"Morning, Louie," he said. "What brings you to us today?"

"Shame, shame on me, Jim. I just want you to know that I've never felt worse than when I did found out what Buck Smith done you all. And I'm the one who sent him you way. It's a sin, that's all, and I apologize from the bottom of my heart." Louie had never sounded more sincere in his life and Stallworth accepted it on its face.

"Louie, you can't take all the blame for this. None of us knew how he was going to mismanage this deal. We didn't see the depth of his greed and larceny. Mrs. Stallworth and I aren't kids, we've been taken before, but we didn't see this coming."

"None of us did, Jim," said Louie. "I know, and I think I know how you feel. You understand I never knowed what kind of a thief he was when I introduced you to him." And that's mostly why I called, Jim. If you'd take just a little time out, I'd like to come up to Waco, and take ya'll to lunch. I've got a solution for you. Just between you and me. Nobody else done gonna be involved. I think I can help get Texas Sun and both of you get out of dis pinch."

"Of course, Louie. You've always been a straight shooter for many years. You've been a good client who paid your bills, and appreciated what we did for you when you were just starting out. Those were the good old days I guess."

"Aw, der's more good old days ahead for all of us, Jim. I'm calling to guarantee it."

"Well Louie, when do you intend to come up? Hell, what are you doing tomorrow?"

"Tomorrow sounds great. It'll be good to visit with you two. Be there about Noon."

"Looking forward to it"

"I appreciate that, Jim, I really do. I'll see you both tomorrow."

Louie leaned back, hit the receiver button and called up to Mona.

"Mona honey," he said. "I want you to go down to the bank and get me a cashier's check for twenty-five thousand dollars as soon as you can. And leave it blank so's I can write in the name. And I'm gonna be out of the office tomorrow. I've got a little trip to make."

Louie didn't like to drive as much as he used to. After his stint in prison, he had an aversion to meeting police, even for a traffic ticket. He didn't like to be alone either. He called up Jack and asked him what he was doing.

"Not a damn thing, Louie. After Buck shut down operations for a couple of weeks, I had been back here in Houston waiting for a call. But now I understand that he resigned as President and gave the company back to the Stallworths. But, what can I do for you?" said Jack

"Brudder, I got to go up to Waco tomorrow and I'd like for you to go along."

"You going up to see Buck."

"Naw, I don't need to see that fat bastard. I'm having lunch with some other folks and want you to go along. I always like to have somebody with me during meetings. Tell the truth, you a good, impartial witness to dis kind of thing."

"OK, you want me to bring my camera?"

"Yeah, come to think of it, that's a good idea. Maybe just bring a little camera and a flash. You done need you whole rig."

"Alright, anything else?"

"No, jus' be here at the studio 'bout eight in the morning, I might want you to drive my car. I'm gonna have some papers to look at."

"See you then." As he was talking with Jack, Louie pulled open his lower desk drawer and pulled out a packet of legal papers that had arrived the day before from his Houston lawyers. They were a local office of the New York firm that handled his legal business.

"Let me see," he mumbled to himself. "I got the letters, gonna have the money and my ride's set. Gonna do some bidness tomorrow."

The next morning Louie threw his briefcase in the Lincoln and arrived at the studio at seven fifty-five. Traffic had been light from his home which was close to downtown, on the Northwest side. His home was in one of the oldest neighborhoods in Houston and one time one of the most prestigious. But this was over thirty years later and it was a bit run down. It made for some good values in big, older homes that needed some loving care to return them to their earlier glory. Louie had been careful restoring his home in the Heights neighborhood since he moved in a year earlier. It was costing him a small fortune but he didn't mind. It was old but comfortable.

Jack was waiting, having only beaten him there a couple of minutes earlier. Louie moved to the right-hand seat and Jack put his small camera bag in the backseat and slid under the wheel. It was quite different than the Pontiac. He would have practically paid to drive this car to Waco. It felt like a battleship with couches.

Nobody had asked for the Firebird back, so Jack kept driving it. He knew that sooner or later the leasing company would track him down and demand its return.

But, that was going to take a little work on their part and he might have a few weeks. He parked in a far corner of the studio lot, behind the van. The Firebird was barely visible from the street.

They got on Highway 225 and made their way downtown where they could pick up Interstate 45 to Waco. The subject of the record company didn't come up. Louie didn't mention the purpose of their trip and Jack decided to keep his mouth shut until Louie broached the subject. A little less than three hours later they were approaching the outskirts of Waco and Louie dropped the small talk.

"Tell you what's up Jack," said Louie. "I'm glad you came along. I know I said I wanted you to be an impartial witness, but I also think you might learn something today. That alright with you?"

"I'm always ready to learn something when I can." Jack said.

"Good, that's the smart answer. Here's the truth, Buck done bankrupted Texas Sun Records. Buck's out of the picture."

"I knew that was coming, bankrupted." Jack said. He felt a little sick but it passed quickly. I shouldn't be surprised, he told himself. He had seen enough of Buck's shenanigans.

"Nope, he ripped off all he could the past year and done gave the place back to the Stallworths. Dey should've never made him the President. He collected all that money and put it in his hind pocket instead of the business. Ain't nothing dey can do about it 'cause he's had dis fancy lawyer right by his side the whole time making sure he stayed legal."

"Man…I knew he was the CEO of the company. Buck told me that was part of the buyout. They made him President because he said he needed that authority to collect all those past due bills. He brought in a load of money they had been owed for years."

"Yeah, he brought a lot in alright, but ain't nobody knows where it is."

"So my job's fried."

"That's right. I always knew Buck was gonna fuk dis up. He's got dat larceny in his soul. You remember me telling you that a while back? You ain't never gonna wanna go back to work in Waco, never. But don't worry; I'll help all I can. You come out alright for the experience, didn't you? You been true and I appreciate that." Jack didn't tell Louie that he had already made up his mind and moved back to Houston. He wasn't going to talk to Buck or Shag again. He'd seen enough.

"So where are we going?"

"You drive us right up to the record company," said Louie. "We gonna take the Stallworths, the old man and his wife Eileen to lunch."

They arrived and he parked his car near the door. There were only two other cars inside the gates which were only partially open. They went into the office and Louie introduced Jack to the Stallworths. Louie gave Faye Stallworth a hug. The couple looked like they were both in their seventies and very tired. They went through the formalities and Louie guided them to the car. They got in the back and Louie shut the door. He had told Jack that they were going to Luby's Cafeteria and Jack knew the way. Louie kept the conversation on small talk about the weather and their grandkids until they arrived there. After they had gone through the buffet line, he led the way to a large corner table. As the group ate, Louie told them about his recent success and how the studio was progressing. He invited them to come down next time Hidalgo recorded so that they could meet him and watch. After they finished the meal, the foursome sat around and pondered their coffee cups.

"I wanted to visit with you about dis situation you in," said Louie. "You fine folks and you deserve a lot better than dis. I been doin' some studying on the problem you got."

"Louie," said Mrs. Stallworth, "I've always done the bookkeeping for our company. When I left, when we turned over the operations to Buck, made him President, truthfully, we were in debt about ninety thousand dollars. That wasn't too bad for a company that did $1.4 million two years ago. We grew a good, solid record company over the past years. But, we had nearly five hundred thousand dollars we couldn't collect from customers. Unpaid invoices that went back a couple of years. That's half a year's sales and Jim and I were in a pinch. It was going to cost a lot of money to sue them, if that was what it was going to take to collect."

"Dat's just about what I figured," said Louie.

"Most of them were our best customers, and if we tried to sue, we thought they'd just take their business somewhere else after the dust cleared. Then where would we be?"

"It's a shame that folks take advantage of situation-- honest people like you. I'm sorry. I don't understand it. I don't understand what Buck did to your company. It's a waste! What happened to the integrity of a handshake in

Texas?" Louie seemed really upset at himself after hearing what had happened after he gave Buck the opportunity.

"So now," said Mr. Stallworth, "We're the proud owners of a company that we allowed to be taken to the cleaners. After going through the books the last few days with our secretary and accountant, we found that we now owe a hundred and twenty-odd thousand to our suppliers, for paper, vinyl, utilities, and at least another seventy-five thousand for past due payroll and bank fees. We've only got eight thousand or so in our company checking account. We're looking at complete bankruptcy and the state and the IRS are all over us."

"Oh my goodness," said Louie. "You worse den you was before."

"I don't know what we're going to do," said Mrs. Stallworth. We've got our house and a little property in Wimberly near the lake. I'm afraid were going to lose it and what we've got invested for retirement will be gone. It's horrible!" Tears had been building up as she talked and she reached in her black vinyl purse for some tissues and snapped the gold bead latch back shut.

"I know what you mean, darlin'," said Louie. Mrs. Stallworth couldn't help the tears and Louie reached out and took hold of both their hands. There, for a moment their hands remained motionless on the table. It was a sad scene as Louie comforted her. He wiped his right eye on his sleeve.

"Trust me, Jim," Louie said pulling back his hands, "Eileen, you know sometimes things happen that jus' bring you to the brink. Dat's the way life is. We all makes plans, and the Lord jus' laughs at us."

"I know," she said quietly. "We've seen tough times before, but we should be through with them by this time in our lives. We'd should, you know, have it made, or at least be comfortable with our future." She dabbed at her left eye.

"I said to your husband yesterday," said Louie. "And now I'll say it to you, I'm gonna help."

"I can't imagine how Louie, we made this mess and we're gonna clean it up," Jim said. "We don't blame you. We went into the deal with Smith with our eyes withe open. We were fools."

"I want to make da fool out of him," said Louie. That got Jack's attention.

"You don't have to dig your way out of this," said Louie. "You tired of workin' and I done blame you. Listen, when my day comes, I'm just gonna retire and buy me a property wit' a big lake full of catfish and a swamp wit' crawdads and frogs. Den I gonna relax and catch all I can eat."

"But dat ain't what I want to do right now," Louie said. He leaned toward them. "I want to buy Texas Sun Records from you. Buy it right now, jus' like it is, warts and all"

The Stallworths and Jack just were stunned. Who would want a company that was so disrupted and broke? Texas Sun was in debt, with several hundred thousand dollars in uncollectible receivables and a staff that had been run off carrying bad paychecks. The staff was gone and the vendors distrustful.

Mr. Stallworth spoke first. "Louie, what are you talking about, didn't you here Eileen a minute ago, our company's ruined. What's left to buy? You have nothing to feel guilty about."

"It ain't guilt," said Louie. "I can handle it. Look, I buy you out and you can go home and relax. Live out on that property so your grandkids can visit the country. You retirement money will be yours. You maybe got most of dat couple of hundred thousand that Buck paid you before he disappeared. You got dat, your savings, your home and property. You can walk away clean."

"What's the catch Louie?" said Mrs. Stallworth.

"No catch, Eileen. Dat's da truth. I buy you out and assume the debts and all the accounts. Gonna put all dem good people that loved you two back to work so de can support der families."

"Really?" she said. One of her biggest regrets in the whole fiasco was the way the workers had been mistreated and defrauded by Buck Smith. I hated that." Faye had once felt like the mother of the whole family.

"I ain't in dis to lose money. You probably know, Louie Thibodeaux don't go into anything to lose money. No sir!"

"It might work, dear" said Stallworth to his wife. "Louie, if you're serious, I don't know how we could turn the deal down as long as it's clean. But we want out completely, buy us out, no strings or contingencies. Real simple, you buy us out and we go home with no liabilities."

"How much are you going pay us for this mess, Louie?" said Faye. What do you see as a fair price?"

"I dun thought about that Faye," he said. "I thought 'bout it all last night, layin' in that big old bed of mine. You gonna be bankrupted. The company, dat's you, owe 'bout two hundred thousand bucks to all dem people you buy stuff from. You old customers still owe you maybe three hundred thousand dat Buck didn't manage to collect and steal. But we don't know if de's ever gonna pay up, right. You sue dem and you gonna lose forty per cent to da damn lawyers, even if you win. That's a hundred and twenty thousand lost out of your three hundred."

"You've about summed it up Louie," said Stallworth. "Whether it's us or you, the new owner's going to be in the hole for about a hundred thousand dollars to get the company back on its feet.

"Yup," said Louie. "That's about how I figured it on the way up here. Tell you what. Louie reached out and took their hands again. "Da place is worth about a hundred thousand dollars as it sits. I mean the real estate, the buildings and the old equipment. I don't think you'd get a dime more if you was to auction it off. But like you said, da owner would still be thousands short in the end."

"OK," said Stallworth cautiously. "You're sure you are serious about buying us out."

"Oh yeah," he said. "Jack, would you go out to the car and bring in that brown envelope I was workin' on in the front seat." Jack made a quick trip out and hurried back to the table. Louie took the envelope and pulled out some documents. He stood up and walked around behind the couple and laid a sheet before them.

"Dis here's letter of intent my lawyer done drawn up yesterday. It says jus' what we've been talking about. I'm very serious." He lightly gripped Mrs. Stallworth's shoulder. "I want you both to read it. Ain't much to it for what dat attorney of mine charges. I want you to take it to your attorneys as soon as you can."

They skimmed through it for a couple of minutes. Louie quietly waited. He turned and winked at Jack. The attendant trolled by and Louie had her refill everyone's coffee cups. It was a simple commitment letter declaring that Louie, through his company Thibodeaux Enterprises, would buy Texas Sun Records from the Stallworth's. That was it, real simple.

"Louie, your lawyer left the date blank and didn't fill in any amount," said Mrs. Stallworth. It looks good to me on paper except for that."

"If we sell it to you," said Mr. Stallworth, "In the condition it's in, and don't take on any further obligations, what were you thinking of as a fair price?"

"Jim, Eileen, like you said before, you're 'bout bankrupt and gonna be in the hole for a hundred thousand or more. Right? It's gonna ruin you and destroy your retirement plans." They looked at him, both vulnerable. He had them defenseless and Jack didn't figure he'd give them much of anything for taking Texas Sun off their hands.

"I told you before, I feel bad about dis whole affair. It's partially my fault." He released his grip on her shoulder and sat down in front of them. He paused and then reached over and took the letter off the table, holding it. "So I'll give you one hundred thousand for the whole mess; land, buildings and equipment. Just like it sits."

"One hundred thousand dollars to us and you get the company, bad debt, in debt, shut down and all?" said Mr. Stallworth. He was shocked and this was all he could come out with at the moment.

"And you two can go on your merry way with you retirement intact. It's all I can do."

"I think that's very generous, Louie, and I really can't understand why you are doing this." said Mrs. Stallworth. "What do you think, dear?"

"Louie, I don't know what you may have up your sleeve. There ain't no oil under the land. We've already been screwed once trying to sell it. But if what you say is true, I think we'll take the deal. I don't have enough years left to worry with this thing. I'm tired. You get us out and get us our money and I don't give a damn what you do to recoup your investment". He paused for a moment. "I can't be as sentimental now as the first time we sold it. It would be nice if you could put our people back to work, but that will be your business."

"It's settled then," said Louie. Louie stuck out his hand to shake. First with Mrs. Stallworth and then Mr. Stallworth. He gave Mrs. Stallworth a bear hug as well. Everyone was smiling.

"I'm so happy for ya'll, sometimes things do work out for good, honest Christian folks like you. Now I know what Santee Claus feels like."

Jack felt good as well, watching the deal being closed and he shook the Stallworth's hands as well, congratulating them on the outcome. They all set back down and Louie waved at an attendant.

"We need a big piece of pie for everybody, all around," he said. Mr. Stallworth ordered pecan and Mrs. Stallworth strawberry shortcake. Jack got apple and Louie ordered chocolate with whipped cream on top. He gave the attendant a twenty and told her to keep the change. More coffee was poured and the letter's blanks were filled out and Louie signed his part. Mr. Stallworth and Louie traded names and phone numbers of the attorneys for both sides. Louie told the Stallworths that he would phone his attorneys in New York and get a special delivery sales contract to them and their lawyer. He wanted to close the deal as soon as possible.

They went back to the car and Jack started up the engine. Louie turned as they pulled out of the parking lot.

"One more thing," he said. "I forgot dis."

"What's that," said Mr. Stallworth. She sounded a little tentative, like he was thinking, "what's the catch."

"Dis," he pulled a check out of the white envelope on the seat between himself and Jack. "I forgot to give you da down payment. He handed it back to Mrs. Stallworth. "I believe you is the bookkeeper so you gonna need dis."

"Why, this is a cashier's check for twenty-five thousand dollars," she said. "I don't believe it."

"Yes Mam," said Louie. "I dun told you in the beginning I was serious. I'd appreciate it if you'd keep dis whole conversation and our deal to yourselves and your lawyers 'til you get the second check. I don't like to put my bidness on the street."

"That's not a problem, Louie. We have a deal and nobody's going to know until it closes. I'll just write in our names on this check."

"Yes sir'ee."

They got to the record company and they got out and shook hands and Louie gave her another hug. The

Stallworths looked like twenty years had fallen from them during lunch.

"Don't it make you wanna dance, don't it make you wanna cry, dey was down, down, down and I know the reason why." Louie sang to himself as they pulled out of the lot.

"Where'd that come from," Jack said. "I never heard you sing before."

"Aw, one of dem boys from Austin that sent me a tape, maybe, I ain't sure."

"You did an amazing thing there, Louie. You knew they were going to go for it, didn't you?"

"I don't see how they could have refused," said Louie. "I saved their asses."

"I'm surprised they didn't ask for more," said Jack.

"Me too. Just shows you how desperate people will jump in a lifeboat full o' sharks. Hell, I probably paid too much, should of offered fifty. Truth is, I did feel sorry for them. But, de getting' a square deal."

"Well, the way you explained it, it was a logical offer I guess," Jack said.

"It's a good day, Jack," he said. "Don't fret about your Waco gig. I'll try to help you out."

"Are you going to open it back up?

"Not me," he replied. "But I wouldn't be surprised if Texas Sun lives on. I got a plan."

The next week, Jack received an unexpected phone call from Buck late one night, a few days later.

"What's up," Buck said without introducing himself on the line. It was like Buck to expect everyone to recognize his voice. It took a few moments for Jack to snap to who was calling. He responded carefully. He really wanted to hang up on him. Curiosity kept him hanging on.

"Not much. How's it going?"

"Pretty good. Wanted to let you know Jack, I'm getting the record company finances back in order. We're taking this thing a new direction. A few more weeks and we'll be reopening." That of course was a lie, but he didn't challenge Buck. Jack didn't let on that he knew Louie was now the owner and Buck was history. Buck might know about Louie's new deal, but Jack doubted it. Louie had a plan and wasn't likely to share it with Buck. Not now. But he wasn't sure what Buck was up to. He waited for Buck to pick up the conversation.

"Still got that Firebird?" said Buck. "I thought I might borrow it for a while." It sounded like Buck was drunk.

"No man, the lease company picked it up a while back. They said the payments were behind." He didn't mind meeting a lie with another.

"Those bastards," said Buck. "Those payments must'a got screwed up by the accountant when we were closing for at the Christmas break. Well, hell."

"So you're gonna open back up," Jack prodded him for more.

"Oh yeah."

"When?

"A couple of weeks. Listen Jack, I want you to come back to Waco when we get it running. It's going to be better than ever."

"I don't know, Buck. I don't think so. I don't think I take to the way you operate"

"What's the problem? I paid you well didn't I?"

"Yeah, good paid for shitty work. I'm going to lay it out, Buck. I'm tired of your bullshit and lies. And, I didn't appreciate getting roped into that deal with Terry and Big Adolph beating the crap out of Jocko."

"What are you talking about? He deserved it didn't he?"

"You're right about that. But you ram-rodded me into that deal and I don't appreciate being in the middle of a felony. You may be ready to go back in the penitentiary for a night of fun, but I'm not."

There was a pause. "I thought I could trust you. Can I trust you Jack? We been on some adventures this year haven't we? You gonna wimp out on me now?"

"Hell yeah you can trust me Buck. But I'm not going to jail to save your ass. I know I could expect the same or less from you if it got down to the nut-cutting. What if Jocko had wound up in a hospital or jail and implicated all of us? Perjury ain't my bag, or jail!"

Another pause.

"So that's how it is? You owe me for pulling your ass out a crack with your picture business, am I right." Jack could feel the chill in Buck's voice. "You're gonna pussy-out on me." Jack felt like a beer about to be iced down.

"You can trust me never to say anything, Buck. And that's all. I can make it on my own, sure as hell without your help or a new car. Jocko got what he deserved. But, he should have gone to jail. But that wasn't good enough for you. Buck, I think our business is over. I'm not coming back!"

"Some fukin' buddy."

Jack heard the phone click off.

Chapter Twenty-Seven

All Right Now

Two weeks later, Louie sent the Stallworths a check for seventy-five thousand dollars, closing the deal. It was early in the year and a wet, blue northern had blown into town. Texas Sun Records was now all Louie's. The parties had closely held the deal and Louie asked the Stallworths to keep it to themselves another week or so. They locked up the place and mailed the key to the front gate and office to Louie.

Both parties felt it was a good end.

The next morning Louie picked up the phone and placed a long distance call to Laredo.

"Buenos Dios, esta es Vaquero Records," a Hispanic accented young woman answered. "At you service."

"You bet darlin'" said Louie. "I'd like to speak with Juan Gomez please. Tell him it's Louie Thibodeaux calling him from Houston, dear."

"Yes sir, I believe he's in," she said switching off the Spanish and the accent as well. "Just let me check."

There was a minute's pause followed by a couple of clicks.

"Louie?" a man's voice bass came on the line. "This is Juan Gomez. How are you me amigo viejo?"

"I'm doin' jest fine, Juan," he answered. "It's been a long time compadre. I hope you' bidness is good. I don't think we've talked since the Tex-Mex Music Awards in Austin a couple of years ago."

"Yes, too long. But the music business has been good to us, has it not?" He had a rich, deep Spanish accent, well-schooled, like one of those Mexican TV announcers.

"Yes, it has. I won' beat 'round the bush, Juan." said Louie. "I got a real good reason for calling. I got dis record deal dat's just come up. I think you'd be real interested into it. Wonder if we could meet, maybe in San Antone in a day or two. Let's have some lunch and let me lay it out on the table for you. It's a money maker."

"Louie, I know you wouldn't waste my time. I can be in San Antonio this Friday if you wish."

"Dat would be fine. Why don't we meet at that La Tierra in the Market about 11:30 Friday? Beat the crowd, you know."

"I'll see you there. Would you mind if I bring my son Antonio, I'm trying to teach him the business."

"No, Juan, dats fine, see you der. I'm hungry already."

Once again, Louie gave Jack a call.

"What you up to?" Louie said.

"Not too much, I'm taking some proofs over to a fiddle player dat's under contract to old man Piedmont," he replied.

"I'd like for you to go with me to lunch tomorrow in San Antonio if you can." He had paid Jack hundred dollars for accompanying him to Waco and much more to Las Vegas and picked up all the expenses, so Jack was available.

"I can do that," said Jack. "What time should I be at the studio?"

"Well, let's see, we got to figure about four hours from Pasadena so we better get out of here about 7:30. I'll meet you den. Lord, I hate to get up that early." Spring was still far off, and it was about half dark at that time. At least the sun would be behind him driving west out Interstate 10. Jack was glad that it was a straight shot from Houston.

They met and Jack again took the wheel as they left town. After fighting their way fifty miles across the metropolitan downtown and suburban west side, they were on the open turnpike where they could make time. The last city they passed on the outskirts of Houston was Katy. That brought Buck to Jack's mind.

"Heard from Buck lately?" said Jack. He had not seen him at the studio or spoken a word to him since the late night phone conversation. He didn't want to see him again.

"No," said Louie. "I think he's hiding' out somewhere's. I don't even know if he's in town. His old lady runs real estate bidness out here in Katy, I think. At least dat's what he's told me."

Jack offered. "Maybe he took all that money and went to Mexico or the Bahamas."

"Oh, I doubt it," said Louie. "He don't want to break his probation, can't leave the country or he'd be violating. He ain't dat dumb."

"Think he's in trouble with the law over his Texas Sun deal?"

"Don't know and I don't wanna know," said Louie. "I don't care to do no more bidness wit' him. Dun told him he ain't welcome at the studio no more." He gave Jack a serious look that Jack could feel while looking down the road. He turned his head briefly looking into Louie's eyes. The snake's eyes were back. "You've always been smart around the studio. You're not one that asks too many questions…dat's using your head, Jack. If I was you, I'd just avoid knowing too much. It'll keep you out of trouble. I know dat fo' sure. Value of a *college* education. The less you know, the less you got to answer for. You really don't wan' to know too much about Buck and his goin's on."

"I guess not," said Jack. Lesson learned. Louie was right; some things were better left unsaid, unseen and unknown.

"When I was up in college," said Louie, "der was dis fellow in the next bunk dat escaped one night. We weren't in no, cell but in the hospital. I had a stomachache. I heard him get up and ask dis other guy if he was coming.' He said no. The fellow sounded scared. So the next morning dis first guy was gone, and da shit hit the fan."

"Dem guards told me he had escaped in the night," said Louie. "De took me into a little room and asked me if I seen or heard something."

"I said, oh hell no. I'd tell you, but I was in the can all night with a case of the shits. I didn't hear nothin'!" Louie laughed. "De caught the guy in the laundry room dat afternoon; he didn't even get out of the joint. I didn't want no part of it. Be smart. Somethings you just don't want to know. I'm just tellin' you for you education you understand."

"But Buck probably gonna come out of his hole sooner or later," said Louie. "He had that downtown lawyer with him every minute of the day during dis whole Texas Sun bidness. I think he just slid along right on that edge between the shady and the sunny side of the law. I guess somebody could sue him. But I don't think he actually broke no laws. I own the place now, and the Stallworths are out free and clear. De ain't gonna sue him for no fraud. He probably just got to watch for the IRS boys and get straight wit' dem if de come snoopin' around. That's why he's got his attorney right der."

"That's a lot of money he kept," Jack said.

"Aw hell," said Louie. "He probably spent it all livin' high on the hog. Probably all gone by now."

Louie had brought along a box of demo cassettes and he played one after another sampling the music. Some were horrible and some had a song or two with possibilities.

They spent the next few minutes talking about music and recording techniques.

"I haven't seen Jocko since the concert in Baton Rouge," said Jack.

"No you ain't," said Louie. "He probably left town after dat. Jack, that fool was stealin' the money. We caught him red-handed."

"So he's in jail?"

"Not from that night. I tell you once, den we ain't gonna mention it again. You meet Big Adolph, that crazy German?

"Yeah, he's one big muncher. Where'd he come from?"

"College boy."

"Well, I know Buck an' Terry fixed him, that stealin' bastard, Jocko. I know it was you was drivin' dem back to the concert dat night. Sorry 'bout that. I didn't tell Buck to heist you off and into it. I know dey put a bad whippin' on him. He ain't gonna be coming round anymore."

"That's probably all I want to know."

"Aw, he ain't dead, but a whippin' from Adolph ain't something you ever forget. Dat's for sure! Jocko Dove wish he he'd been taken to the cops."

"Yeah, I guess you're right."

"Yup, der's you lesson. You been careful to stay out of the inside action. Dat always been fine with me. And I admire your smarts for layin' out sometimes."

Jack was quiet for a while as Louie kept sifting through his box of tapes, punching them into the cassette deck one after another. It was everything from blues to country and lousy rock. He changed the subject.

"When you listen to all this stuff," asked Jack, "how do you figure out what to do with it? I mean some of its terrible and it's easy to throw it out. But some of the music has something, the lyrics or the tune isn't bad. You get boxes of this crap."

"Jack, you jus'listen for the feel. It's my job. It's got to have the sound dat's popular. I don't care if it rock or country or soul, it's got to sound like what radio stations are playin' today. You can't hardly get a record played otherwise. If you can't get it on the air with a strong rotation all over the place, you' sunk. Den its gets' to have some soul, something that moves you. It can be happy or sexy or sad, but the words or tune got to move der hearts. I think I was just blessed by the good Lord to hear these things."

"Yeah, that makes sense"

"And most good songs got to build. Got to have a climax. You can fix everything else later. Lots of songs got that thing. Dis *Bridge Over Troubled Water* dat's shootin' up the charts. Man, the producer jus' blows the lid off at the end. That Beatle song, *Day In the Life*, I know you've heard that, it's another one. Dem's the extreme, but I done dat on lots of hits. You got to build it up and leave them hangin' at the end. Jus' drain 'em. It's sex man"

"Yeah," Jack said. "Guess it is."

"Den, I also look at my acts and I asks myself which song might work with dis or dat one? I try to match 'em up. You get a good song and sometimes you just get everyone to record it. Maybe one of dem will make a hit. You never know for sure."

"Den you got to sell it to the big label and line up the DJ's or station managers and all that. You get that one that you thinks gonna be a monster and you take it to New York or Nashville or LA. That's when the work begins. The rest is fun."

They jumped off Interstate 10 where the freeway lunged right into downtown San Antonio. La Tiera was in the Mexican Market and practically under the I10 freeway as it cut through San Antonio. It had been there since the forties and was one of the best traditional Mexican food restaurants in town.

Juan Gomez and his son were right on time, and were not hard to spot outside the restaurant's door. Juan was looking distinguished in a silver-gray, western cut silk suit and bolero tie. It matched his longish gray mane which he combed back in a businesslike pompadour. His son was dressed more casually. Juan looked exactly the same as he did on his popular Hispanic TV show which presented an assortment of his artists every Sunday. Louie introduced Jack and Antonio gave Jack a less than cordial handshake and expression. The old man was different. Tony may have remembered his face from the day in Buck's office. Jack couldn't be sure and made no reference to meeting him before. Juan was more than friendly and the staff obviously knew and greeted him and Antonio as celebrities. They were led to a semi-private table set into one wall. The surroundings were traditional old San Antonio with beautiful wall decorations from Mexico setting the atmosphere. Jack was looking forward to a great meal.

"Did ya'll drive up this morning," asked Louie.

"No," said Juan. "I had some business here last night so we came up earlier."

"Where do ya'll like to stay?" said Louie. "You got a hotel you could recommend?

"Louie, usually the St Anthony or the Menger Hotel," he said. "I like the traditional hotels. The warmth of old, elegant lobbies and gracious woods and rugs. These new hotels are all cement and plastic. They have no heart, no style. They look the same in every city in America."

"Amen," said Louie. "Stayed at the Menger before myself. I love dat old Teddy Roosevelt bar in the Menger Hotel. Done a lot of business der. And de got da best breakfast biscuits and gravy in town at the restaurant."

"You love good food?" said Juan.

"Too much," said Louie, patting his stomach. "Damn near as much as young chicks."

"Well La Tiera cooks some specialties for me when I'm here. Please allow me to order for all of you," said Juan, assuming the host role. I promise you a feast."

The courses began arriving and they began to enjoy a magnificent South Texas lunch. Louie and Juan discussed their earlier days and talked about the people and hits they were a part of over the prior decade. Both of them seemed like comfortable old friends or scoundrels. Jack and Antonio sat silent as the history unfolded. After the waiters brought the entree and laid it out on the table, Louie brought up the business.

"You're gonna like what I'm bringing to da table today, Juan," said Louie smiling at him and Antonio. Antonio had kept the same sour look on his face all morning. Jack didn't think he liked playing second fiddle to his father. He was a spoiled brat who enjoyed his father's name and wealth without any of the responsibility.

"Juan, you and I have some common interests…we like the music, right? And we like making money and good food, and beautiful ladies." He smiled. "We all have those interests. Ain't nothin' wrong with dat." Juan looked amused and a little interested. He was letting Louie go on without interruption. Louie looked over to Antonio and back to Juan. It was obvious that the son was masking his own ignorance with some macho posing.

"You and I make records," said Louie, "dat costs a lot of money that we have to pay out before the sales profits come back in. I got a point here."

"I know you had a run-in with Buck Smith at Texas Sun Records a while back." Antonio suddenly sat up straight and froze. He got Juan's full attention also. What was this? Antonio flushed; surprised that Louie would bring up his humiliation at Buck's hands. This had been a cordial lunch so far.

"From what I learned a while back, Buck came back from Eagle Pass that day and collected about two hundred thousand dollars on your account." Juan did not acknowledge the truth or fiction of Louie's statement. He was going to keep his cards close to his chest and see what was coming. "I know things got rough. I'm sorry. I hope you have fully recovered from your illness."

Antonio looked ready to spring on Louie. "I'm well again, Louie," said Juan. "But as a result. I am taking a little more care with myself." He seemed comfortable saying this.

"Look, I'm just telling it like it is," said Louie to Antonio. "I'm sure you was taken by surprise by Buck, Antonio. You didn't know he was gonna show up. He's a mean bastard with a prison record. Look, we understand dat in our bidness, sometimes we gotta cut some corners." Louie was getting to his point. "Ain't one of us that don't take advantage of some situations, right? I ain't talking outta church here."

"I'll grant that there are situations that we work to our advantage. Yes," said Juan. "You say you have a point?"

"Yes, Juan, I have a reason here. You still owe Texas Sun Records about two-hundred and twelve thousand dollars by my count." said Louie.

"I will never pay that son of a bitch, Buck Smith, another dime!" said Juan. "I will see him dead first. Am I making myself clear! I will not tolerate him a second time." A sinister side emerged from an otherwise old, apparently courtly Spanish gentleman.

"You won't have to."

"We won't? So you guarantee this?" said Antonio.

"I guarantee it if you listen to my deal?"

"What is this deal?" said Gomez.

"Buck ain't with Texas Sun Records anymore. He done quit and left da Stallworths holding the bag when he left town. Took the money like a damn pirate. Looted the place and now dey was more in debt than before dey made him president. He never paid dem off for the place, so de still owned it when he disappeared with the cash."

"He is a very disreputable man," said Juan. "A thief and a brute who belongs in a jail. But I must say, Jim Stallworth is a good man."

"I'd shoot the bastard if I had the chance," said Antonio. "He damn near killed my Dad."

"I'm sorry for that, Antonio," said Louie. "But it's a new day and there's new deal like I said. We are gentlemen here and sometimes you just got to let the past be the past, and move on."

"So, what is this new deal?" Antonio was skeptical of any idea from Louie.

"The Stallworths don't own Texas Sun Records anymore," said Louie.

"Is that right?"

"Yeah, I do."

There was a long pause and Juan sighed and leaned back from his plate. He looked Louie in the eyes. "So, my friend, you bought them out?

"Last week, we closed the deal."

"So now you are going to tell me *I* owe you over two hundred thousand dollars."

Antonio tightened up. He leaned toward Louie. "Vaquero Records ain't gonna pay nobody, not ever. We don't care what gringo owns it. You'll never see that money."

"You ain't gonna haf'ta pay dat damn debt, Antonio. Now jus' sit der and enjoy your iced tea. Just listen up. Louie gave him an intense look. Their eyes met and Jack could see Antonio retract slightly. Something in Louie's eyes moved him back."

Antonio also leaned back from the table but held onto his fork like he might use it as a weapon. He didn't like being talked down to.

"Like I said, I own it now, lot stock and barrel,' said Louie. "But I don't want da damn thing. I'm a record producer, not a record plant operator. Nowadays I get my records made in the big record plants with da latest technology. The big labels won't have it no other way these days. And, I don't know nothin' about managin' a place like Texas Sun. I bought it right so I'm gonna sell it cheap."

"And then I'm gonna owe somebody else?" said Juan.

"Tell you why dis is a good deal, Juan," said Louie. "'Cause I think you ought to buy it."

"You think we're stupid," said Antonio. "You said it was bankrupt."

"Juan, follow me for a minute. There's about four hundred thousand dollars out der owed to Texas Sun by record producers. Hell, half of dat debt is yours. The other half's a bunch of half-ass producers and lots of them are your compadres along the border, both sides.

"The place is in debt to suppliers for 'bout a hundred grand. Dat's chicken feed for what you gonna get outta ownership. Your own record pressin' plant, Juan. How 'bout that. First, you forget about the debt you owe yourself. Your account payables jus' drops two hundred thousand dollars. You pressure da other producers that owe you to pay up. Maybe you buy them out. Most of them don't have the cash. Maybe dey pay you with recording contracts of der best artists. Shit, I don't know. Think about the power you can have when you own dat record factory in Texas. You got you' competitors by the balls, overnight. Dat staff in Waco is mostly Hispanic and dey gonna love working for Vaquero. And your fans don't care if the records are made out that old black vinyl. It's a different market than LA and New York rock 'n roll. Am I wrong?"

"I don't know, I must think about this," said Juan. "Louie, whenever your name comes up in conversation in Los Angeles or Chicago, my other markets, they speak well of you."

"Hell, you make young Antonio here, or one of your other sons, da plant manager. You'll own the Tejano market!"

"How much Louie? It is yours now. So, if you sell to me--how much ?"

"Here's how I figure it. Da real estate's worth a hundred thousand dollars. I had it appraised. My best guess is dat the buildings and equipment is worth another fifty thousand. Da name, dey call it goodwill. It's worth at least a couple of hundred thousand. The business did about 1.4 million year before last. Dat ain't bad. Add dat up and you got assets worth three hundred and fifty thousand that can produce over a million a year in revenue. And don't forget about da receivables and da power they can bring you."

"I don't know, Louie," said Juan. "You're not leaving out anything?"

"Well, da company does have bills of about seventy thousand. Look at the alternative. You don't buy and me, or some bank muderfukers, and don't foget the IRS are gonna come after your ass to pay the bill. You'll lose. You'll pay them and da lawyers. It could threaten your bidness. Dis is a good deal." He lowered his voice so that no one outside the table would hear.

"You don't want to jeopardize your bidness or upset those fella's cross the border, and up north. Da funny money thru your record sales.

"What," said Juan? He wasn't expecting this.

"You know what we're talking about. Da importers you does bidness with. Washing da money."

"I don't know what you are speaking of," said Juan.

"You better shut up," said Antonio giving Louie a threatening look. Antonio looked around the room to see if anyone might have been in hearing range.

"I won't say nothin' mo'," said Louie. "I think I've made my point. It won't go no further but let me tell you. Some of my friends know your friends and everybody just wants to keep things runnin' smooth."

There was a long silence while Juan paused and dipped a tortilla chip into the salsa. He took a long drink off his Carta Blanca and looked up at Louie.

"What are you asking for Texas Sun Records, the entire property, as is," said Juan.

"I didn't come here to insult or take advantage of you Juan," said Louie. "Just want what you owe me as the temporary owner. Three hundred and twenty thousand dollars. You gonna haf'ta pay somebody something sooner or later. Why not pick up a record plant instead. Hell, you can take it off you income tax."

"I don't like this intimidation," said Antonio. "Father, I don't know why you listen to his shit. Lies from one gringo after another!"

"Silencio, Antonio!" said Juan. "Wealth and power come from listening and being reasonable. We will soon own our own record manufacturing plant. Louie Thibodeaux is not our enemy, he is not robbing us. He's right. This is a fair price. Stop and think. I hope someday you will learn to see through your anger at the world and act like a businessman. You're emotional as a teenage girl sometimes."

Louie let that pass for a few moments to clear the air after Juan's insult to his boy.

"So it's a deal my friend?" said Louie. "We both know we hav'ta put our profits somewheres."

"Yes, it is a deal, Louie. Am glad you came to me first. But we will not speak again of my associates, yes?

"What associates?"

"And him?" said Juan gesturing at Jack.

"He's safe. Jack's been tested true." Juan looked Jack in the eyes and nodded. "I'll have my lawyers send you the books and the contract immediately." said Louie. "Maybe we can wrap dis up before the end of the month. You gonna make more money dan ever."

"You know my young friend," Juan turned back to Jack. "In the land of the Vaquero, unfortunate accidents happen to a man with no character. Working in cowboy country can be a dangerous business. Snakes, rogue bulls, especially for one who crosses his amigos."

"A man needs his friends, Senor Gomez," said Jack. "I value that, and sometimes they need him. Maybe we can do some business in the future. I think Louie would vouch for my work."

Jack was actually ready to leave. Again, he was hearing too much. Veiled as it might be, Vaquero was also involved in the drug running business. Buck had told him as much, and now Louie had verified it."

"Possibly," said Juan. "We'll see."

Louie had just turned two hundred and twenty thousand dollars profit in a month on the transaction. As they finished the lunch, Louie regaled them with Hidalgo's success and how it broke new barriers for Hispanics and Latin music. Louie figured that they all would profit from his crossover into pop music. They finished a pitcher of Margarita's and said good-by. Louie gave Juan an *embracio* and Antonio a handshake and they went out of the restaurant under blue skies.

"How old was this plan of yours, Louie? If you don't mind me asking?"

"I'll tell you Jack, but don't ever let nobody know. Maybe a couple of years I guess. Ever since I found out those old folks were going to sell it."

Jack and Louie got back into their car and pointed it back to Houston. "Think I left anything on the table?" Louie laughed after the question.

"I doubt it. He even picked up the tab."

Chapter Twenty-Eight

Going To the Country

Jack was back in Houston, but not to stay. Waco and Buck were behind him now and he was knocking around day to day waiting for something good to happen. He hadn't heard anything from the studio so he decided to drop by one afternoon. He parked and was walking down the back hallway to Mona's reception room when he heard someone in Studio A. He saw Travis at the piano but decided not to bother him. He seemed focused on his work. Travis's head was bent low and he was plunking out some notes and writing on a tablet.

Jack walked into the reception room to find Louie and Mona with a couple of guests. There was an attractive young black woman in some tight green jeans, an orange tube top and a load of costume gold jewelry. She didn't look over thirty. She stood next to the couch with a girl who looked twelve or thirteen seated beside her. Jack figured her to be the Momma. Louie turned to greet Jack.

"How ya doin' Jack?" he asked.

"Pretty good all things considered."

"Been up to anything since I sold Texas Sun.?" said Louie. His eyes looked bloodshot.

"I'm back in town to figure out what I'm going to do next. Did the Gomez's take possession of the plant?"

"Oh yeah," said Louie. "It's a done deal. Don't have much I can offer you at dis time; we're a little slow dis month. But I know things are gonna pick up soon. Just rappin' with des two lovely ladies about makin' sum music. Are dey hot or what?"

Jack nodded their way

'Dis is Miss Ester Lemonde and her daughter, Leann." said Louie. "They is both auditioning with me today."

"It's nice to meet you," said Jack. "We can always use more talent." He turned to Louie. "Just thought I'd drop by for a minute. I saw Travis back in Studio A on my way in. You been doing OK?"

Louie gave him an inquisitive look, slightly suspicious.

"Yeah," said Louie. "You know, dis and that. Kinda lyin' low and waiting for da next ting to come along. It always does. Most of my bidness lately, been out a town." He put his fingers beside his nostrils and sniffed hard. "Damned sinuses."

"Well, something's bound to pop around here. Hear anything from the other guys from Blackplanque?"

"The tour is taking a break, said Louie. "You ain't been 'round, so I guess you ain't heard da bad news. Sorry Jack, it's somthin'' real sad. Jus' broke my heart."

"What's that?" said Jack.

"You tell him Mona," said Louie. "I can't talk about it without goin' to tears."

"I'm sorry Jack," she said. "It's about big Mombo," said Mona. "We heard last Monday. He was playing with a little band down in a joint near Lafayette. Some fool's wife started flirting with him between sets Saturday night. Apparently Mombo spoke to her but that was all. Just being friendly like, you know."

"Yeah," said Louie. "Dat boy wasn't in to chasin' no tail. He was very devoted to Dee Dee, his wife. I told her dat Wednesday after da funeral."

"The funeral?" said Jack

"Mombo's dead," said Mona. "After the show this gals' drunken idiot husband came up to him while they were loading equipment back into the van and stuck a knife in Mombo's side. The other guys jumped on the jerk and held him until the police arrived, but poor old Mombo bled out on the way to the hospital."

"He's dead?" said Jack astonished.

"Jus' like a big old beached whale," said Louie, "layin' in dat casket. I loved dat boy. I cried all da goddam day. We used to have a studio together, years ago."

"Oh man, you're kidding." said Jack. "Man, I hate to hear that. He was such a nice, friendly guy. Hell of a musician too."

"I hate to lose him," said Louie. "I had big plans for him, like a son you know."

"He really was a sweetheart," said Mona. "Louie's paid for his funeral in Hattiesburg. Him and Dee Dee didn't have any kids and that's where their family's from. I hate it. That's why Travis is moping around by himself in the studio."

"Dis kinds shit happens on the road to musicians all the time," said Louie. Fan's relatives get jealous, planes an' bus's crash, sickness or some other craziness happens to dem. It ain't an easy life traveling all the time like dat."

"I'm really sorry," said Jack. "I really liked him. Louie, you remember that time you asked him to drive Queenie back to the airport." Jack started laughing as he told the story. Louie and Mona smiled at the memory. "He took him back in the van. Mombo didn't know about Queenies personal preferences you know, his lifestyle should I say. About an hour later Mombo comes back into the studio and walks up to Louie and says completely deadpan. 'What's wrong with that boy?"

Louie and Mona began laughing at the memory.

"So Louie says, 'what do you mean, Mombo'. Mombo says, about halfway to the airport, he put his hand on my leg and says, 'my, you're a big one aren't you.'"

By then they were all getting hysterical at the picture.

"Mombo never knew he'd been set up by Louie," said Jack.

"Dat was a gas," said Louie. "Never could get Mombo and Queenie in the same room again. Aw Jack, glad you remembered dat. Remembered da good times. Why done you come by dis time next week, Jack," aid Louie. Maybe I'll have some bidness for you by then."

"OK"

Louie turned back to the young black woman. He put one finger beside his nose again and sniffed hard. "Sinuses," he said. "Excuse me." He smiled and looked at Momma. "Honey, let's you and me go back to da office and discuss ya'll's future." He looked at the young girl. "Child, der's a break room down the hall on the left and I think we got some cokes and cookies back der. Why done you check dem out. You need anything and jus' let Mona here know. OK?" She nodded and went off to investigate the break room. Louie opened the hall door for Momma and they disappeared into the back.

That left Jack and Mona alone in the reception room.

"Something tells me this may take a little while," said Mona. "Guess he's gonna do some negotiating. Come up with some recording deal with her and the kid."

"Is the girl a singer?" Jack asked.

"Well, I guess, or at least her Momma thinks so. That's why she's back there in Louie's office working out the details.

"I figure Mommas got a lot to bring to the table" Jack laughed.

"Uh huh," said Mona, "Or the couch. She's very determined. I think she really wants to be a singer herself. Maybe Louie can get two-for-one." She seemed unhappy at the situation and spoke bitterly.

"I see, the daughter looks a little young."

"I know -- well who knows, Jack. I wish Louie wasn't Louie, but he is. Someday it's gonna come back to bite him. There's a lot changing around here since you've been gone. It's getting a little weird." She lowered her voice. "You know, Louie's girlfriend packed up and went back to New York City about the time you left for Waco. His hearts really been screwed up since then. I feel sorry for him."

"That's too bad," said Jack. "I've been noticing that Louie seems a little unfocused on things, kinda distracted."

"Yeah," she continued. "I'm more than worried about him. He's letting the studio business slide. Hasn't recorded anything serious in weeks. That's not like him. I think Shingles got him something to calm down, relax you know, but it's making things worse. He's just getting irrational and he just seems to be letting things slide instead of controlling everything. You know that's not like him. I don't know what to expect of him when he shows up every day."

They'd talked for about twenty minutes when the young singer's mother emerged from the back smiling and called to her daughter. She seemed pleased with herself. She looked at her daughter. "Lee, Mr. Thibodeaux's in the back office, down that hall. You be nice to him. I think we're close to getting you a record deal. I'll be outside in the car when you finish visiting with him. Get on back there and be sweet. He gonna make you a star, baby."

"Thanks Mona," she smiled at Jack and Mona. "I'll be seeing you I'm sure. Ya'll take care. Tell Randy hello for me." She began digging in her purse and walked down the hallway toward the parking lot. Her daughter opened the door to the back hallway trundled back to Louie's office.

Jack really wanted to talk more with Louie and get his thoughts on the studio's future. Today was not going to be the day. He was losing hope for more photography work in the music business. Times were changing. Mona and Jack continued to make small talk for about half an hour when the girl came out. She stumbled once and put one hand on the wall for balance. She went down the hallway toward the back parking lot without looking up at them.

Mona shook her head. "She did not look very happy." A few minutes later Louie came out.

"Dey gone?" he asked Mona looking around.

"Yeah, did you give her a contract?

"We gonna give her a chance," said Louie. "I think dey both got what it takes to succeed in the bidness. Lot a talent for sure. Dat little gal can sing. Let's get dem in next month and get down some tracks."

Louie said good-by and told Mona not to bother him for an hour because he was feeling down and needed a nap.

"You still got dem Hassblebloods, Jack?"

"Yeah, I'll keep them loaded in case anything comes up."

"Good, just keep'em 'til we need them. Leave a number with Mona where I can reach you,"

Louie was headed back to his office as he spoke. Jack told Mona good-by and left the room feeling worse than when he arrived.

He was walking back down the hallway toward the door when he saw Travis, still in the studio. He walked in and Travis looked up.

"Travis," said Jack. "I just heard about Mombo. Man, I'm so sorry. That's such a bummer."

"I know, man. I still can't believe that big guy's gone. He had so much soul." Travis picked up a new Ovation acoustic guitar that was next to the piano stool. He began picking a country style rift for no particular song, as far as Jack could tell. Just a slow C, F, G chord progression picking the bass line as it flowed.

"I just got to get away, Jack," said Travis. "I'm moving out of rock and roll. You know, there's something going on in country music," he said. "Something new."

"I know what you mean. I'm not sure what my next move will be. It's a restless time. What are you thinking about?"

Travis looked him in the eyes, and Jack could sense that he had come back off the road changed. Louie had been right. The road had turned Travis's head around. Playing the blues nightclub for fourteen months had driven Lee and Travis into a rut. It had become a job. The fun had disappeared from the music.

"No man, I'm talking about some *new* music," said Travis. It seemed revitalized and excited about something. His old basement blues were gone.

"Let me tell you, Jack. There's a lot of talk on the road. You know, a lot of the musicians, especially the guitarists and keyboard men are from the South. I don't care who they're backing up, most of them are southern boys. You meet them in Vegas, LA and studios in New York. Lot of them have country music in their hearts. There's a whole country thing in California too. Hell, there's some good old southern boys that back the Beach Boys on their records."

"I could believe that," said Jack. "The South builds musicians that have a lot of feel in their playing. Louie call's it soul. Some of the tightest players and bands around are from Texas, and all the Gulf coast states. Singers have always loved being backed up by that sound."

Travis stopped playing and set the guitar back in a stand.

"Right, it's soul and gospel and country and rock. That's where they're coming from. You see it on the road as you run into other guys and trade licks and stories. Things are changing, the business of music is changing, and it's the artists that are doing it. But, what I'm rediscovering is pure country. You take the classics and rethink the arrangements and sound. You get that feeling and write your own thing from all that shit."

"So that's where your head is at these days. Rock and Country"

"Well, the good old boys who run the music in Nashville, the Grand Old Opry, those producers and promoters are losing control. More of the artists are rebelling and producing themselves. Some big names are tired of putting up with being told what they can play or record. The rebels are writers with a free spirit. They're getting tired of being put in a cookie cutter. More are writing and recording what *they* like, and it ain't all about the money or contracts. This new country's got more rock in it plus even jazz and gospel. Church music has always been a major part of country music. You can call it whatever you want. The country scene is opening up to new ideas."

"Well, it's a sign of the times," said Jack. "Everybody's looking for more freedom. That same kind of thing is happening in rock. Artists get big and start to call their own shots. Look at Dylan or The Beatles."

"Yeah, but there ain't never been no dope smokers on the Nashville stage. Drinkers, yes. Been some come in and play when they were practically knee-walkin' drunk. But no dopers, except maybe old Hank or Johnny Cash. They were tolerated 'cause of their talent and they weren't doing anything too illegal. That's still moonshine land. But now, some of the new writers and pickers have been hanging out in LA and San Francisco, or at least spending time with them rock and rollers and it's rubbing off. Those old timers out in Nashville ain't getting it and don't want to. They've always had sort of a closed empire. But a lot of their most creative writers and pickers are cutting loose."

"So what's the cost? They won't get a spot on the Grand Old Opry?"

"Well, hell, even Elvis played the Grand Old Opry and so have a few other rock and rollers. But they were still in the grasp of the old timers." He paused and lit a cigarette. "Have you been to Austin lately?"

"No. not since I used to go up there to do a little politicking in college. We thought our student delegation could help get more funding for the school. That was a waste, a joke as it turned out, so we just wound up getting wasted at some beer garden."

"I think it's happening there, 'round the university," said Travis. "There's a whole mess of hippies and cowboy pickers living up there now. Austin seems to attract them. A pretty strange mix. We played there and had an extra day to hang out with some of the local musicians. You know, some are former Texas University students and others just seem to settle there. Now, a place called the Armadillo World Headquarters has opened. It's a crazy scene. There's hippies and rednecks, real cowboys, surfers and congressmen hanging out there, listening to the music. I visited one night at The Vulcan Gas Company. It's a dump, but everybody's there doing their own thing."

"What do you mean?"

"Everybody's getting off on all kinds of music," said Travis. "You got traditional country music and Bob

Wills type swing. A little jazz and a lot of rock and roll. They even bring in soul groups and acid rock, whatever. Man, people are just relaxed and take it in -- whatever the bands serve up. Everybody digs it. You can dance or just lay on the floor like at Love Street. Austin's going to be where it's at in Texas and I hear some country artists are considering moving there, leaving Nashville."

"Country rock," Travis continued. "That's where it's at for me. I think I'm going there when I wind up this Hidalgo gig in a few months. I'm saving my money so I can buy a little place in Austin. Maybe set up a garage studio."

"The world's changing Travis," said Jack. "Is Lee going there also?"
"Nope, Lee and his wife are moving to southern California. He wants to live in a place called Redondo Beach, south of LA. We stayed there during a California break. It's on the Pacific; sun, beaches, and the whole Surf City scene. He's been offered a pretty contract with Capital Records as a studio musician in LA. He's got a Hollywood agent that we met in Vegas and every time we get a few days off he flies to a session in LA. He's gonna get rich for a Lufkin boy."

"Well, that's great," said Jack. "He deserves it."

"Seriously, I think he can make a lot of bucks just doing session work there and they'll have a real home. Wish I played that good. I'm gonna miss Lee. His wife's out there right now looking for an apartment and thinking about a family. Lee and me been together practically every day for a good many years. I was best man at their wedding. I'm gonna call in a favor when I cut my next music in Austin. Have him come down and sit in. You know Jack, I think I'm gonna fit in there. It feels like home, very comfortable."

"Yeah," said Jack. "That central hill country around Austin and Kerrville, it's all really relaxing with the lakes and rivers. Very natural kind of place, and very Texas."

"That's where it's at for me," he concluded and went back to playing. "It's gonna be a while 'til I sign another contract, not that Louie's done me wrong or anything. I've just got to dig deep into myself, soak it all up and start writing. Go back to the woodshed."

"I can dig that."

Mona had told Jack that Hidalgo had an upcoming European tour that was going to go two months and then they would return for a month off. Following that they would do another three month round through most of the

U.S. The Blackplanque guys would stay with him through that leg and then Lee, Travis and Mel would leave. Mel and Travis had begun to write together and Travis had talked Mel and his wife into moving with them to Austin after the last tour. So Travis's big move was about six months off.

Mombo's future had been uncertain. Before his death, Travis told Jack that Mombo said he was tired of touring and wanted to go back to the Deep South and look for a band or gig. He could also get studio work but didn't like to be obligated to anyone.

"Mombo said, 'I just need to do some fishin','" said Travis. "He hoped that some deep fried catfish might bring him back to his sensibilities." Jack watched as Travis rubbed his eyes. "He was through with the tour."

Jack learned of the rest of Blackplanque's plans. Jacob had thrown it all off and gone straight. He had cut his hair like a Republican fundraiser, bought some suits and a tux and played jazz and popular piano music nightly at one of the exclusive private dinner clubs in Houston. Picking up extra work and private parties and weddings. He was doing all right on his own and getting back to jazz, which was his first love.

Louie was apparently working on getting Hidalgo a weekly, one-hour television network show like The Smother's Brothers with whom he had appeared. Louie said one deal would have him being the summer replacement for the Dean Martin show in a year.

He had appeared with Dean Martin and they had done a clever skit where they were twin brothers who had never met. It wound up with a duet that the TV critics liked. Dino had talked with his agent about bringing him back as a regular. Hidalgo was set for life as a celebrity with guaranteed record sales ahead from a solid base of fans.

Hidalgo was in the studio fairly often when he was in Houston and was still the quiet and shy personality he had always been. There wasn't a friendlier and more pleasant guy in the business, thought Jack. Everyone enjoyed having him around and considered his success well deserved.

Mona and Jack were talking about him over coffee one morning a few months earlier.

"You know," said Jack. "He's one of those personalities that is so quiet; you wouldn't ever notice him in a restaurant if you waited on him. Ten minutes after he left the place, you wouldn't remember him. But you put him up on a stage and it's like you plugged in a spotlight."

"Lots of these stars are like that," said Mona. "They've got so little expressive personality in person. They're just dull offstage, like a flat tire."

"Yeah, but their life is on the stage," said Jack. "That's where they're alive. Not down here in real life. I think," said Jack. "When they get off that stage, nothing else compares. I mean, on stage Hidalgo waves his arm or jumps in the air, and forty thousand people go nuts. You don't get off like that working at Sears. They come here for a meeting or something and lot of them look like Macy's Christmas balloon with the air taken out. They seem so tired, so down. I think that's why so many stay on the road all the time. It's like a drug. It's stronger than the money. These artists are emotional wrecks about half the time. I don't know how Louie deals with them."

"You got me," said Mona. "But I tell you the truth; Hidalgo was pumped up last week when Louie told him he was booked to appear on Playboy After dark with Hefner."

"Can't blame him for that. Probably thinking about going back to the mansion for a swim in the grotto."

Jack said his good-byes and went out to his new truck.

So, nothing going on for a month and Mombo was dead, thought Jack. It was hard to believe. Life passes too quickly and mine's passing me by every day too, he reflected on his recent past. No progress and no fun anymore. "What in the hell am I going to do for the next few days," he asked himself out loud, as he drove away. All of his stuff was stored in his brother's garage. On Monday he got a letter from the Houstonian Car Leasing Company demanding that he turn in his tough Firebird at a local bank. Jack had his brother follow him down and he parked the car in the bank's parking lot and put the keys and a brief note in an envelope and dropped it in the night deposit. That finished that. He now felt completely disconnected from Buck, Texas Sun Records and Waco. He went car shopping in his Mustang and made a deal on an almost new pickup.

Jack called Maggie that evening. She answered on the second ring.

"Hi Maggie, it's Jack."

"Good afternoon darling," she said. She had the most soothing voice Jack had ever heard. He needed that sound and thought about it for a moment.

"Maggie, do you know what a great voice you have?" he said. "It just pours over me like warm honey. Did you know that?"

"No," she replied slowly. "But it's a provocative thought. I don't think anyone has ever told me that. The warm honey sounds interesting."

"Well someone should have," he said. "I love your voice."

"That's sweet Jack. Are you drunk or something?"

"No," he said. "Haven't had a thing. Maybe I'm just worn out. It's been kind of rough you know. You know Angie and I broke up not long after I met you in Vegas. Not because of Vegas. It's been a few months coming."

"I'm sorry," she said. "But I'm not surprised after what you told me. I can imagine what you've been going through."

"And now my boss in Waco, at the record plant, he's bankrupted the place and pretty much stole all the money on the way out. He is the one you didn't meet."

"Oh, boy," said Maggie. "Where does that leave you?"

"Unemployed and lost I guess. Yeah, it was bad. He just put about a hundred employees on the street when he ripped the place off.   Anyway, I'm technically unemployed now and I'm going to have to rely on free-lancing again."

"Is that bad?" she said.

"Well, I've got a pretty good wad of money saved. You know, enough for a few months, but I don't know where I'll go from here when it runs out. I'd like to stay in photography but I feel I'm kinda back where I started. Originally, I was going to invest my savings in a small photo studio here in Houston.   Now I don't know.   I think I'll leave town."

"Yeah, I'm sorry for the way things are going.. Maybe my news will cheer you up a little. I'm planning to leave Las Vegas real soon. I've got my stash and I'm quitting the business and going near Denver, just west in Boulder.   I've been accepted into the University of Colorado. I'm going to do it Jack."

"That really makes me happy, Maggie. I can't tell you how much, for so many reasons.   It's what you deserve. You're a smart, beautiful and caring person and you sure need a new life. I know Las Vegas was just a means to an end, but it had to be wearing on your soul. You need to get past it and move on. Maybe we both need to move to a new scene."

"Thank you Jack, You'll never know how much, how nice it is to be appreciated for more than sex," Then she laughed. "Although I have to admit, I'm pretty good at it. But you're right. I hope someday to be doing it for love, not money. Doing it because I want to give it away to the right guy. Lord knows I could use some stability in that department."

"Well, I hope when you find him you'll know it. We all make decisions every day in our lives. Some good, some maybe not so good. I'm sure you've seen a lot of other girls disappear into alcohol or drugs."

"Do you think I made a mistake doing this, these past couple of years?

"I don't want to judge you Maggie," said Jack. "How can I say if it was a mistake or not. Your time in Vegas is almost over. But, I think the Lord's been watching over you. You're the only person who can say if it was wrong, or a mistake. I think you have to work that out with yourself or God."

"Yeah, time will tell. Guess it's time to pray for my future."

"Just know one thing, Maggie. There's one guy out in Texas who does care about you, the real you that I was with that night in my suite. I can pray for that gal."

"So you're going to be there for me.

"You bet. I'm just a phone call away."

"I'll be there for you too Jack. Let's keep it honest. I'm going to give your situation some thought and then I'm going to call you back with advice."

"I could use some. Some smart input." He gave her his new number at his brother's house and they said good bye.

Chapter Twenty-Nine

Desperado

Jack pulled up to the studio the next week to see if he could pick up some work while he decided his own future. He was disturbed over the weirdness of his last visit

But when he arrived, his discomfort was blown away and replaced with shock. The gate was locked with a chain. There was a sheriff's sign on it, barring entrance that stated that the premises were a crime scene. The entire studio was a crime scene. Jack could see yellow police tape across parking lot and the big back door entrance to Louie's studio. It was all locked up. Inside, on the lot sat Louie's shiny Lincoln and the old white van Randy usually drove. He was astounded and wondered what violence or catastrophe had occurred. Where was everybody?

From out of nowhere, a Harris County Sheriff screeched up behind him in a Dodge and stopped suddenly behind his truck. The noise made Jack jump and he spun around. A cop car. Jack turned to see the deputy step out of the car like Broderick Crawford on *Highway Patrol*. The sheriff left the car running and approached him with one hand firmly on his holstered gun.

"Need to see you ID son," he said. You didn't mess with a Harris County Sheriff. They had a rough tradition that dated back to the previous century. The sheriff was at least a foot taller and a hundred pounds heavier.

"Your ID," the sheriff said.

Jack reached in his hip pocket and pulled out his wallet and showed him his driver's license.

You are John Alvin Clifford?"

"Yes"

"What are you doing here in front of the gate? It's a crime scene."

"I didn't know that," said Jack. "What kind of crime? When?"

"I asked what you are doing here."

"I'm a photographer. I do some free-lance photography jobs here."

"What kind of photography?"

"Publicity shots, record album covers, show business stuff."

"So, you know Louie Thibodeaux?"

"Sure, he owns the place. He's a famous record producer."

"You ever take pictures of him with kids?"

"Kids? Nope. Just musicians and singers"

"You don't look like a long hair, seen anybody doing drugs at this place?"

"Nope, seen some drinking, but no dopers."

"Uh huh."

The sheriff wrote down the statistics from Jack's driver's license and his truck's license plate. "You live at his address?"

"Yes," Jack lied. He didn't want to start a conversation concerning his string of semi-permanent residences. He couldn't see how it would matter in the long run and he didn't want to confuse things. He gave him his former phone number in Houston. It was local and seemed to satisfy him. Jack damn sure didn't want his brother and sister-in-law to get a call.

"You're not an employee of the studio?"

"No."

"Well you're buddy Louie Thibodeaux has been arrested. He's in the Harris County Jail facing several counts of child rape, child molestation, possession of child pornography, lewd behavior and possession of cocaine; 'bout half a pound."

"Holy shit!" said Jack.

"Watch your mouth. This is a public street."

"I'm sorry sir, I was just surprised. I had no idea." Don't irritate the sheriff, Jack thought. He thought about his darkroom equipment, now locked up behind the police tape. He'd rather not lose it, but it was expendable.

"If I was you son," said the sheriff, "I'd look for work elsewhere in the future. I don't want to see you around here anymore."

"I think you have a fine idea." The sheriff gave him an unforgiving look as a reply.

"Don't be smart with me. Get your butt out of here, son."

The sheriff turned and got back into his idling car. He threw it in reverse and then into drive and sped around the corner like he was late for a bathroom break. Jack got back in his car but noticed that there was an old Cadillac in front of the shack where Randy and Suze lived.

He moved his truck around the corner and parked across the street from the Cadillac. Jack went up to the door and knocked.

Suze answered. He hadn't seen her for a several months, and she looked like she had gained some weight.

"Hello, Jack," she said in her usual monotone. Her personality was always the opposite of Randy's.

"Hi Suze," said Jack. "How are you? Is Randy here?"

"Yeah," she said. "He's in the kitchen trying to screw the legs off the table."

"You're moving out?"

"Damn straight. We're moving to Miami, Florida to stay with his cousin. Randy's going into the real estate sales business with him. His cousin's been there forever." They walked toward the back kitchen to see Randy.

"Miami must be really nice," Jack said. "Sun and beaches and waves."

"And hurricanes," she said rolling her eyes. "This Watts girl ain't never been seeing no hurricanes."

Jack laughed. "They ain't so bad Suze. I've been through a number of them and I'm still here."

"Uh huh."

"Hi Jack," said Randy. "How's it goin' brother?" Randy gave him a big smile and a soul handshake. "Ain't everthing's gone to shit or what?"

"It's terrible, Randy," Jack said. "Buck's busted the record company. Then Louie sells it to the Tejano mafia. Louie's headed for prison again and the studio is a crime scene. It's all gone to hell at once."

"I know man," said Randy. "Ain't no good nowhere. You know Louie was screwin' this gal and her daughter. Momma didn't seem to mind. The woman was crazy, had to be. So she been dealin' dope and getting' Louie some coke. Then she gets busted with speed, smack, cocaine, all kinds of shit. Louie don't know it. She knocks down a plea deal with the cops about Louie's pictures of her daughter and says he raped the kid. That was all it took. The feds have been after him for so long, it's pitiful. That little gal was just thirteen. He's fucked up big time. Man, they got the dirty pictures of him and dope in his office. So we're leavin' today. I don't want none of this. But how about you?"

"I just got hassled by the sheriff outside the studio gate. He took my name and told me to get lost and don't come back!"

"Wow, I'd take that to heart."

"I'm just lost, unemployed and my girlfriend's just married another guy."

Randy laughed. "It tests your faith sometimes don't it?"

"Yes sir," said Jack. "It's a test. So I hear you're headed for Miami."

"That's right. Just as soon as I can get the legs off this table and stick it in the back seat. We're all packed. How you like my new car?"

"The Cadillac? I like it. It suits you two."

"Yeah, said Randy. "I got it out of Buck. His Mom's been driving it for years, but it's in good shape. He owed me big time for some jobs I did for him. I think he was afraid I'd talk about some of his deals, after Louie got busted. I didn't blackmail him you understand. Nothin' like that. But I reminded him that he owed me."

"I just hope you got the title in your name."

"I did. Momma didn't raise no fools. I'm gonna get rich in Miami, Jack. You just watch and see. I'm real fortunate, my cousins doin' well out there, and he ain't got nearly my charm. It's a real job Jack. That's a first for me."

"Randy," I wish you and Suze all the luck in the world out there. I really do." Jack grabbed the screwdriver and had the legs off in a few minutes and helped Randy and Suze finish loading.

They all shared hugs and promised to keep in touch. Jack left them to lock up and headed back across town. He knew he'd never see them again despite all the promises. It was another page of characters turned.

Chapter Thirty

Splash One

There's a time when you say Enough, or to Hell with It, or something else that emphatic that suits your frustration.   You have to stop. A time when you need to look around, figure out where you are, and where you're heading next.   Maybe this is my time, thought Jack.   It wasn't a time for going back. That was not a consideration, there was no back possible.

He had told his brother that he was heading south and would be in touch. He didn't try to stop him. They were close, but had never tried to control each other's life or dreams. They just accepted their differences and wished each other luck. Jack promised him he'd let them know where he landed. I think I'm finally getting my head together, he told himself. South meant small bay front towns, beaches, and endless ranch land with warm breezes in the winter. After the past year, it seemed peaceful and beckoning. Enough of the fast lane!

Jack sat in a Prince's drive-in next to the Houston's I45 Gulf Freeway looking at his hamburger. They had over-loaded the red sauce and it dripped out of the back. The uniformed carhop had just delivered it to him with an order of onion rings. Prince's made the best onion rings in town as far as he could tell. They were the last hold-out in the local drive-in restaurant business that still had uniformed carhops to take your order and deliver it to the car. He had seen pictures of this Prince's carhops from the 1930's on their walls inside. Back then they wore roller skates and it still seemed like a good idea to Jack.

He sat in his almost new Ford pick-up and had a small U-Haul trailer hitched to the back bumper. Jack was proud of his deal, trading in his old Mustang at a Ford dealer for a year-old short-bed, V-8 F-150 with a three speed on the column. He was sitting in everything he owned except for the trailer behind him.

But, he pondered the wisdom of his next move. The first consideration was that Louie was in jail facing an enormous bail, if any. Jack's future doing business with the studio over and it was the base of his music business work. Buck was apparently in hiding, leaving a trail of creditors behind. For all Jack knew, the Rangers would be looking for Buck next. Randy Sun had taken off soon after Jack talked to him and was on the road to Miami. Jack figured that with his golden tongue he'd make a million selling homes.

And then there was Angie. Jack had talked with her best friend and got and ear- full of the wedding. Angie was happily married now with a home in the Sharpstown development at the southwest edge of Houston. Jack spent a few moments trying to be happy for her but couldn't work up much enthusiasm.

Jack knew he could stay in Houston, his hometown. He could get a straight job again and continue to do photography on the side. That would bring him back full circle to where he was at a year and a half ago. But, Houston didn't feel the same. He'd lived there since elementary school and was tired of it. Tired of it all. He felt he needed a change, a fresh restoration of his spirit. He had found Corpus Christi on the map. It seemed big enough to find a job but small enough to find some peace and space to relax.

He had no desire to get back with the same crowd of buddies, doing the single dating and partying thing. That seemed like a step backward. The thought just made him tired. It was a place where he did not want to do a second round.

"I guess I'm just depressed," he said out loud to himself. But, he knew he had never been able to stay in that state of mind, even if he tried. Optimism was a problem he couldn't seem to overcome, even in times like these.

Jack had managed to catch up with Mona Sinclair at her mother's house the day before. She was happy to see him. Not surprisingly, Louie's lawyer and Moonie were now running Louie's business. They had retained Mona to handle the day-to-day accounts and paperwork. Bills still needed paying, there were royalties and offers that came in every day, and someone had to handle the office and take the money to the bank. Louie asked them to take over while he was "out of pocket."

Mona said she was still making good money and figured it would continue until at least the end of the trial.

"Then, who knows," she said. "His family and a dozen others are suing to get hold of Louie's properties. There are millions of dollars there and money is still rolling in."

"Moonie said he'd like to buy it all out if an arrangement can be made with that bunch of Cajuns," said Mona. "He offered me a job in Nashville. I might take it. My girl's old enough to understand a move, but I don't know how Momma would feel about it. I'd probably want to take her too."

"I'm afraid Louie's going away for a long time this go 'round," said Mona. "His attorney is a heavy hitter but they've got him with cocaine, pornography and child rape charges. Now there's other parents with kids he has under contract trying to charge him with sexual exploitation, statutory rape, the whole thing. They even found color photos in Louie's office of him with some young girls."

"Wow," Jack said. "I didn't know. I mean, I knew he liked young chicks, but not the little girls." So there was more than one.

"Yup," she said. "It's not only the girls, but their star-struck, pushy-ass stage mom's in a lot of cases. Louie was ballin' them all. Now they're all after him. After the money. But it's Louie that done it…it's all his fault."

"I talked with Louie one time," said Jack, "about the lengths some people would go to, to be famous. The money, the fans and living a star's life. They'd sell their souls…a lot of them."

"Well, they traded off their little girl's innocence and a lot more. Louie's weak spot has always been the gals. But I never thought he'd be after them that young. He didn't used to be that way. I know Louie like nobody else. Jack, there was a time when I thought I loved him. In those early days, when he first gave me a job. He left me with a lot more than just memories from those days, if you know what I mean. But now, I mean the drugs, heavy stuff, and my god, ruining little kids. I don't know what changed him. I think it was just like his soul getting sucked in like quick sand."

"Maybe so," said Jack. "This business…I don't know if people like Louie start out crooked, or they just get tempted, and greedy. It can all come so easy once they get on a roll."

"Jack, people like Louie have power. That's all artists know. All of the folks that want to be singers or writers or musicians. All these aspiring artists come to him. They invest all their hopes in him. It goes to their heads, these producers and music big shots like Louie."

"You've got to be a strong person for it not to get to you eventually."

"That's not Louie," said Mona. "He's plenty weak to the sins of the flesh, as the preacher's say. And the paybacks are hell. He's gonna be gone for a long time after this. The lawyer says Louie's gonna need to sell the studio just to pay the legal fees. They're already looking for a buyer."

"They ought to call Buck," Jack said joking.

"That fool," said Mona. "He called me late one night, last week saying that Louie owed him two thousand dollars. I told him to get in line. I don't think Louie owes him a dime. More likely the other way around. Buck's desperate. I think he must have been drunk. Don't waste your time here, Jack," said Mona. "It's over. I wish I could offer you some work, but it's all over."

"Yeah."

"You'll find something to keep going. This is a big city. Lot's of opportunity."

"Thanks," said Jack. "I know. Louie's tent is folded up, probably forever."

"Yes sir, that's about the size of it. I could try to set you up. Put in a good word with Moonie, but you'd have to move to Nashville. He knows how good you are. He's not a bad guy actually."

"I'll keep in touch, Mona." Probably another lie, thought Jack. They were coming easier the more time he spent around the business.

Jack pondered their conversation while he munched on the crisp onion rings. He thought about how he was going to get the onion smell off his fingers.

And how was he going to get the smell of the music business off his soul. It did stink, just like Angie warned him. Now there was his opportunity for him to escape. Escape the seduction and leave it behind. Forget Moonie, Houston and Nashville. He had plenty of money and no ties left to break.

He got out of the truck and carried his scraps in the paper sack to a trash can near the restaurant door. He went into the Prince's, through the dining room, and into the restroom.

He washed his hands twice with the industrial strength cleaner in the dispenser. The smell was gone from his hands. Easy enough, fresh hands. He went back to the truck to finish his Coke. It was just past noon.

"So long Houston," he said out loud. "I'm leaving y'all behind." He cranked the key and started to pull forward out of the drive-in's lane.

"I love you but I'm southbound."

Then he stopped and took the truck out of gear. He thought about Maggie and shut off the engine and stomped on the emergency brake. Hell, if I'm going to be this melodramatic, I better share the experience. I ought to tell her I'm finally leaving, he thought. I'm going to be out of pocket for a while, at least until I'm settled, somewhere.

She had never called him back with her advice.

He got out of the truck and locked it. He had seen a phone booth at the corner of the drive-in. He went into the restaurant and got a pocket full of change before going into the booth. He dialed Maggie's number, hoping she'd answer. He needed to talk with her and get her thoughts, or at least her blessing.

She answered on the second ring.

"Hello, who could this be?"

"It's me, you're Texas lover."

"Hi Jack, what are you up to?" said Maggie. "I've been waiting for a call. In fact, I was about to call you." She sounded excited, bubbling.

"I'm leaving Houston!" said Jack. "I've had enough of the music business."

"When is this happening man? "

"Right now, I'm about to head for the city limits. I've got all my stuff loaded in a trailer behind my truck. The guy I work for, Louie, remember him? He got busted for dope and raping juveniles. It's all over."

"Really…that's a bummer. Well guess what?" she said. "I've got good news. I'm done with Vegas. I had my last date last week. I'm at the end of the month and the end of my entertainment career. I've sold my furniture, fancy clothes and I don't own a thing I can't fit into the 'Vette. I'm moving out," she laughed. Maggie was jabbering with excitement.

"I'm really happy for you. I've decided that I'm done with the music business and these bastards."

"I'm sorry, Jack. I'm off to school in Colorado. Jack, where are you going to go?"

"I'm not sure," said Jack. "But I'm headed way south. Someplace more peaceful and slower paced. Maybe along the coast like Corpus Christi, or maybe all the way to Brownsville."

"And then?"

"Maybe I'll just fish or learn to sail. I don't know. But I do know I'm leaving here. Maybe I'll go back to school and teach school or something."

"Leaving your bad memories behind, Jack, things you want to forget?" said Maggie.

"No, I don't think so. I don't want to forget a damn thing. Some of those memories are precious, some are just crazy, but they're all mine. You know, I love the city and the music. I'm just burned out on it."

"You'll probably starve to death down there. I think it's some kind of cattle desert. We drove to Brownsville once from Dallas, it took two days. You might as well be in Mexico."

"Well, I won't starve anytime soon. I've got about ten grand saved up and a cool new truck."

"Is that the future you want?" said Maggie. "Where are you *really* going?

"Me? That's a hell of a personal question? I don't know. I'm working on it."

"I'm personally involved with you, Jack, like it or not."

"I like it. That's why I called."

"Then listen to me. We've spent hours on the phone since Vegas. I know you and I just don't think you can run away, man. You know, I really care about you and what you do next."

"I know. You're about the only one who gives a damn these days, outside of my family. You're my best friend. But Maggie, I've got to do something. I can't stay here."

"I've got a much better notion, something beautiful Jack," she said. "I've been giving it and you a lot of thought."

"Then tell me. I need something beautiful."

"Move up to Colorado and be with me, Jack. Join me in Boulder?"

"Near the Rockies, this Houston boy will freeze." said Jack.

"Not if you're with me, I promise. It's at the edge of the mountains, it's perfect for us. Exactly what you say you're looking for. In the summer, we can drive up in the mountain woods where it's cool with icy streams. It's just minutes from town. And the winter's for skiing and Irish coffee by a fire. And Jack, there's going to be a lonely, lovely twenty-four year old waiting for you up there. She's a Texas girl, looking for a fresh start too. Sound good?"

"Maggie," said Jack. "You're serious aren't you. I have to admit, I've thought about us being together. You've always asked for honesty Maggie, so here it is. The past few weeks I've thought about two things, getting out of Houston and you. Not necessarily in that order. I've leaving everything behind, but I can't get you out of my mind. I'm crazy about you."

"I hoped so."

"It seems so far out, so unlikely."

"Don't be so logical," she said. "You said you only have about thirty hours left for your degree," said Maggie. "That's only a year or so. Come back to school for a photography degree and I'll get mine in psychology. We've got plenty of money between us for four years at least. It doesn't cost that much when you live like poor students. It's not that far out if we can admit we love each other."

"Maggie...I do, you're like sunshine to me, even when we talk on the phone. I do love you. And I'll find myself really, completely in love with you…it can only grow. Could you handle that?"

"Yes, it could happen for both of us, Jack, and time will tell if this is real," she said. "I feel the same way. I think I love you. All the time, I find myself wondering where you are and how you're doing. It's a little nutty, really. I've become possessed. We've actually only been together for about twelve hours. I know I would love to be with you and see where it leads. I just want to try living what I already feel. Please meet me in Boulder."

"How are we going to get together? Where can we meet?"

"You're such a guy, always thinking about logistics. I'm too excited to think," she was bubbling again. "Wait, I know. Monday, we'll meet Monday on the campus of UC. I'll meet you at ten o'clock in the morning in front of the school library. That gives you four days."

"I don't know where it is, but I'll be there. I can't wait to hold you again."

"Neither can I. We can make this work, Jack. It's time for us to roll the dice."

"I'll see you at ten," said Jack. "I love you!"

"I love you, Jack. We'll find an apartment," said Maggie. "We'll buy an old, squeaky bed and make passionate love between classes."

"I love squeaky old beds," said Jack. "They make beautiful music."

"It's settled then...so will we."

"Yes, I'm just reeling at the thought of having you with me, and maybe going back to school."

"Jack, I think you're one of the greatest guys I've ever known. I'm sure of that. You have a good soul, real soul," she said.

"I've got soul? I've got tell Louie."

"What are you talking about?" she said.

"I'll explain later," said Jack. "I love you and I'll see you soon."

"Jack, don't break my heart. Please be there at ten," said Maggie. "Monday."

"I will!"

"Bye-bye."

Jack hung up and went back to his truck. His mind was racing. He fired it up and got Cullen, turning onto Interstate 45 heading north. He felt strange, excited, but with a little hesitation. It might not work in Colorado. South Texas seemed like the easiest answer, no strings, just escape. He drove along crossing over the downtown Houston streets on the Pierce Elevated and approached the Highway 59 interchange where I45 would continue north and Highway 59 would swing south toward the Texas valley.

It seemed a little like a dream, a little surreal. He thought about Maggie, her energy and empathy. What should be his course for life and love; the more familiar life in Texas beckoned? His decisions had not been stunningly brilliant over the last year. His truck sped down the center lane, closing on the split overpass ramps which V'ed ahead to the North or South. He wished he could slow down and think this over. He found himself briefly straddling the solid, wide white line, hesitating. Then he turned the wheel slightly and leaned into the curve. His decision made; he was off.

November, 1995

Over twenty had passed when Jack went to visit. Louie was out on parole. Jack had read that he was living with his estranged wife near Sour Lake on her family rice farm. Jack wasn't sure why he did it, either curiosity or nostalgia. Who knew? He made the trip that late fall day from Austin. After they had gotten their degrees, he and Maggie had moved there from Colorado. They had both been drawn back to Texas. A local quick-stop store attendant in Winnie told Jack where Louie could be found.

"Don't know what you can get out of him," the clerk said. "They tell me the old cuss is getting a little senile from all the drugs and lechery. 'Course, that's only what my wife tells me, she goes to Mass with his daughter."

Louie was a notorious celebrity in the community and everyone knew where he could be found and had heard rumors of a huge stash of money buried in a strongbox out somewhere in the rice fields.

It was one of those cold and overcast days in East Texas that could chill you. A light mist seemed to be suspended in the air that wet everything. Jack found Louie sitting alone by the catfish pond on the property. His son-in-law met Jack at the farmhouse and Jack told him who he was and he just wanted to tell Louie hello. The guy directed him to a pond that was about 300 yards from the house. The wild grass and was crunchy from earlier frosts and crackled under his feet as Jack walked over a couple of levees in the field. Louie didn't see Jack coming up behind him as he sat in a lawn chair, hunched slightly forward with a five-foot fiberglass rod in his hands. He held his arms close to his sides like he was a little cold as he waited for a bite. Jack could see his cork floating about fifteen feet off the bank. The water was perfectly calm that morning and the cork caused occasional rippling circles that ran away from it.

"Hi, Louie," Jack said. Louie turned and a slow, broad smile came on this face. He looked much older than the picture in Jack's mind.

"Jack?" Louie said, his voice a little wearier than Jack remembered. "Jack...my friend. It's so good to see you brother. How the hell did you find me?"

"Well," Jack said. "Somewhere I heard you were living back up here with your family so I just looked you up."

"Hope you didn't bring no police," he laughed.

"No, I didn't see a one."

"Naw, dey leaves me alone dese days and I leave dem alone. I'm thru wit' my shenanigans. Nadine and my granddaughter takes care of me and her kid's don't fuk wit' me. Dey all got most of my money. You know, we never divorced -- me and Nadine. She's a good Catholic and never quits praying for me. Good woman. Got to be good if she forgives me and my mischief."

"Louie, I just thought I owed you something. Wanted to see you for some reason," Jack said.

"Oh," he replied. "I know why."

"You do?"

"Yeah, it's cause all that shit that happened back den. The stuff you went through. Maybe you wanted to thank me for schoolin' ya. Man, you were jus' growing up. I was watchin' you back den. You was just beginnin' to see things da way dey are. You just wanted to come visit me to make it all real again, so you don't tink you dreamed it. Dat's why."

His words took Jack aback for a moment. They ran through his mind and he considered whether they were true, or just some of Louie's Cajun country psychology. He still had the gift to make people see things his way.

"But we had some fun and we heard some great sounds didn't we?" Louie said.

"I remember the sounds. Some great music. Some talented, crazy people."

"You married?"

"Yeah," said Jack. "Almost twenty years now. You remember that trip we made to Las Vegas to see Hidalgo?"

"I do, dat was a good one."

"You remember my girl, the one that Moonie fixed me up with that night?"

"Yeah, she was a little firecracker redhead, right. I god a good memory for da ladies."

"She's my wife now. We got together and lived in Colorado about ten years and finished college up there. We moved back to Austin and we've got a couple of kids."

"You shittin' me! She a good wife?" said Louie. "Wished you brought her."

"She's the best. We're happy."

"Ain't life peculiar? Dat's nice for you. You never know where life's gonna lead you." He reeled in his bait and rebaited with a big, dead grasshopper he pulled out of a small, brown paper sack. He looked up at Jack and smiled. "My grandson catches 'em for me."

"That's nice."

"Jack, you was always a soulful guy."

"My wife says so."

"Does she really; dat's cool. You dug the music just like me, and you know, you never broke your word. You never put my bidness on the street. I'll remember that, when I forget everthing else 'bout you. I'm gettin' old Jack."

"I didn't know you liked to fish?"

"I don't, but my pappy always put a lot of faith in its healing powers. I do like to eat 'em."

"You need some healing?" Jack asked. Louie gave a flip with his rod and the cork and bait flew back out in the lake.

"Some would say. Anybody dat really lives is gonna need some healin'. Never knew many people who didn't try to hide somethin'. Lots a dem got no idea what der after or what dey gonna do if dey get it. Dreams are hard to handle when dey come true. It makes a lot of people crazy sometimes."

He paused for a while, considering his own words and Jack decided not to break the silence with more questions.

"I got a few folks prayin' for me. But, like I said Jack, you was true to you'self, I think. And you was true to me."

It was quiet out in the field. The rice plants were knocked down and gently rotting on the soggy land. It felt like another cold front was approaching. Jack felt enveloped in the emptiness, like the deadened sound of old Studio A.

"Thank you Louie. It was some trip."

"Yes sir.

Jack thought he knew what Louie meant even though his words hadn't made particular sense. He was beginning to feel sad seeing the loneliness Louie had brought on himself. So this was how Louie's dreams would end.

"I could never figure out why you wanted to be in the middle of all dat shit, 'cept for da sounds," said Louie.

"Yeah, it was the sounds, the music."

"Well," said Louie, "You know it was all my bidness, dem sounds, the music, da acts, all of it. It was all my bidness and I've kept it all up here." He tapped one finger against his head. "If I was younger, I'd go back and do it again. Start clean. I god a feeling about it. I hold all those sounds way deep in my heart, down to the last note in my ears. I always held that secret. I had that magic, the soul, I was borned with it. I'll always have the sounds in my heart."

Louie looked back at the gray water and began silently planning out how he would do it, if he had another chance.

Jack felt finished. He turned and walked away.

Made in the USA
Charleston, SC
11 May 2012